THE ANOMALY

A. Triceratops

NEWMAN SPRINGS PUBLISHING
320 Broad Street
Red Bank, NJ 07701

First originally published by Newman
Springs Publishing 2024

ISBN 979-8-88763-800-3 (Paperback)
ISBN 979-8-88763-802-7 (Hardcover)
ISBN 979-8-88763-801-0 (Digital)

Illustrations by Johnathan Hudson Jr.

Printed in the United States of America

All glory to God and His Son, Jesus Christ

CHAPTER 1

Philadelphia, Pennsylvania

Hi there. Listen…I'm gonna be honest with you, okay? Gimme ten minutes of your time, and I will tell you the *craziest* true story you have ever read! *I promise!*

Well, okay, the story is not *entirely* true because that would be impossible; but despite certain parts obviously being fictionalized, it still holds *some* truth to it while remaining highly entertaining. Complex, layered, intense, ups and downs, twists and turns, you name it! Just give me ten minutes of your time to properly set this thing up for ya, and I promise you'll be hooked. You're already a li'l bit intrigued as it is, right? Don't be dumb enough to stop reading now! Trust me, you'll thank me later. ☺

Here we go…

A. TRICERATOPS

A green Chevy Blazer with an 85 percent tint sat parked across the street from the bank, engine running, no air conditioning. (The AC was broken.) The inside of the car smelled like fresh *and* stale cigarette smoke mixed with the scent of yesterday's "weed." The two men inside the vehicle were having *this* conversation:

Anthony: Get your head in the game, Vinnie! Remember, we're in and out! *Absolutely* no casualties! We *just* want the money. We're not gonna kill anyone!

Anthony wiped sweat from his forehead, sweat that was arguably caused by nerves just as much as the ninety-two-degree metropolitan heat.

Vinnie: What are you even worried about, bro? I'm with you, man! Just the money. Nobody dies. I got it!

Vinnie was a nineteen- or twenty-year-old kid with black hair, which was tied back into a very short ponytail. When let loose, it would spill into chin-length hair. His complexion was peppered with skin impurities like mild acne and random cuts and bruises, implying he had been engaging in petty confrontations like fistfights or semiheated arguments

2

with Selina Kyle. He was wearing a black hoodie that had the words *Sotally Tober* on the front and hole-in-fested jeans that hadn't seen the inside of a washing machine in at least a year, if not five.

Anthony: I'm serious, Vinnie! We can't have any [Anthony paused] this time!
Vinnie: I SAID I GOT IT!

Anthony stared at Vinnie in silence for five seconds. Distrust was thick in the air, thicker than the exhaled menthol cigarette smoke swirling around the driver's sun visor. As the five seconds (which felt like 3.5 years) went by, Vinnie sensed the distrust from his buddy and became visibly angry. He gawked back at Anthony with an icy stare that could freeze Arnold Schwarzenegger to his Mr. Freeze costume. The tension was palpable. Another three seconds went by, which felt even longer than the previous five seconds. Something bad was almost certainly about to happen. Then suddenly…

Vinnie let out a disgracefully loud fart and began to laugh with the kind of grating, obnoxious laughter that a 1987 B movie street thug with a Mohawk (and a thin chain attached from his nose to his earring) would exhibit after pushing an old lady to the ground and taking her purse—before RoboCop shows up to save the day, of course!

Anthony shook his head in disapproval without cracking a smile. He had known Vinnie almost all his life; and even though he had redeeming qualities, the kid was always in trouble, in and out of juvenile deten-tion centers, serving short stints in county jails, etc.

Vinnie had no real family of his own, having grown up in a foster home where his adoptive fam-ily despised him, so Anthony's mom was more of a mother figure to Vinnie than his own mother (whom he did not know) ever was or his foster mother (whom he hated). He was always well-behaved whenever he was around Anthony's family, which was why they had high hopes of reforming the wild street kid; but they were unaware that their own son was far from an angel, influencing Vinnie to get into the types of activities like the ones that were about to unfold that particular day.

Having gotten himself involved with the Marconi organized-crime family of Philadelphia as an entry-level "enforcer," Anthony had taken on active duties like making sports-betting "collections" and "leaning" on guys who needed extra "convinc-ing" with regard to important matters. He had even begun "kicking up" a fee every month to his high-er-up in the organization, a heavyset man who shall remain nameless.

The bank robbery that was about to take place had the purpose of bringing Anthony up to date on his monthly "kick-up." As for Vinnie, it was just a quick means to fund his heroin drug habit.

After "letting one rip" (as he called it), Vinnie continued to laugh like an imbecile for another four or five seconds, after which he settled down to light up another cigarette. Anthony stared at the side mirror on his side of the car while deep in thought, the uncertainty and distrust he had in his heart prior to the ignorant flatulence remaining unchanged. Finally, he muttered these words: "At least take the round out of the chamber of your 9. I saw you rack the slide. There's no need to go in there with a bullet in the chamber. We've been staking the place for three months, and sixty-five-year-old Mr. Atlas is the *only* guard on duty right now. The man has a metal hip and glaucoma. He won't resist."

Vinnie exhaled as if annoyed and said, "Fiiine!" then pretended to remove the 9 mm bullet from the chamber of his gun but left it in when Anthony turned his head to look toward the bank. As you might guess, Vinnie boy would come to regret that dearly.

3:17 pm

Both men exited the vehicle, wearing black ski masks over their heads, and hurried inside the bank. The crisp air-conditioned air slammed against their sweat-soaked skin like a wave of cold ocean water against an overheated and overweight tourist on a Fort Lauderdale beach. The two bank robbers might have noticed this phenomenon, but the adrenaline coursing through their veins had commandeered their bodies, leaving any other sensation by the wayside.

Anthony: Nobody move, this is a robbery! You behind the counter, let me see those hands!

Vinnie: Old man [referring to the short and chubby Mr. Atlas], keep your hands off that crusty old revolver, or I'm putting your brain on marble!

Vinnie took the revolver from the old man's holster after he put his hands up.

Exactly three minutes passed. The robbery was successful, and the two criminals were heading toward the door. But before they could reach the outside, Mr. Atlas decided to give them some "sixty-five-year-old Black man" wisdom to take with them: "I better not see either one of your punk asses in the street!"

Anthony ignored the short, bald man and continued walking toward the front door; but Vinnie stopped in his tracks, turned around, and responded, barely containing his laughter, "What you gonna do, ol' man? Hit us with your walker?"

Mr. Clarence Atlas uttered his last words on planet Earth: "Yea, you're real tough with that gun in your hand!"

Vinnie turned to Anthony while pointing to Mr. Atlas with his gun and said, "Can you believe this old fool?"

However, somewhere in the middle of the word *fool*, the gun had a negligent discharge, hitting Mr. Atlas in the face. Parts of his brain splattered against the marble floor, and the bank employees immediately started screaming. Anthony's and Vinnie's jaws dropped, and as if those events were not tragic enough, the day was about to get far worse for these two men.

What neither one of them knew was that one of the bank tellers triggered the silent alarm exactly fifteen seconds into the three-minute robbery. As they stood there in shock at the instant death of Mr. Atlas, whom they had known for several years from the ol' neighborhood and had grown to like, four police cruisers pulled up in front of the bank, screeching their tires. Vinnie was the first to snap out of the state of shock he was in as he barely heard the police cars through the ringing in his ears, caused by the gunshot. Before Anthony even knew what was happening, Vinnie panicked and rushed through the front doors of the bank, desperately trying to flee the scene of the accidental murder. But since he was still holding his 9 mm pistol in his hand, the Philadelphia PD greeted him with multiple 40-caliber rounds from their Glock pistols as he ran toward them through the bank doors. His life ended almost as quickly as Mr. Atlas's.

Anthony saw his friend drop from the barrage of bullets, and then he fell to his knees while being overtaken by monumental dread mixed with the kind of adrenaline only shock can muster up.

Police officers rushed inside the bank, screaming, "Drop the gun!" And upon compliance, they handcuffed the stunned Anthony James Tricerra and took him away. He did not resist. Vincent "Skid Mark" DeRossi would never resist anything ever again.

CHAPTER 2

Jefferson, Texas

I would give you the exact date and time of the following conversation between Granny Carter and her beloved granddaughter; however, for all intents and purposes, these particular details are irrelevant to the story. Suffice it to say, it was happening in a suburban home in one of the more blue-collar neighborhoods of Jefferson, Texas (population: 2,512). Taking place in 2009, it was exactly five years after the disturbing events that unfolded in the previous chapter.

So then, dear reader, let's give our full attention to Mrs. Cordelia Carter, affectionately referred to as Granny Carter by her only grandchild. Granny was speaking to her granddaughter while lying on her hospice bed, in her son's modest Texan home.

Granny Carter: Morgan, honey, listen to Grandma very closely because the time is coming where I won't have the strength to tell you the things I need to tell you, dear!

Morgan: No, Grandma, you rest. You're going to be just fine. I'm sure that—

A. TRICERATOPS

Granny Carter: No, dear, you listen to *me* now!

Morgan looked at Granny silently while tears formed in the corners of her eyes.

Granny Carter: I have a gift for you, my dear, as well as some advice.
Morgan (with a trembling voice): Okay, Grandma…

The unusually thin, gray-haired old woman reached under her pillow, then took out and opened a small cardboard box that had been yellowed by time and had the appearance of something that might smell like old newspapers. From the box, she removed a 24-karat gold brooch, which had been fashioned into the shape of an ornate flower with ten petals. Five petals were placed over five petals, with the first five petals arranged to be in between the others. Five small blue sapphire stones were also placed between each of the top petals, and one large blue sapphire stone had been placed in the center of the brooch, which resembled the sun at the center of our galaxy except for the deep-blue color of the expensive sapphire.

Granny Carter: This, my dear, is a very special item. It is a brooch modeled after an anemone Rosea, or an anemone rose. It is our family crest, and this brooch was hand made by a Swiss jeweler in 1905 at the request of your great-great-grandmother Ophelia Rose. She worked for seven years to save up enough money to pay for this brooch, Morgan, and no matter how tough times got, she refused to sell it because she intended to pass it down to her daughter, Iris, who then passed it down to *her* daughter, Eva, my mother, who then gave it to me in 1947.

This brooch has made it through the most difficult and dangerous times because of the dedication of our past family members, who risked being arrested for refusing to turn it in and then hiding it during the gold-confiscation executive orders of the 1930s. It laid wrapped in newspapers underneath floorboards and inside walls that had bricks removed from them to create hiding places during those times. And during the Great Depression, when food was so scarce that people were eating snails off the pilings at the Philadelphia docks and licking maple trees for the sugar, this brooch was well preserved by Iris Rose, who refused to sell it even while her family made do with only dry bread and kidney beans every night. It has survived World War I, World War II, and many of the most difficult trials you can imagine, Morgan and you must do your best to guard it and pass it along to your children one day.

The blue sapphires in this brooch are flawless, and the gold working in it is one of a kind, custom-made by the Swiss jeweler for Ophelia in 1905.

I am now eighty-nine years old, Morgan, and it is time for me to pass it on to you. I gave

it to your mother when you were only two years old, but she passed away only six months after. So now that I feel *my* time coming to an end, I want to give it to you, Morgan.
Morgan burst into full-blown tears.

Granny: This brooch is a symbol of our family's strength, honor, and endurance through the toughest and most unforgiving times. You must never sell it, no matter *what* kind of hard times or financial hardships you encounter. Our bloodline must remain in possession of it, and it must be passed down to the next descendant after you whether he or she carries the name Carter or not. It has been in our family for five generations, and it is my gift to you, Morgan. And along with it, I'm going to give you some advice as well.

Morgan sniffled through her tears.

Granny: I know that in a few weeks you will be leaving this small town behind and moving to Los Angeles to start working on that new movie you auditioned and got the part for, but all I can tell you is *this*, Morgan. You are a good-hearted, beautiful girl from a small Texas town. Never *ever* change who you are, regardless of what kind of success or fame you encounter out there in Hollyweird. Just be who God made you,

Morgan, because you are one of a kind, just like that brooch.

Morgan was bawling uncontrollably by that point. Granny placed the brooch in her hand and took the two plastic breathing tubes out of her own nose so she could more comfortably lean forward to kiss her granddaughter on the forehead. Morgan hugged her grandmother assuring her that she would do *all* that she asked.

Morgan: I promise, Grandma, I will *never* change who I am or forget where I came from. And I will always take care of this brooch for as long as I live!

The two women continued to embrace while sobbing as Morgan's father walked into the room. Upon seeing the touching moment taking place, he decided to give them a few more minutes before coming to call his daughter for dinner.

Two weeks later, Cordelia Carter passed away peacefully in her sleep, three days after her ninetieth birthday, and she had a beautiful funeral service where she was surrounded by her family and friends.

Three weeks later, the beautiful and talented Morgan Carter moved to Los Angeles (operating under the stage name Cordelia Rose) and began working on her newly landed Martin Scorsese picture. She also began to slowly forget the promise she made to her beloved grandmother.

CHAPTER 3

Morgan Carter, Hollywood Starlet Extraordinaire

Once again, it had been exactly five years since Ms. Carter—or should I say Ms. Rose—moved to Hollywood to pursue her dreams of becoming a big star. It was 2014, and in just five short years, Morgan had achieved a tremendous amount of success for a previously unknown actress. Morgan's limited part in the Scorsese movie was indeed her big break, but it was only the beginning.

You have to understand, dear reader, that Morgan Carter was arguably one of the most beautiful female specimens on the planet. At five feet and seven inches tall and 132 pounds, with long blonde hair and stunning green eyes, she was a jaw-dropping beauty whose raw acting talent and Thespian skills were virtually impossible to match. The soft features of her angelic, fair-skinned face; her small, perfectly sculpted nose; her perfectly shaped eyebrows; her full natural lips; her picturesque but very kind green eyes; and her long eyelashes *immediately* drew the attention of Hollywood directors, not to mention the fact that the 36:26:36 ratio (which she had) was considered a big-screen gold mine (according to Harvey Weinstein's piggish protégé). And with an acting range mirroring that of Leonardo DiCaprio, Morgan was quickly on her way to the top, all while forgetting the promise she had made to her grandmother.

She followed the Scorsese film with a role in a picture called *Alice*, in which she played the role of Alice Weaver, the best friend of Kate Winslet's character, Samantha Simmons, a forty-one-year-old survivor of the Columbine school-shooting tragedy. What made the film unique was that in its stunning conclusion, Samantha Simmons realized Alice Weaver and herself were the same person and that the trauma of the events at Columbine had fractured Samantha's psyche, forcing her to create and rely on help from an imaginary friend named Alice to get her to safety on that tragic day, and she remained "friends" with Alice ever since. The picture, shot in mostly flashback sequences, revealed that Samantha only realized Alice didn't exist during the film's final act. The movie did a great job of portraying her interactions with Alice as her best friend for years, and the twist of discovering that Weaver was not real, shocked audiences. The film was met with raving reviews and tremendous financial success. Cordelia Rose (Carter) won a Golden Globe Award for Best Supporting Actress, and *Alice* quickly cemented her reputation as a pro in Hollywood.

However, Morgan's greatest achievement in her short five-year run in Tinseltown came in the hard-hitting two-hour-and-forty-minute drama called *To Hell and Back*, in which she shared the screen with Hollywood heartthrob Chris Hemsworth, who at the time was in his late twenties, which initially caused a bit of a concern for the casting directors, who wondered if Mr. Hemsworth, playing the love interest of then-twenty-year-old Ms. Carter, would be an issue with audiences. It was not an issue, and their great on-screen chemistry as well as Morgan's amazing performance not only led to top-notch reviews but also her winning an Oscar award for the portrayal of Mellissa Green, a twenty-one-year-old small-town girl turned addict, turned criminal, turned reformed model citizen and mother to Chris Hemsworth's character's son.

This role not only granted Cordelia Rose the Oscar for best actress, but it also made her the *only* twenty-two-year-old woman to ever win an Oscar. Needless to say, it instantly made Morgan a massive star, complete with many endorsements like a Dior clothing line, a Chanel perfume line, a Valentino Garavani shoe line, a Smirnoff Vodka branding deal, etc. Yeees, life was good for the gorgeous and talented Cordelia Rose.

But the millions of dollars and millions of fans also came with a price. Morgan forgot who she was (the girl who promised Granny Cordelia Carter she would never change), and she allowed fame and money to go to her head. Not only did her opinion of herself change into that of an entitled, snobby brat, but her behavior morphed as well. She began spending night after night in the high-class nightclubs on the Sunset Strip, drinking, partying, and doing drugs (mostly cocaine) with her young famous friends until…

One night, exactly one year into being a twenty-two-year-old Oscar winner, she left the Playhouse Nightclub on Hollywood Boulevard, intoxicated beyond belief; entered her 2013 Bugatti Veyron; attempted to drive home (after doing a line of cocaine off the car's center console); and hit another car head-on, causing the accidental death of a Los Angeles woman named Carla Romano, a little-known exotic dancer in Hollywood. This tragedy caused Ms. Romano's "long-lost family," who hadn't been in contact with Carla in years, to suddenly come out of the woodwork and sue Morgan Carter in civil court for her role in the vehicular manslaughter.

After paying the Romano family almost $20 million in damages and paying high-profile, shark-toothed Hollywood attorneys millions as well to plead down her criminal case to only feature punishments that did not involve prison time, Morgan lost all her money and all her endorsements and became almost instantly blacklisted in Hollywood. After her role in the death of Ms. Romano, Morgan Carter became a name that Hollywood writers, directors, and producers started running from like the plague. And just like that, as quickly as she rose to the top, Morgan crashed to the dreadful bottom.

She liquidated her remaining assets like her Hollywood home, her cars, her jewelry (except for her grandmother's brooch), etc. to pay for her legal fees. Furthermore, in order to escape the paparazzi, who were hounding her every day and night, she decided to move to a very small town where she thought people wouldn't know her. She couldn't go back to Texas because she was so well-known there as the infamous Hollywood star who "killed that stripper while boozin' 'n' drivin' [spits chewing tobacco into spittoon]," so Morgan did the only thing she *could* do. She used the remaining bit of money she had to buy a house with an acre of land in the smallest town that a thirty-second "small town with nice scenery" Google search rendered. Therefore, the gorgeous blonde, who was still an entitled snob despite killing someone with her car in a drunken stupor, had no choice but to escape to Sky Haven, Pennsylvania (population: 1,115).

CHAPTER 4

Anthony Tricerra, Jailbird Extraordinaire

Let's for a moment put Morgan Carter on the back burner and go back to the life of Mr. Anthony Tricerra.

For his role in the deadly shooting at the bank in 2004, he was charged with being an accessory to a second-degree murder and armed robbery and sentenced to twenty years in prison with the possibility of parole after ten years. The district attorney's office attempted to offer him a plea bargain in return for his testimony against the Marconi crime family, a well-known Philadelphia criminal organization for which he was a suspected foot soldier, but A. J. (Tricerra) turned down the offer and chose to do his time instead.

In prison, he met James "Pitts" Montero (or Jimmy, as A. J. called him), who was a "made" Marconi enforcer and was doing life for first-degree homicide. Pitts's was a very unique case, however, because while he also refused to cooperate with the feds to reduce his sentence, he renounced his life of crime while in prison and instead spent his days reading the Bible and professing the ways of Christ to other inmates. Because he believed that his past crimes/mistakes were his own and that nobody else but he was responsible, he never "rolled over" on the Marconi family. This gained the respect and appreciation of the Philadelphia Mafia enterprise, which was sad to see him go but considered him a loyal ex–family member for the rest of his life.

But Pitts wasn't always a devoted follower of Christ. In fact, two years prior to A. J. Tricerra arriving at the prison, Jimmy Montero beat an inmate almost to death; and when three guards tried to stop him, he bit a piece of one of the guards' ear off, then knocked the second guard unconscious and severely injured the third guard in a way that involved a hand rail and a food tray, which I don't care to get into.

Yes, in the past, Pitts Montero was a big, violent, virtually unstoppable animal. Not only was his demeanor that of an angry rhinoceros, but also, his overwhelming six-foot, eight-inch height and 320-pound stature was enough to intimidate *any* inmate. So why and more importantly *how* did the change of heart and drastic change of behavior happen?

Well, in 2003, a man named Vito Mancini, who belonged to a rival crime family from New York, was picked up in Philadelphia on an illegal gun charge when a random traffic stop done by "regular schmo" Philadelphia PD officer Scott Kildare resulted in the police officer noticing the firearm sticking out of Mancini's underarm holster. While being questioned about the pistol, Vito offered the officer a bribe in hopes that he would "fugget about it." But since Kildare was a regular schmo and had no idea who Mancini was, he refused the bribe and took him into custody. Vito, who had once made a pass as well as a veiled threat to Pitts Montero's nineteen-year-old daughter Isabella in a restaurant (while Pitts was incarcerated), found himself waiting at the Philadelphia prison to be extradited back to New York on a half dozen charges of murder, assault, racketeering, extortion, etc., and he was mistakenly put in the same cell block as Montero because of the negligence of the Philadelphia penal system. Needless to say, within twelve hours, the two men had a violent encounter that left one of them dead from fourteen stab wounds and the other man bleeding out on the rec room floor, unconscious. *That* particular man was Jimmy Montero. And whatever he saw on the "other side" as he was dying on the cold prison floor terrified him to a degree that changed him *forever*. He would often tell Anthony "A. J." Tricerra with a horrified look in his eyes, "Lemme tell you somethin', pal. That Jesus stuff? It ain't no joke!"

That was how the infamous James "Pitts" Montero came to be a completely different man. After being revived and treated in the prison infirmary, he would never return to being the angry rhinoceros that all the guards knew and hated. He would even apologize to the guards he injured, especially the poor man he…did that thing with the food tray to.

A. TRICERATOPS

This new man was the one who Anthony Tricerra had the pleasure of sharing a cell with for ten years, listening to his words, hearing his testimony, and taking it to heart. Before long, Anthony started making sense of what the ex-rhinoceros on the bottom bunk was telling him; and he, too, renounced his life of crime, becoming a Christian while at the same time refusing to "snitch" on any of his old Marconi associates for the same reason as Pitts Montero. This did not go unnoticed by the crime family either, and Anthony was privy to the same protection Jimmy Montero was as a loyal ex–family member of Marconi "Enterprises."

After ten years in prison, at thirty years of age, Anthony was granted parole and released for being an exemplary inmate. During his last day in lockup, he shook the gigantic hand of Pitts Montero and promised him to never return, before leaving the prison that was his home for ten years. Not wanting to go back to the corrupt hustle and bustle of the big-city life, he did a Google search for "small town with nice scenery" and found himself intrigued by a place called Sky Haven, Pennsylvania, with a population of 1,115 people.

CHAPTER 5

The Secrets of Sky Haven

So both Morgan Carter and Anthony Tricerra ended up living in Sky Haven for different yet similar reasons. Unfortunately for them, however, it was no ordinary small town. On the surface, it certainly *seemed* like an ideal place to live a quiet, crime-free life. But Sky Haven had secrets—many secrets. And *one* secret in particular was so horrible that it could *never* get out. In fact, this secret was so extraordinary that the FBI had gone out of its way to permanently monitor the town to make sure it would never get out.

The mysterious town was located in the Pennsylvania mountainous region known as the Poconos. Because of its location, the area was quite conducive to coal mining and therefore contained a plethora of new and old mines and quarries. Some of them were still active, but some had long been closed for safety reasons.

One such mine deserves a closer look and a proper introduction, but in order to truly understand its mystique, we must travel back in time to the summer of 1953, when coal miners living in Sky Haven who were working inside Black Rock Mine (as it was dubbed by the locals) discovered something very extraordinary at a depth of 482 feet.

It was never properly reported by the newspapers because a fringe division of the FBI known simply as the Meta Division would not allow the information to get out. Legend has it, however, that at almost five hundred feet into the earth, the miners discovered a…metal structure. Only parts of it were visible because it was buried beneath tons of volcanic rock, but the miners believed that it was very advanced technology that had never been previously encountered, technology that simply could not exist in 1953. The legend says that as the miners attempted to dig out the structure, they awakened something within it and met their ends with violence and blood. The story goes on to say that two miners managed to flee back up through the dig-site shafts after igniting a pallet of dynamite in the caverns below them. This caused a great explosion and a massive cave-in, trapping whatever was awakened from the metal structure at a depth of nearly five hundred feet belowground.

As if the story wasn't strange enough, the two surviving miners made it out of the mine alive, but both suddenly died two days later. One of them was cremated, while the other was buried by his family in a closed-casket ceremony shortly after. The names of those brave miners were Emitt Clydesdale and Johnathan "Johnny" Embers. The Clydesdale family had long relocated from Sky Haven, and details of their whereabouts were lost in history. But the descendants of Johnny Embers, who was buried in the Sky Haven cemetery, still lived in the town to the present day.

In fact, these descendants were the infamous Embers boys, known all over town as the kind of scum you ought never to run into. Having their hands in everything from methamphetamine production and distribution to armed robbery and alleged murder, these boys were the worst of the worst. Two of the Embers boys, Jethro and Reggie, had active attempted-rape and home-invasion cases against them in Lackawanna County; and the oldest, Deek Embers, was a wanted suspect in two homicides in Upstate New York.

Deek was the brains of the operation as well as a bona fide emotionless sociopath who viewed human life to be as expendable as flies on a windshield. He was a tall, good-looking blond-haired man with no facial hair and arms like Colossus from *Uncanny X-men*. His fists were nearly the size of a slightly smaller-than-average human head. He was instantly liked by women who didn't know him, and he instilled fear in most men everywhere he went.

Reggie and Jethro, on the other hand, were shorter than Deek, thin, and almost always dirty-looking, with greasy chin-length hair. Since they were identical twins, they attempted to differentiate from each other by doing subtle things like alternating days when they wore baseball caps as well as Jethro having a big stupid-looking mustache that covered up most of his mouth, which was actually a good thing since his teeth looked like he had been eating dirt sandwiches since about the age of three.

Suffice it to say, everyone in Sky Haven knew what the Embers boys were capable of, and all the townsfolk were afraid of them. Everyone in town also knew to stay off the Embers property, which consisted of the Embers "mansion" and its fifty acres of land. The reason for placing the word *mansion* in quotation marks is that, yes, it was a house built to the dimensions of a mansion. Right size, right design, but *wrong* everything else. Imagine if you will how a mansion would look if the *Texas Chainsaw Massacre* family lived in it. *That* was the Embers mansion. It was massive but dirty—no, *filthy*—dilapidated, and infested with the desires of depraved men with no conscience. Also, the decrepit centuries-old building, with its deteriorating rooms and moldy corridors, smelled like dog feces, meth, cigarette smoke, and liquor and was an unnerving eye-sore even from a distance.

And speaking of meth, not twenty-five feet from this architectural marvel lay the ol' Embers meth lab, a rickety shack where Jethro and Reggie spent most of their time (when not committing atrocities against humanity). *This* is the main reason townsfolk knew to stay clear of the Embers property.

Everyone in Sky Haven knew what went on there, including Sheriff Charles Bouchard, aka Charlie Bumper, of the four-man-deep Sky Haven PD; but because the Embers boys were such savages, nobody dared bust up their meth lab, not even the sheriff, who was actually a good man. Apart from Charlie and Bumper, some townsfolk referred to the sheriff as Tommy (behind his back) because he looked a little like an older Tommy Lee Jones, and his demeanor was that of TLJ in every single movie where he played a law enforcement official. This was not intentional. The elderly sheriff just happened to be a no-nonsense type of guy who was also smart and to the point. And he knew that unless he managed to arrest all three Embers boys at once, he would be putting his own family members' lives in danger by risking retaliation at the hands of any Embers man who was not picked up in a raid on the meth lab. Not only that, but even *if* Sheriff Bouchard managed to arrest all three Embers boys at once, they had an uncle in Pittsburgh named Elmer Embers who was arguably even worse than Deek. And Elmer was not alone. He had a cult following in Pittsburgh of a small army of methheads who would kill on command without a second thought. In other words, the Embers boys were "connected" and virtually untouchable by local law enforcement, and Sheriff Bouchard knew that.

But let's not get ahead of ourselves, and just focus on one story at a time. So Black Rock Mine had been closed since the early 1950s and sealed off by the Meta Division of the FBI under the guise of being too unstable to be properly excavated. Furthermore, the FBI drafted a contract in the mid- to late-1970s to place direct monitoring on the closed mine and, if it was disturbed, dispatch Meta Division agents to

Sky Haven immediately. This contract was drafted after a few troublesome teens discovered a back way into the sealed mine in 1975 and almost made it in before being caught by Sheriff Bouchard's father, who spotted their dirt bikes outside the hidden entrance.

Now you might ask yourself, "If the FBI was monitoring the Sky Haven mine already, why wouldn't they just monitor and build a case against the Embers boys as well?" Well, there are two particular reasons for that: (1) the Meta Division of the FBI did not deal with conspiracies of the distribution of narcotics or other "run of the mill" criminal activity; it strictly dealt with matters of the occult, otherworldly, or metaphysical and the beyond, and (2) the last thing the agency wanted to do was draw attention to the town because of the sensitive subject matter in the mine; therefore, sending federal agents to the tiny town just to raid the Embers was out of the question. It could draw too much national attention to Sky Haven, putting the spotlight on its creepy legends of "haunted" coal mines. This, along with Elmer Embers's connections in Pittsburgh, pretty much gave the Embers boys freedom to operate with local and federal impunity.

So yeah, Sky Haven had it all: murderous drug dealers, meth labs, federal conspiracies, mysterious mines containing who knows what, FBI monitoring said mines, and a fallen Hollywood star as well as a reformed criminal whose shady connections were arguably more sinister than those of the Embers boys. Fun, right?

CHAPTER 6

Anthony and Morgan

Now then, I'm not particularly fond of wasting my time or yapping aimlessly (that's not entirely true), so you might have guessed that there had to have been a reason I gave you A. J.'s and Morgan's backstories, right? Of course, you've guessed it! They were going to meet. But remember, despite having accidently killed someone with her car, Morgan still blamed everyone else for her problems and had retained the stuck-up attitude and demeanor of a snobby *B* word.

A. J., on the other hand, was a completely changed man after spending ten years in prison, listening to Pitts Montero's testimony, becoming a Christian, and leaving the life of crime behind.

At this point in our story—well, *my* story since you're doing nothing but reading it and occasion-ally chomping on a snack—it was 2015, and both A. J. and Morgan had lived in Sky Haven for a year. Morgan had not ventured out of her house much out of fear of being recognized and hounded, but on occasion, she did manage to put on a wig and dark sunglasses and head over to Sky Haven's shopping center to pick up necessities. And by necessities, I mean mostly cold cuts and Smirnoff vodka.

Having been stripped of all her achievements and status, Morgan had sunken into the bottle even further, living off residual checks, cold-cuts sandwiches, ramen, and liquor. She only drank a Smirnoff brand vodka because, when she did so, it made her feel like she did not lose her Smirnoff endorsement for some reason. She also had enough money left over after her legal troubles to outright purchase a small house, and the residual checks from her three movies provided sufficient funding to pay her monthly bills and feed herself. And, as per the details of her court-ordered rehabilitation, she had to give a clean urine test once a month for one year and avoid getting arrested at all costs. The clean urine was no problem since she had stopped doing all drugs, but the only time Morgan didn't drink was when she went to see her probation officer in Sicklerville. Apart from that, she was almost always intoxicated. In fact, despite being afraid of being recognized, she did muster enough nerve (with vodka courage) a few times to wander into the local hangout known as The Caboose (a bar with the exterior of a short train caboose) and have a few drinks there while sulking in a dark corner and looking down on the locals in silence, disgusted by how far beneath her they were. She didn't interact much, but she did like listening to the stories the townsfolk told tourists—stories and legends about haunted coal mines. She certainly thought such legends would make a good movie. Or perhaps a good novel. 😌

On the other side of the spectrum, A. J. was greeted by the Marconi family with a care package immediately upon leaving prison, a "thanks for keeping your mouth shut for a decade" gift, no doubt. Or, as the dark-haired, sinister-looking gentleman who knocked on his motel door the very day he got out put it, "from yer friends in Philly. A li'l somethin' to help you get back on yer feet."

A. J. never saw the dark-haired gentleman again but had no trouble finding the $250,000 in the envelope he was handed. He also never saw that same motel room again as he used the money to buy a house on two acres of land in Sky Haven as well as a used pickup truck, and then he used whatever money was left over to open a general store in town, making sure he had steady legal income from then on out. It wasn't glamorous, but things were good for A. J. They were quiet and serene.

That was until the day when a gorgeous stuck-up blonde who smelled like Smirnoff vodka walked into his general store.

The tiny bell hanging from the front door handle jingled to signal that someone had entered the store, and Morgan instantly filled the entire front room with the scent of clear liquor. Anthony immediately recognized Cordelia Rose from an exposé done by *60 Minutes*, which he watched with Pitts Montero and other inmates in the prison rec room about six months before his release. He politely greeted her but did not let on that he knew who she was. Morgan wasn't even gracious enough to respond to the greeting before starting to look around at the items for sale.

A. J. pretended to go about his business of stocking shelves with merchandise, but he couldn't take his eyes off the beautiful green-eyed blonde. He was a great judge of character and could tell that she was trouble, but he could not help feeling waves of warmth all over his body as his heart rate sped up.

She was oblivious to what was happening to him and continued to browse the store while touching all the merchandise and sporadically rolling her eyes, unimpressed with it all. A. J. saw her behavior and quickly deducted that she was a snob. "I hate snobby women," he told himself. "But this one...I dunno, though. She has *got* to be the most beautiful woman I have ever seen in my life. No exaggeration. There may not be a woman on this planet prettier than this stuck-up, drunken blonde."

His thoughts were interrupted by the sound of glass breaking. Morgan had picked up a glass dolphin with blue liquid inside it, and it slipped out of her hand, shattering on the floor.

"Oh crap!" she exclaimed. "Sorry about that." The apology sounded nonchalant and insincere.

"It's okay, don't worry about it," responded A. J.

Morgan was visibly not worried as she quickly moved on to picking up another item that she ended up not being very impressed with.

Her cell phone rang, and she rushed out of the store and picked it up. A. J. came closer to the front door to see if Morgan was leaving and ended up hearing the conversation she was having on the phone as she stood in front of the store.

Morgan: Heeey, Gabby! What up, girl?... No, I'm not busy!... I know, I miss you too, doll... Tell Marcel I said hey... I know, right? Haha!... Yea, I hear that!... I wish I was at Avalon, partying with you guys right now! Ugggh!" [There was a longer pause as Gabby managed to string together a few sentences before Morgan interrupted her again.] No, not at all. I've been here for a little over a year, and there are, like, no hot guys in this town *at all*!... Well, I just walked into this general store a few minutes ago, and the owner has a...Depp slash Momoa thing going on. And Mama like, Mama like, but he's probably some country bumpkin who's lived here all his life and whose parents lived here all their lives, and their parents' parents etceteraaa, HAHA! Girl, you know I like bad boys. What am I even gonna do with a guy like him?... What?... Yea, I'm sure you *would*, you tramp! Hahahaha! Okay, boo, call me later! Love you! Tootles!

A. J. ran back behind the counter before Morgan walked back into the store and acted as if he did not just eavesdrop on her conversation, but in his haste, he stepped in the blue liquid that was in the glass dolphin Morgan broke and left footprints from the door to the counter. As Morgan entered the store again, she saw the footprints and realized that the "country bumpkin" probably heard her conversation. Slightly embarrassed, she tried to make small talk. She pointed to her phone.

Morgan: My girlfriend from Hollyw—err, Montana.

Morgan let out uneasy laughter.

A. J.: Right. How *is* Montana this time of year?
Morgan: How the hell should I know?

A. J. thought, *She is so annoying.*

Morgan (with a condescending tone): Anyway, cute little store you have here. Do you sell cigarettes?
A. J.: I'm sorry, but we don't.
Morgan: Ugh! Fine. See ya!

Morgan turned to leave.

A. J.: Wait!
Morgan: Yeah?
A. J.: What's your name?
Morgan: Morgan.
A. J.: Nice to meet you. I'm Anthony, but my friends call me A. J.
Morgan: Well, nice to meet you…*Anthony* [not A. J.]. Bye!

Morgan started walking toward the door.

Anthony: Wait!
Morgan: What?
Anthony: How about I take you out do dinner some time, blondie?

Morgan paused and smiled, visibly flattered. She thought about it for a good four or five seconds, appreciating Anthony's confidence, while tapping on her teeth with her fingernail and making an uncertain *ummm* sound.

Morgan: No, I don't think so.

Morgan turned around and walked out the front door.

Anthony, through the store window, watched her walk to her car and smirked because Morgan couldn't help but turn her head to look back at him and wink with her right eye before she got in her car and sped off in search of cigarettes.

CHAPTER 7

The Embers Boys

Let's be clear. Anthony was fully aware of who Morgan was and what she had done, but at the instant their eyes met, he could tell that there was something really good in her heart even if *everything* else about her attitude and behavior said otherwise.

It is often said that the eyes are the windows to the soul, and on looking into her eyes, he saw something kind and good buried deep in the recesses of Morgan's soul—something that she had not yet managed to suffocate or drown with alcohol, something that she had brought with her from Texas and did not manage to destroy yet. It was the same quality that Morgan's grandmother knew existed.

During Anthony's time with the Marconi crime family, his ability to read people, more specifically their eyes, had proven to be a very valuable skill, one that even saved his life once or twice, and because of this, A. J. learned to trust and rely on this instinct. Not only was Morgan by far the most beautiful girl he had ever seen (and this guy had seen a lot of girls), but her eyes gave away a kindness and depth that someone without Anthony's ability to read people would have never sensed. Furthermore, A. J. had never experienced love at first sight before because he just wasn't that type of guy. But the second he looked into Morgan's eyes, that statistic changed; and in the next few days, he would not be able to stop thinking about her. I believe the term is *walking into walls*, and if it's not, then it should be because that was what Anthony was doing. He was unable to focus on anything other than replaying their encounter in his mind while the words "Mama like, Mama like" kept echoing in his head. No matter how hard he tried, he just couldn't get her out of his thoughts. And saving her life two days later certainly did not help matters.

That's right. You read correctly. Anthony James Tricerra saved Morgan Carter's life forty-eight hours after formally meeting her. But how? Why? Where? Well, hooold your horses, li'l impatient dawgie. We will get to that soon enough, but *first*, let me throw a bunch of filler at you and pointless descriptions of things you don't care about. Just kidding. Here's how it went down, fam.

As I've mentioned before, Morgan found herself with enough courage once in a while to visit The Caboose and set up shop at a table in the darkest corner of the room. She didn't like talking to the townsfolk, but she loved hearing about the haunted-mine legend. So she would drink her vodka on ice, smoke her menthol cigarettes, and just listen to the drunken old men spin yarns of the supernatural. And theories about the mine were as many as the grains of sand on a beach. Monsters, goblins, ghosts, aliens, and even the Grim Reaper himself were talked about in these extraordinary tales of grandeur. And silly, intoxicated Morgan ate them all up quietly. That was until someone in the bar would eventually notice she was there and try talking to her, which freaked her out since she didn't want to be recognized, so she would immediately walk out. This phenomenon happened more than once, and a few of the regulars noticed, prompting them to nickname her "the gorgeous retard [spits in spittoon]." But I digress.

Two days after meeting Anthony, Morgan found herself in the bar during happy hour again, but this day was different.

Deek Embers was there too, and one thing about sociopaths is that oftentimes they are incredibly smart and cunning, and they know exactly how to manipulate situations and people to get what they want. Deek was no different. Noticing Morgan's wide-eyed interest in the mine legend, and being the good-looking, charming, and calculated psychopath he was, he managed to disarm her enough to sit at her table and engage her by telling her that his great granddaddy Johnny Embers was the first man to ever see the anomaly in the mine with his own eyes and was even able to "best the beast."

Naturally, Morgan fell right for it.

Deek: Not only did he slay that foul creature with
dynamite, but... And here is the biggest secret
this town has ever hosted [there was a long

pause as Deek faked being worried]. I dunno if I can trust you with this, darlin'…

A single tear formed on the inside of Deek's right eye. (He was almost as good of a thespian as Morgan.)

Morgan: I will *never* say a word to anyone!
Deek (after a pause): Well, okay. A rumor has been passed down through the Embers family that [Deek gave an even longer pause] Great grandaddy John didn't die after escaping the mine. They faked his death. And to this day, my uncle Elmer says that if we were to dig up that coffin, John Embers's body would not be in there.
Morgan (gasping): Whattt?
Deek: Yeah. I've never told this to anybody outside the Embers family. Please, darlin', don't make me regret it.
Morgan: You have my word.
Deek: I've always wondered if it was true. Heck, I…

Deek gave another long, tearful pause.

Morgan: What?
Deek: Nothin', nothin'…
Morgan: No, what? You can tell me!
Deek: Well, it's just that… Oh, I shouldn't be telling you this.
Morgan: No, really, it's okay.

The bartender, noticing the cat-and-mouse game that Deek was playing and knowing what kind of dangerous animal he was, tried to interrupt out of concern for Morgan.

Bartender: Hey, Deek, can I get you another lager?

Deek Embers never uttered a single word to the bartender but instead fixed his eyes on him with the coldest, most piercing and sinister look any man had ever seen. Every fiber in the bartender's body *knew* it was in grave danger. He also knew without Deek ever having to say it that if he uttered another word to him or Morgan, the oldest Embers brother would gut him like a pig in the middle of the night in his own bed, next to his sleeping wife. He walked away from their table.

Morgan didn't catch the psychotic exchange because not only was she intoxicated already (at four twenty-three in the afternoon), but she was also too busy downing her frosty vodka beverage.

Deek: Like I was sayin', darlin', I've always wanted to see for myself but never had the courage to.

Morgan was really feeling the effects of the last drink she dumped down her gullet.

Morgan: What do you mean? Like, you wanna, like, you know, dig up a dead guy?

Morgan hiccupped.

Deek: Well, my great granddaddy's coffin was never buried. It is in a mausoleum in the cemetery here in town. If somebody wanted to see if his body is in there, all they would have to do is break through the stone wall on the inside of the mausoleum. I just never had the courage to do it on my own.

Deek made puppy-dog eyes at the floor.

Morgan: Well, what if there was someone, you know [she hiccupped again] to, like, help you?
Deek: Who? Who would want to do such a morbid thing? Even *if* it would settle an almost-century-old question for my poor family...

The bartender looked over at them again but didn't say a word because Deek's eyes snarled at him in silence.

Morgan (her words slurred): Well, look... If it will, like, help your family or whatever, I'll help you.

Deek: You would? Oh, bless your heart. I'm so glad I trusted you with this. C'mon, let's go. The cemetery is only a few minutes from here!
Morgan (agreeing without giving much thought to what she was agreeing to): Okay.

They both got up and headed for the door of The Caboose. As Deek passed by the bartender, the demon living behind Deek's eyes smiled at the barkeep.

CHAPTER 8

Disaster in the Cemetery

Morgan had no idea at this point, but her life was in terrible danger. Both Jethro and Reggie were standing outside The Caboose, smoking cigarettes, when Deek, their older brother by three years, walked past them with one of the most beautiful blonde women anybody had ever seen. The two twenty-eight-year-old sexual deviants froze in their tracks and threw away their cigarettes while mentally drooling at the possibilities presented by their depraved brains.

"It's not even my birthday," mumbled Reggie as he and his twin brother, Jethro, followed Deek toward his pickup truck.

Morgan and Deek got in the cab, and Reggie and Jethro hopped into the bed of the truck, smirking at each other. Morgan was completely oblivious to the danger as she lit a menthol cigarette and put the window down. The ugly doo-doo-brown Ford Ranger pulled out of the parking space and headed toward the cemetery.

But another truck followed right behind it. In *this* truck was Anthony Tricerra, who just happened to be sitting directly behind Morgan and Deek's table in the bar, where he heard the *entire* conversation and was now following the Embers brothers to the cemetery. As he passed by the front of The Caboose, A. J.'s and the bartender's eyes met through the front window. The bartender was holding a phone receiver to his ear, and he seemed very concerned as he spoke.

Fifteen minutes later, Morgan, Deek, and the other two Embers hyenas were walking through the Sky Haven cemetery. Morgan finally noticed the presence of the twins and asked why they were there.

Deek: Oh, they're just here to help us pull out the coffin. It's very, very heavy. Mahogany coffins were built very differently in the 1950s than the ones built today.
Morgan: Right?

Morgan took a mini bottle of Smirnoff from her purse, opened it, and drained it into her mouth in one shot.

One minute behind them was Anthony, who pulled up in his truck next to the massive Sky Haven cemetery. He opened the glove box and took out a .357 revolver that had its serial number scratched off as well as a ski mask that only had eye holes but no mouth hole.

Now, why would a former criminal and currently reformed Christian man be driving around with an illegal gun and a ski mask? Well, the gun was in the same Marconi care-package envelope that contained the $250,000, and A. J. kept it just in case, knowing that he could not legally own a firearm since he was a convicted felon. As for the ski mask, it was the same ski mask that Vinny DeRossi wore during the bank robbery in 2004. It never left the glove box because it belonged to his friend who died that day, and it was the only thing A. J. had to remember him by. It was also a stern reminder of the kind of heartache that a life of crime could bring. So cool your jets there, Mr./Mrs. Judgmental! 😉

Anyway, A. J. (who knew all about Deek's and his brothers' reputations) was aware of the fact that if *any* of the Embers brothers saw his face, not only would his life be over, but also, his parents, who lived in Philadelphia and were the only living family members he had, would be in danger too. If he was going to help Morgan, he had to remain anonymous.

Speaking of Morgan, she and the dangerous riffraff she was with made it to a large stone mausoleum with green mold growing on the outside, where the name Johnathan Harvey Embers was displayed in ornate but unkempt letters on the front. The mold could easily be attributed to the small frog pond that was located next to the mausoleum. A neat walkway made of cut tree stumps that stuck straight up out of the water and were one foot apart from each other went all the way across the frog pond to the other side. Small frogs were heard splashing from the tops of some of the stumps into the green algae-covered water as soon as Deek spoke.

Deek: Here it is!

Morgan: Wow!

Deek: Shall we go inside and find out if the legend of
the empty coffin is true?

Morgan splashed another mini Smirnoff into her
throat and followed Deek into the tomb after Reggie
broke the old rusty lock on the heavy metal door.
The inside smelled damp and moldy, as expected.
Cracks in the stone structure gave way to ants, centi-
pedes, and much creepier insects. The three Embers
brothers stood there, motionless, staring at Morgan,
who had her back to them now.

Morgan (looking at the back wall): Well, are we
gonna break it open?

Deek: No, we are not.

Morgan turned around to face Deek.

Morgan: What do you mean?

Deek: We are only going to break *you* open!

Jethro and Reggie started to laugh like the
grotesque hyenas they were. Pure fear penetrated
Morgan's bones all the way to the marrow like an icy
dagger. She was now instantly sober and realized she
had made a fatal mistake. She started trembling, and
her life flashed before her eyes.

Deek (to his brothers): Do what you're gonna do. I'll
dispose of the body.

Morgan (through tears of desperation): No! Wait, you can't!

Her words were drowned out by hyena laughter. The laughter got closer and closer to her. Closer. Closer still. She took a step back, but her trembling legs wouldn't hold her up, and she fell backward. Jethro's dirty hillbilly face and his gross mustache were suddenly three inches from her face. She tried to scream, but a filthy hand that smelled like meth smoke covered her mouth. She screamed anyway, but nobody except the people in the mausoleum could hear her when suddenly...

"STOP!"

Deek, Jethro, and Reggie all turned around to find a man wearing a ski mask pointing a .357 revolver at them.

Masked man: Give me one reason to end you, you worthless parasites!

Deek: Easy now. Do you know who we are?

Masked man: Shut your mouth! Everybody out! SLOWLY!

Morgan got up, and everyone exited the mausoleum.

Masked man (talking to Morgan): "*You*, go on. Get out of here!

She tried to run; but Reggie yelled, "No!" and grabbed her shirt, ripping it and causing her grand-mother's brooch, which she wore that day because it matched her blue form-fitting Dior shirt, to fall on the soft, damp ground. The masked man shot Reggie, hitting him in the left shoulder. He let out a hyena squeal, released Morgan, and grabbed his gun-shot wound while falling on his left side. Morgan ran like a bat out of hell toward the cemetery exit, leaving everyone in her dust.

Deek and Jethro bum-rushed the masked man after the initial shot, and he fired two more times at them as they ran toward him. A hot slug hit Jethro in the fleshy part of the thigh, and the other struck Deek's face, splitting his cheek wide open as it passed clean through his flesh and embedded itself in the bark of a nearby sycamore. Morgan heard the gun-shots, but she didn't stop running as pure adrenaline carried her to the cemetery gates.

Jethro went down, screaming in pain, from the .357 round lodged in his thigh, but Deek head-butted the masked man in the chest like a ram, send-ing him flying through the air. When he landed on his back, the revolver went twirling out of his hand into the nearby frog pond. Before the masked man knew what had happened, Deek was on top of him, dripping blood from his wounded cheek onto his ski mask while ferociously striking him in the face five times with his gigantic fists. His nose broke instantly, his lip split like snappy red licorice, and his left eye swelled up with blood on the spot. After the barrage of hits, he was still conscious but barely. Deek gave out a maniacal laugh and reached to pull his ski mask off when suddenly…

Sheriff Bouchard: Deacon Embers!

Deek froze.

Sheriff Bouchard: Do *not* make another move!
Deek (with blood squirting out of his split-open cheek): Whatever you say, Sheriff.

Deek put his hands up, seeing that the sheriff had the drop on him and that his Beretta 92FS, 9 mm pistol was pointing directly at him.

Sheriff Bouchard: Now slowly get up, take your brothers, and get the hell out of here! Now!

The Embers brothers propped one another up, forming some kind of limping, bleeding gimp trio, and hobbled away from the scene (presumably to the closest hospital) while hurling profanity-laced death threats to the masked man. When they were long out of sight, A. J. took off the mask, revealing his mangled, bloody face.

Sheriff Bouchard: Next time you're in The Caboose, make sure you thank that bartender. He saved your life today.

Sheriff Bouchard put his Beretta back into its holster.

A. J. laid his head back down on the soft moss.

A. J.: "Ugh. Thnks, Shrf!"

He couldn't pronounce the words with a split lip and blood in his mouth.

Sheriff Bouchard: Now you listen to me, kid. I read your jacket, and I know who you are. I was skeptical about you when you moved to this town, but what you did for that girl today took a lot of guts. And I don't know if you're still the same guy who does Marconi's dirty work, but I intend to find out. In the meantime, a word of advice. Don't go to the hospital in Sky Haven. The Embers boys will be looking for a guy with a busted face, and they have connections at Sky Haven Memorial Hospital. Stay clear of it. By the way, your nose looks broken even from here. [The sheriff took out and lit a Parliament cigarette.] I was a medic in the army, and I can reset your broken nose if you want. As for everything else...a lot of ice and prayers, kid. [He took a couple of drags of his cigarette.] By the way, don't show your face in The Caboose until your wounds heal either! You *don't* want the Embers brothers knowing who you are. You saved that girl's life today and shot all three of them. They won't soon forget it. Speaking of which, where's the gun?

A. J.: What gun?

He spat blood on the ground.
Sheriff Bouchard shook his head while rolling his eyes.

Sheriff Bouchard: All right. Come here, and I'll reset your schnoz, kid.

A. J. sat up and let the sheriff snap his broken nose back into place. A quick but very painful crack, and he could breathe again. The sheriff headed back to his vehicle, leaving A. J. to dust his clothes off and try to wipe some of Deek's blood out of his hair, when suddenly A. J. spotted a blue sapphire shinning from a gold flower on the ground.

Anthony: Morgan's brooch.

Anthony picked it up and put it in his pocket.

CHAPTER 9

The Aftermath

Morgan had escaped physically unscathed thanks to the masked man, whose identity she did not know. She also never witnessed the extent of his injuries at the hands of Deek Embers. In fact, for all she knew, he was not injured at all because she heard three shots ring out from the cemetery as she frantically ran to safety. In her mind, the three Embers monsters were probably dead, and there was a mystery man to thank for saving her life. But who was he? And why was he there? Would she ever see him again to thank him?

Morgan spent the rest of that day in the solitude of her home, with the curtains drawn. She took a hot shower, which made her feel a little bit better, but then ended up drinking herself stupid to numb the lingering shock of what had happened, especially once she realized that her grandmother's brooch was gone. She would have gone back to look for it, but considering she ran all the way home from the cemetery, it could have fallen anywhere. Also, she was terrified to go back and look for it, so she accepted it as gone forever. The consolation of being alive and unharmed was only a temporary distraction from the broken heart of losing the brooch, as the thought came in and out of her mind.

Morgan (to herself): Five generations of Rose women managed to keep that brooch safe, and I couldn't even keep it for one decade. (Through tears:) I'm so sorry, Grandma!

She cried for a while, and at one point, she turned on the TV in an attempt to escape from her thoughts. Unfortunately, she channel surfed onto a program titled "Where Are They Now: Cordelia Rose."

After introducing her full vodka glass to the television's flat screen with a loud crash, she then broke out into hysterical tears and continued crying until she fell asleep.

*****

Elsewhere in Sky Haven, A. J. was icing his entire face and chest to diminish the injuries he suffered at the hands of Deek Embers, who not only broke his nose, split his lip, and fattened his eye real good but had also left a skull-sized purple mark over his sternum area. He, too, stayed indoors the rest of that day, but he struggled to remain there after twelve hours passed. He found himself to be restless and unable to stop thinking about Morgan. Not knowing how else to get a hold of her, he decided to go to The Caboose, risking being discovered by the Embers brothers as the culprit who shot them, in hopes of running into Morgan there. And sure enough, he was right.

*****

After waking up the next morning and seeing her multicolored cracked TV screen, Morgan murmured, "To hell with this," grabbed her Armani purse, and made her way to The Caboose, where her favorite back-corner table was calling her name. On arriving there, uncertain of the fates of the Embers brothers, she looked around to see if Deek or his hyenas were inside the establishment, but they were not. She started heading toward the back corner table; but for some reason, she stopped in her tracks, pivoted, and headed toward the bar instead, where she took a seat next to an old man with a trucker hat and a long gray beard, drinking a Miller Lite.

The bartender, who was wiping a beer glass with a manila-colored dishcloth, was happy to see her unharmed, so he smiled and asked, "Smirnoff on the rocks?" to which Morgan replied, "No, gimme a beer! And give him [she pointed to the old man with the gray beard] another one too!"

"Much obliged," said the old man, and he raised his glass. There was nobody else in the bar besides Morgan and the gray-bearded fella (since it was 11:00 AM); and the two of them and the bartender sat in silence, watching the news on the TV for a while, until the front door of The Caboose swung open and

a badly injured Depp slash Momoa-looking gentleman came through the door, smiled, then made his
way over to the bar, grabbing a seat next to the pret-
tiest blonde in town.

A. J.: Gimme a beer, will ya, Randy?
Randy, the bartender: Sure thing, kid.

Randy was a good-hearted middle-aged man
with a dad bod who sported a brown mustache and
slicked-back brown hair. He was the type of person
who appreciated courage and honesty in today's fallen
world and despised the Embers boys with a passion.
Knowing their reputation, he was thinking about
just how lucky A. J. was to be alive as he poured a
cold Yuengling beer into a glass and put it on the bar
in front of him.

A. J.: Thanks, Randy!

A. J.'s and Randy's eyes locked, and Randy nodded with a serious look on his face, understanding
that Anthony was thanking him for the beer *and* for
calling the sheriff the day before. Randy had spoken
with Sheriff Bouchard shortly after the cemetery
incident and received his gratitude for saving A. J.'s
life as well.

Morgan (addressing A. J. while turning toward him):
    Shouldn't you be at your store? And...*oh my*!
    What the hell happened to your face, townie?

What did you do, try and hit on your cousin, but she wasn't having it, and she literally hit on *you* instead? Hahahaha!

Morgan found her question quite amusing, and she laughed obnoxiously, completely unaware of just how inappropriate it was.

A. J. and the bartender looked at each other once more. A. J. smiled, while Randy shook his head with a half smile on his face. Anthony made up some story about being beaten and robbed on his way home from the store and then continued talking with Morgan while never letting on that he was the masked man who saved her life. A few times during their conversation, he gripped Morgan's gold brooch, which was in his pocket, but he could not bring himself to give it to her because in doing so, he would reveal himself as her rescuer. He did not want to rely on that to gain her favor. He wanted Morgan to like him for who he was, not for what he had done for her.

And it was working. They actually had great chemistry together, and the conversation never stopped or felt awkward. They spoke of their families, similar interests they both had, their outlooks on life, etc. A. J. was also famous back home (in Philadelphia) for his sense of humor, and he continuously made Morgan laugh during their conversation, even a little to his detriment, when at one point one of his witty zingers made her laugh so hard that she spat out her beer all over the front of his leather jacket.

"Oh no! I am so sorry!" exclaimed Morgan, who proceeded to wipe the beer off his jacket while laughing with embarrassment.

"Don't worry about it," said A. J., "but if you really want to make it up to me, how about saying yes to that dinner invitation?"

Morgan stopped wiping his jacket; stopped laughing; looked directly into his swollen, blood-filled eyes; and, with no hesitation and a serious look on her face, answered, "It's a date."

The rush of endorphins through Anthony's body made the room feel ten degrees hotter. His heart pounded like that of a race-car driver inside a car that is flipping over multiple times on the track. He wanted to shout with joy, but he played it cool and instead said, "All right! Drinks for everybody!" And since there were only four people inside The Caboose (including Randy, the bartender) that order would certainly not have broken the bank.

"Much obliged!" once again said the old man with the trucker hat and long gray beard, who was sitting at the bar, next to Morgan and A. J.

"You're welcome, sir." responded A. J., who was feeling extra generous and friendly after winning over Morgan (while looking like hamburger helper) with *just* his personality and sense of humor and *without* telling her that he was the masked man who had saved her life.

A. J.: What's your name, buddy?

The skinny old man downed the entire beer A. J. had bought him, then he put down the glass, stood up, and walked over to the front door. Before walking out, he replied, "The name's Elmer. Elmer Embers."

CHAPTER 10

Cat's Out of the Bag

The infamous Elmer Embers was only in Sky Haven because Deek had called him. He was there to assist with Deek's masked-vigilante problem (having been made aware of it the night before), and even though he hadn't been in town for twenty-four hours yet, he already knew who the vigilante might be. Elmer seeing A. J. Tricerra and Morgan Carter in The Caboose bar and recognizing her from the movie *To Hell and Back* as well as the fact that every single one of A. J.'s injuries could very well correspond with Deek's details about their encounter was exceptionally bad for Morgan and Anthony. Elmer was about 90 percent sure that Anthony was the culprit, but he wanted to be 100 percent sure before putting out a "hit" on him and his entire family. This was because with one phone call, Elmer could unleash a small army of methheads on the Tricerra family. There was no doubt that soon the other three Embers boys would know about Anthony too, as told by their uncle. They would certainly know who Elmer was describing because there weren't a ton of long-haired, bearded, Johnny Depp– or Jason Momoa–looking gentlemen in Sky Haven.

Anthony's life, store, and home would be in danger as well as his folks in Philly if and when Elmer made the call to Pittsburgh. A one-hour flight time and a three-hour drive would ensure the small methhead army would reach Sky Haven quickly, so once that call was made, time for defensive preparations would be very limited. This put Anthony in a race against time from the moment Elmer Embers left The Caboose.

Immediately upon hearing the name Elmer Embers, Morgan's face sunk, and she got up and excused herself to go to the ladies' room. Visibly shaken, she splashed water on her face and tried to control her trembling.

Anthony's heart was racing as well while he spoke with the bartender.

Randy: You gotta get outa town, kid! Now!
Anthony: If I leave, they will go after Morgan and my
　　　family. I can't do that.

　　Randy uttered an expletive.
　　Morgan walked out of the bathroom while trying to keep it together. She went back to the bar, where she then excused herself by pretending she had just received an urgent text and started walking toward the door. Feeling like the walls were closing in on her, she simply had to get out of there.

Anthony: What's your cell number, Morgan?
Morgan: 555-057-0507.

She walked out the door without much resistance from Anthony, who was trying to figure out his next move as well. After a couple of minutes of focusing *only* on the seriousness of the matter and how to fix it all, Anthony finally spoke, asking Randy a question.

Anthony: Randy, do you know where Morgan lives?

Randy: I think it's the old red brick house on Towanda Street, across from the baseball field. I drove by once, and Hollywood was getting her mail from the mailbox in her underwear, so it's kind of stuck in my memory…

Anthony: Okay, look, I gotta go. If Morgan comes back in here, don't tell her… Wait, you know who she is?

Randy: Of course, kid. I'm not an idiot, and I do have a TV, you know!

Anthony: Fair enough. If she comes in here, don't tell her I'm the guy from the cemetery, okay? I'll tell her eventually, but I wanna do it on my own time line, not anyone else's, okay, Randy?

Randy: You got it, kid.

Anthony ran out the front door of The Caboose. He looked up and down the street to make sure nobody was watching who might tail him before he got in his car. He took out his cell phone, and after a few minutes of hesitation, he decided the only option was to strike first. So he pulled up the only name he could think of in that situation: Paul Marconi.

CHAPTER 11

The Crooked Cavalry

After explaining the situation to Mr. Marconi, Anthony reached the conclusion of his phone call.

Anthony: You know I hate to ask for help, Mr. Marconi, but it's an emergency.
Marconi: Don't apologize, kid. It'll be my pleasure to help you out.
Anthony: Thanks, I'll be in touch.
Marconi: All right, kid. Talk soon.

After ending the phone call, Anthony started his truck and drove right over to Morgan's house on Towanda Street while trying to reach her on the phone with no success. He hustled up the steps of her porch and rang the doorbell, which, to his surprise, played the Mexican tune "La Cucaracha."

Morgan opened the door and was surprised to see Anthony standing there. Her cat was running around the living room very quickly for some reason.

Morgan: Heyyy…wha-what are you doing here? And how did you…

Anthony: The bartender told me where you live. Listen, there's… Really, though? "La Cucaracha"?

Morgan: I know. It was like that when I moved in, and I was gonna change it. But it makes my cat crazy when it goes off, and she runs around the house really fast, which is hilarious. Plus, I kinda like—

Anthony: Randy told me about your run-in with the Embers boys. He said he called the sheriff on them yesterday, and then somebody shot all three of them in the cemetery. But they're still alive, Morgan! Do you have *any* idea how dangerous they are?

Morgan's jaw dropped.

Anthony (speaking fast): And you don't know the half of it. Listen, you're in serious danger, Morgan! Get whatever stuff you can and come with me right now!

Morgan formed a questioning look on her face.

Anthony (speaking faster): Ugh! They are coming after you! And I'm not a country bumpkin. I've only lived in *Sky Haven* for a year. I'm an ex-Mafia associate from Philly, and I did ten years in prison for being an accessory to murder.

Morgan looked even more confused.

Anthony (speaking the fastest he could): I didn't kill anyone! My friend Vinny and I robbed a bank, and his gun accidently went off, killing the security guard, an old man named Clarence, who we both knew and liked. He was a nice old man from our neighborhood, and what happened was an accident. I did ten years in prison for being there that day, but I left the life of crime behind me and moved here to start over. And what I'm telling you about the Embers boys is completely true. Unless you get your stuff and come with me *right now*, you might be dead by tomorrow. This is not...

Morgan grabbed Anthony's (who was frantic by this point) hands and stopped him in mid-sentence. She looked him dead in the eyes, and with a serious and doubt-free tone, she said, "Okay."

Twenty minutes later, after seeing Randy about a shotgun, they were both on the way to a hotel, while Anthony kept looking in the rearview mirror to make sure they were not being followed. Morgan sat in the passenger seat, petting a fat calico cat named Pepp while she smoked a menthol cigarette.

Morgan: So what's the plan once we get to the hotel?
Anthony: All we have to do is just lay low for a few days and wait for a phone call.
Morgan: A phone call?

Anthony: Yes. I will explain everything to you later, I promise, but for now, I'm just gonna need you to trust me, blondie!

Morgan was a bit excited by the circumstances and, if she was being completely honest with herself, even a little turned on by the situational danger and Anthony's ability to deal with it all.

Morgan: Okaaay, geez!

Anthony took out his cell phone and dialed a number he knew by heart.

Anthony: Hey, Ma? Yea, it's me. Hey, listen. You remember little Ralphie Vagnozzi and Fat Donnie Oso? Yea, that's right, the kid who ate a whole shoelace before realizing it wasn't pasta. Well, listen, they're gonna come stay with you guys for a couple of days and keep an eye on things… Yes, that's right… No, nothing is wrong. They're just gonna be there for a couple days, that's all… Yes, he still eats pasta… No, Ma, I'm sure he won't mind if you make spaghetti and gravy for dinner… Yes, put them up in the guest room and stay away from the windows for a few days, okay? And tell Dad I said hello and that the Juventus defense looks real good this year. Chiellini and Buffon aren't letting anything through… Okay, okay, I'll call you in a couple of days. All right, love you, Ma. Bye!

Anthony hung up the phone.

Morgan: An entire shoelace?
Anthony: Yeah, the guy's dumber than centipede feces, but he's a good guy to know. Plus, his partner is the brains of the duo.
Morgan: I bet.

Morgan smiled, feeling important.
Anthony looked at Morgan twice, noticing her smile.

Anthony: Are you getting a kick out of this?
Morgan: I've always had a thing for bad boys, townie.

She looked him up and down like a lioness staring at a rack of lamb.

Anthony: (shaking his head): Unbelievable.

Anthony and Morgan checked into the Days Inn Hotel two towns over, under the fictitious names Mr. and Mrs. Bumpkin, and after settling in, they passed the time by getting to know each other better.
Anthony confessed that he knew who she really was and that he had known all along but that he didn't want to admit it to Morgan because he didn't

want her to think he only liked her because she was famous.

Morgan talked to him about the fateful night of her accident, how she thought about it every day, and how it was part of why she drank so much. She told him that the weight of the guilt was unbearable and that alcohol was the only way to lessen it. She explained that she didn't think she deserved for the guilt to ever go away but that sometimes the pain of killing that young woman was too intense, and drinking was the only thing that numbed it.

Anthony told Morgan stories from his time in prison and revealed to her how his Faith in Christ had changed him for the better. They each had instances where they teared up in front of the other, and they also had moments where they laughed uncontrollably. Morgan spat out Mountain Dew on the front of Anthony's shirt while laughing and he forgave her—again. They both let their guards down and shared intimate and personal matters with each other that not many other people were privy to. Anthony even shared his nerdy love for reading cowboy books, especially his favorite book—*Winnetou* by Karl May. He not only confessed to reading all three volumes several times but also to making extensive notes on them while reading. Morgan smiled at his prospective geekiness and then admitted that she loved the song "La Cucaracha" and was the culprit who purchased and installed it as her doorbell ring tone.

At no point during the entire time Morgan was with Anthony in the hotel room did she have or crave alcohol. In fact, she never even thought about it for a moment.

Morgan and Anthony were getting along so well that he decided to let their natural chemistry take its course and save telling her about his presence in the cemetery and the brooch for another time.

The next day, Anthony got a text message from an unknown number that said, "Pay phone, 555-839-1119." He left Morgan alone in the hotel room with the Mossberg pump-action 12-gauge that he had gotten from Randy, the bartender, and went to the pay phone on the corner of Twelfth and Monroe. He called the number in the text message, and a voice answered after one ring, "Have you seen the Sky Haven newspapers?" The dial tone came on.

After running back to the hotel room, Anthony took Morgan with him and drove to the Dunkin' Donuts on Mundy Street, right over the Sky Haven city limits, where he bought a copy of the *Sky Haven Gazette* from the kiosk next to the Dunkin'. There on the first page, in bold letters, an article said METH LAB EXPLOSION, KILLS FAMILY OF 3, 1 STILL MISSING.

CHAPTER 12

Where's Deacon Embers?

Back in Sky Haven, roughly seven hours earlier, a gruesome scene was unfolding on the Embers property.

The Sky Haven fire department had its hands full despite having every volunteer on deck while an ambulance, three police units, and the coroner's van were all on the property as well. A Sky News 10 helicopter from nearby Sicklerville was orbiting the blaze while reporting in real time.

Apparently, a massive explosion had completely decimated the meth lab and eaten roughly half of the Embers mansion, which was still in flames, and the Sky Haven fire department was diligently trying to extinguish it.

Anthony and Morgan had spent all their time talking and getting to know each other, so they had not turned on the television in their hotel room or seen this local breaking news.

Once the fire department subdued the flames, Sheriff Bumper and his deputies cleared the rest of the house and property, allowing the reporters to come close enough to photograph the wreckage without going inside the mansion. After a close inspection of what was left of the meth lab (which wasn't much) done by the Sky Haven Police Department and its forensic team, aka Dr. Alexander Spetzil (a forensic pathologist and local egghead), Sheriff Bouchard announced in a press release that based on the DNA remains found in the meth-lab wreck and tested by Dr. Spetzil first thing that morning, Sky Haven PD believed that Elmer, Jethro, and Reggie Embers were all decimated by the explosion, which was most likely caused by mixing chemicals incorrectly while high on crystal meth. Deek Embers (who often drank but never used crystal meth) was believed to be missing. The Sky Haven newspapers published the breaking story less than one hour after Sheriff Bumper's press release, putting a hold on all other front-page news leads. This also caused a special afternoon edition of the *Sky Haven Gazette* to be printed—because of the huge developing meth-lab story in the tiny town. That was the edition that Anthony and Morgan picked up and read at the kiosk next to Dunkin' Donuts.

Sheriff Bumper did not elaborate to the press beyond those statements, but he believed that Deek had escaped from a fire that was raging inside the meth lab only seconds before the massive explosion. Bouchard based this theory on blood DNA evidence found fifty feet from scene, which continued into the nearby woods and stopped about a quarter mile in.

If the sheriff's theory was correct, Deek might have feared bleeding out in the forest and then covered his injuries somehow, which would explain why the blood trail stopped suddenly. It was uncertain why he ran into the woods, but Sheriff Bumper suspected that he was either being chased, or he feared that someone was following him.

On returning to the hotel room, Anthony and Morgan would receive the same details they read in the newspaper again by watching replays of Sheriff Bumper's statements to the press on television from earlier that morning.

They both sat in silence, watching the local news while a hundred thoughts swam through their heads. Morgan's thought process went something like this: *Was it really an accident? Who is Anthony Tricerra, really? What have I gotten myself into?*

A. J.'s thought process, on the other hand, went more like this: *This is definitely Marconi's work, but his goons let Deek escape, and Morgan and I are still in danger. Elmer is dead, and Deek doesn't have the clout in Pittsburgh to summon the methheads, which means my family is safe. But where is Deacon Embers now? And when will he come out of hiding to make his move?*

Anthony was also feeling guilt and remorse over causing the deaths of the other three Embers boys, but he knew that if they had lived, innocent people would have died. And that included people who had nothing to do with him, Morgan, or his family.

During the year that he had lived in Sky Haven, he had heard all the stories about the Embers boys (including Elmer and his meth army) and all the people Jethro, Reggie, and Deek had assaulted and supposedly raped, murdered, and made disappear. Strangely enough, over the years, not a single body had ever been discovered that would tie the Embers to a homicide, with the exception of the two bodies in the Upstate New York case where Deek was a wanted suspect.

There was no question that the world was a better place without the Embers, but "Thou shalt not kill" was not a commandment that Anthony took lightly. His conscience was heavy, and his heart was in pain on the realization that he had allowed his fears to motivate him to reach out to Paul Marconi for help instead of God.

Furthermore, in doing so, he had botched the situation and most likely enraged Deek even further, who would undoubtedly now try and hunt Morgan and himself down like a depraved, wounded animal with nothing to lose. Because of this, Anthony and Morgan could not return to Sky Haven, not until Deek Embers turned up from whatever hole he was hiding in.

Morgan, who had no problem admitting that she had a thing for bad boys in the past, was now starting to understand the gravity of what that actually meant. She couldn't help the fact that she had feelings for Anthony, but now three people were dead. And despite the fact that all three of them were monsters, she was starting to understand why a bad boy might not be the best option for a serious relationship. At the same time, she was starting to really like Anthony (after getting to know him on a much more personal level) despite the fact that his face still looked like Stallone at the end of *Rocky 2*, which meant that it wasn't just a superficial attraction. There was definitely something very different and worth liking about this…mysterious and probably dangerous ex-criminal.

"At least he's reformed," she consoled herself and lit up a menthol cigarette.

Morgan: So…what do we do now?

Anthony: We wait a little longer. Deek has to surface sooner or later.

Morgan: And then?

Anthony: Don't ask questions you don't want to hear the answer to, blondie.

Morgan continued smoking her cigarette in silence while staring out the window.

The silence was interrupted by "La Cucaracha" as a cell phone ringtone. Morgan answered the call while trying to stop her cat from running really fast around the hotel room.

Morgan: Hey, Dad. Yes, I just saw it on the news, but how did you see it in Texas?… Wait… What? You're *where*? What are you doing in Sky Haven?… A surprise visit? [Morgan looked at Anthony, horrified.] Dad, I'm not home right now… No, I'm [she looked at Anthony, who made a horse-riding motion] riding a horse? [Anthony slapped his forehead.] Yea, I'm horse-back riding…because…I…do that. Are you at my house? Oh, you *were* at my house, and now you're at The Caboose? Okay, give me thirty minutes, and I'll meet you there… Okay, Dad, see you soon.

Anthony: You can't seriously be thinking about going back into Sky Haven right now!

Morgan: I don't much have a choice now, do I? And what was all that horse-riding stuff?

Anthony: Horse riding? I was trying to tell you to say you're at the carnival. There's a carnival happening in Eastside right now. It's two hours away from here, and your dad may have just said not to worry about it and then gone back home if he thought you were that far away.

Morgan: How would I deduce *carnival* from you riding a horse?

Anthony: They have a carousel there!

Morgan: Are you serious right now?

Anthony looked at the ground while scratching his head.

Anthony: Well, it's too dangerous to go back to Sky Haven right now. Deek Embers could be watching your house and waiting for you to return, for all we know.

Morgan: What choice do I have, Anthony?

Anthony was going to say something else, but he paused because the sound of his name rolling off Morgan's tongue made him feel warm and tingly inside. He smiled at her like an idiot.

Morgan: Focus*!*
Anthony: "Right! Look, what if you just don't go back to your house? Just meet your dad at The Caboose and then take him out to dinner somewhere, but don't go home.
Morgan: How am I going to tell my dad that he can't come to my house, *Anthony*?
Anthony: Okay, okay, look… I will come back with you, and when you get back to your house, I'll sit outside, in my truck, keeping an eye on the street. If I see anything out of the ordinary or anybody watching your house, I will handle it, blondie.

Morgan once again found herself to be a little turned on by the take-charge tone of "I will handle it."

Morgan: Okay…I guess that could work.
Anthony: Let's go, then!

The two immediately started packing, checked out, and headed back to Sky Haven. They stopped at Morgan's house first, and after quickly clearing the entire building and deeming it safe, Anthony allowed Morgan to go in to drop off her cat and belongings and make the house look presentable. They then quickly headed over to The Caboose. Before letting Morgan out of his truck to go into the bar, Anthony warned her, "Morgan, I just cleared your house no more than five minutes ago, but every minute you're in The Caboose is more time that Deek could show up at your place, rendering my sweep of it pointless. Get your dad *immediately* and head back home. *Do not* linger in there!"

Morgan: Linger? Okay, Legolas.

Anthony audibly exhaled.

Morgan: I'm just kidding, babe. I understand what's at stake. I will be quick in there. Don't worry.
Anthony (to himself after Morgan left): Did she just call me babe?
Morgan (to herself while speed walking toward The Caboose): Did I just call him babe?

Anthony waited in his truck for no more than two minutes before Morgan and her dad came out, got in her father's car, and went back to her house. Overall, no more than ten minutes had passed between the time they left her house and returned there with her father.

Arriving back at Morgan's, she and her dad went in the house, and Anthony did a full sweep of the street by driving up and down it, inspecting every car, and carefully looking into the neighbors' alleyways. Not finding anything out of the ordinary, A. J. parked a little ways down the street, in a spot where he had a good view of her house and could keep an eye on things. Within a few minutes, Morgan texted him, "We are ordering pizza and staying in for the night. My dad will be leaving in the morning."

"Ok, blondie," responded Anthony. "I'll be out here, keeping an eye on things."

"Ok, townie. (Winking face emoji.)"

Anthony physically smiled while sending a smile emoji back to Morgan through text.

A. J. sat in his car for a few hours without noticing anything suspicious, and as the sun finally set, he started thinking, *Maybe we're in the clear.*

He had very little idea of just how wrong he was.

CHAPTER 13

Meta Division, FBI

Still with me, dear reader? If you want to take this time to use the lavatory facilities, re-up on soda pop, or call your *abuelita* back, now is the time. But it *would* be best if you just sat your silly ass down and let me dive further into this story because this is where things take a *really* interesting turn.

I already told you that the FBI was monitoring Black Rock Mine in Sky Haven, but I didn't tell you how.

In 1976, when the contract to monitor the mine was drawn up, cameras were set up and hidden in the forest around the mine; but back then, surveillance equipment had limitations. The images captured by the cameras could only be broadcast within a short range, and an FBI utility van had to constantly be in Sky Haven to receive the images through a transmission receiver. So if you lived in Sky Haven in the mid-'70s, you were likely to see a strange van on your street, labeled Alberta's Cakes, Mookie's Cleaning Supplies, or Bobby's Butt Candy. Okay, I made that last one up. In fact, I made them *all* up, but you get the idea.

Well, as decades passed and technology improved, the primitive equipment was replaced with state-of-the-art technology like satellite imaging as well as something called digital trip wire.

Small electronic chips the size of ladybugs were placed in the forest, in strategic locations very close to and surrounding the mine, and they formed a laser-beam parameter that acted like an actual trip wire. When the laser beam was broken or interrupted by something, it would send a signal to a satellite orbiting the Earth; and that satellite would instantly zoom in on the area, sending images back to FBI headquarters, showing what or who tripped the laser.

If it was something worth pursuing, the Meta Division of the FBI would send agents to Sky Haven to investigate, and they would arrive within an hour on a direct personal flight from Washington, DC.

One such agent who was always on call was agent Frank Guardavaccaro and his junior partner, Frank O'Neil. Yes, it *is* funny that both their names were Frank, and the other agents would often make jokes at their expense—although never to Guardavaccaro's face. He was not known for his sense of humor or patience for silly games.

O'Neil, on the other hand, was constantly the butt of their jokes as he was a rookie who had only been on the force for two years. Despite being a sharp kid, having the status of a rookie all but guaranteed he would be constantly pranked by the other agents and made fun of for at least the first couple of years. After all, it was tradition.

Being assigned with the veteran Guardavaccaro was both a pro and a con. The benefit of having such a seasoned partner was that naturally, he could learn a lot: tactics, procedure, sharpening your instincts, etc. The downside was that Frank G. was a perfectionist and workaholic who expected perfection from himself as well his partner, which was sometimes more than the twenty-five-year-old O'Neil could provide. But Guardavaccaro liked Frank O., often describing him as a "good kid" (to himself). He never said it to O'Neil, though, who sometimes thought Frank G. didn't like him. Young Frank would work hard at trying to impress and gain the acceptance of his partner, but it just seemed like nothing was ever good enough for Guardavaccaro, who had no family and no personal life. The job was the only life Frank G. had.

O'Neil was a very ambitious kid, though. Top of his class at West Point, he was smart and tough and wanted to excel in the FBI, just like he had excelled at everything else he had put his mind to. He was determined to gain Guardavaccaro's respect and make a name for himself in the Meta Division of the Federal Bureau of Investigation.

He was five foot ten, about 160 pounds, and tanned, with short, dark hair, no facial hair, and chiseled Asian features—a good-looking, polite, and friendly kid who was much smarter than other FBI agents gave him credit for as a rookie. He was also a great shot with his Glock 17, gen. 5, 9 mm pistol and a digital-technology genius too, which was why FBI director Pasquale Siphos Ricketts paired him with Guardavaccaro, who was fifty-six years old, six foot two, and 212 pounds (all muscle), with salt-and-pepper short hair and a similarly colored beard. Guardavaccaro was also well trained in hand-to-hand combat and a weapons expert but terrible with digital technology and often frustrated by simple tasks like finding a photo in his cell phone's gallery.

Truth be told, they made a great team, but on first hearing that Siphos Ricketts paired him with a twenty-five-year-old kid, Guardavaccaro protested profusely for several days. But he finally accepted the outcome *only* after nicknaming O'Neil Potter because he "looks like Harry Potter" (which he didn't). Frank O. didn't mind the nickname because he was secretly a Harry Potter geek and even owned the Elder Wand, which he bought on eBay for $498.

The digital-trip-wire technology would often trigger the satellite to zoom in on nothing more than a deer or a fallen tree, but one day it was triggered twenty-three times in a matter of four minutes by animals that were fleeing from a large explosion in the area. This drew the attention of the FBI, who, on looking at satellite imaging from approximately 0.3 miles from the trip wire, discovered the inferno on the Embers property.

Furthermore, because of all the news reporters who were attracted by the meth-lab story, director Pasquale Siphos Ricketts immediately dispatched Frank G. and Frank O. to Sky Haven to investigate, contain the story to only the meth lab, and do damage control if Black Rock Mine entered the conversation in any way. They were only to return when interest in Sky Haven died down and the secret of the mine was again safe.

Within two hours (minimal time to pack for a few days' stay in Sky Haven), Frank G. and Frank O. had arrived in the small town and checked in at the flea-ridden Adelaide Motel as Mr. Frank Paulson and his son, Frank Jr., and were ready to investigate the current events.

Their first stop was going to be ground zero, aka the Embers property, to get an idea of what had actually happened there and how the details could be used to sensationalize the meth-lab story and distract from the mine. Little did they know they would find far more than they bargained for on the Embers property.

CHAPTER 14

A Sinister Discovery

It was a beautiful sunny afternoon in Sky Haven, Pennsylvania. While Morgan and Anthony were making their way back to town from the hotel to meet Morgan's father, Frank Guardavaccaro and Frank O'Neil were on their way to the Embers mansion.

With all the reporters having been cleared out after Sheriff Bumper's press conference and the area sealed off with police tape, Frank G. and Frank O. could go snoop around in peace, without reporters asking them who they were and why they were there.

On arriving at the Embers mansion, they saw that Sheriff Bouchard was still there, giving instructions to one of his young deputies who was to stay behind and keep people off the property for the time being.

Behind them was the picturesque image of half of an old mansion that was charred to perfection. A massive black crater in the ground that had burnt rubble all around it lay no more than twenty-five feet from the house.

A. TRICERATOPS

Frank G. and Frank O. exited their black Cadillac and made their way over to the sheriff and his deputy.

"Mornin'. Can I help you boys?" said the elderly sheriff.

Frank G.: Special Agent Guardavaccaro, FBI. [He showed his credentials.] This is Special Agent O'Neil.

Sheriff Bumper: Sheriff Bouchard. This is Deputy Harris. You boys get lost this mornin' on your way to DC?

Frank G.: We at the FBI take narcotics trafficking very seriously. We just want to look around and get an idea of the scope of this operation.

Sheriff Bumper: Be my guest. There's not much left of the meth lab, and we've already searched the house and found nothing but paraphernalia, booze, and dog @#%. But you boys can have a look if you want to. Careful on the second floor. The fire has really weakened the structure of the entire place. If you need anything, Harris here is your man, or you can call my office.

Frank G.: Thanks, Sheriff.

Sheriff Bumper: You bet.

The sheriff then got into his car and left, leaving Frank G. and Frank O. with Deputy Cameron Harris.

Deputy Harris was a pleasant-looking young man in his midtwenties, with an average body type and curly, short brown hair. His face was almost always clean-shaven, and the young deputy was well-known for respecting his elders and superiors.

Cameron Harris: If you gentlemen don't mind, I'm just gonna wait out here. The smell of smoke really upsets my sinuses.
Frank O.: No worries. We'll let you know if we need anything.
Deputy Harris: Sure thing.

Guardavaccaro and O'Neil made their way into the fried mansion since it was closer to them than the remains of the meth lab. They were both disgusted by the filth in the place and almost glad that the heavy scent of smoke was there to mask whatever else was lingering in the air.

Turning over a half-burnt table, kicking the charred remains of a couch, and poking the fireplace ash to see if anything had recently been burned in there apart from the blaze that engulfed the house, they were pretty much just going through the motions, knowing that it wasn't really necessary to do extensive detective work since their reason for being there was not to solve a crime.

"Has the Sky Haven PD been down to the base-ment yet?" shouted Guardavaccaro to Deputy Harris from the living room of the mansion, taking advan-tage of the fact that there was no longer a wall in front of it.

Harris: Yes, sir. We didn't find anything of particular
    interest. Just more filth.
Frank G.: What do you say, Potter? Want to see the
    basement?
Frank O.: With all my heart, Frank.
Guardavaccaro: Call me Mr. Guardavaccaro, kid.
O'Neil: Not a chance, Frank.

Guardavaccaro shook his head while mumbling something to himself that started with "In my day..."

They made their way to the basement, where, sure enough, there was even more filth than upstairs and tons of junk, trash, and rusty bicycle parts lay disassembled and strung all over the place. At one point, they must have provided hours of amusement for a tweaker or two who, fueled by crystal meth, must have thought they were going to restore the bicycles to their former glory. Clearly, such a day never came.

But on another note, the federal agents couldn't for the life of them figure out why there was so much dog feces down there. Did these lowlives have dogfights in the basement? Yes, that *had* to be the answer—keeping dogs down there to fight.

"What a sickening hellhole!" exclaimed Frank O.

Rusty chains hanging from the ceiling, old mason jars filled with brownish liquid, newspapers thrown all over the place, dirty old plastic dolls with their eyes gouged out, random rusty buckets and bags of sand and cement—what exactly was the meaning of this place?

On reaching the back wall of the basement, both agents froze in their tracks while staring at the wall and then looked at each other.

Guardavaccaro: See that?
O'Neil: Yup! Those marks on the floor, as if some-
    thing scraped the floor and then went into the
    wall. That's a fake wall, Frank. There's some-
    thing behind there.
Guardavaccaro: I'm impressed, kid! Gimme a hand.

The two federal agents started looking around for a lever or mechanism that would move the false wall at the back of the basement.

After a few minutes of poking around, Guardavaccaro noticed that one of the stones in the west basement wall was a darker color than the others, like it had been touched many times by hands covered in motor oil. Pushing the stone inward caused the false wall to open outward like a door, scraping the floor as it moved.

A lever sat on the inside the fake wall. On flipping it, the agents were treated to a domino effect of lights, which came on one at a time as they went further and further down what seemed like a never-ending corridor with only three doors on each side of it. All the lights were hanging from the corridor's ceiling, and neither the walls nor the ceiling were dry-walled. Just dirt and large stones seemed to hold everything together.

A room sat at the beginning of the corridor, before the six doors; and when looking inside it, the agents discovered a bunk bed, a table with a TV screen on it, several firearms, and a folder next to the TV.

Frank O.: What in the hell?
Frank G.: Let me have a look at that folder, kid.
Frank O.: Sure thing, Frank.

O'Neil handed the folder to Guardavaccaro; and on opening it, they were horrified to find Polaroid pictures of young women, each picture with a name written on the bottom. There had to be at least forty or fifty pictures in the folder.

Frank G. threw the folder back down on the table, and both federal agents drew their firearms from their holsters and headed back out the room, to the corridor.

"Stay sharp, kid!" exclaimed Frank G.

Trying the handle of the first door, Frank O. found it to be locked.

Guardavaccaro: I've got your back.

O'Neil kicked the door in without hesitation while Frank G. pointed his pistol at it. It swung open to reveal a filthy mattress covered in dried blood and rusty shackles attached to a radiator.

Kicking open the remaining doors in the corridor revealed the same setup of a mattress and shackles attached to a radiator in each room, but three of the rooms also had showers installed in them, with drains in the middle of the floor. There were only six doors in the corridor despite the fact that it looked like it went on forever. Since the ceiling was fairly low, O'Neil looked up and noticed two small dark marks in a large stone that was embedded in the ceiling, which resembled bullet impact marks.

O'Neil: What do you make of this, Frank? They were obviously kidnapping young women and torturing them. But where do you think this corridor goes?

Frank Guardavaccaro put his pistol back in its holster and sat on the floor of the corridor with his back against the stone wall. He took out a Marlboro Red cigarette while shaking his head, placed it into his mouth, lit it, took a huge drag, and exhaled all the smoke. And then, looking at O'Neil, he said with authority, "The mine, kid. The corridor goes to Black Rock Mine."

CHAPTER 15

Quality Time

At the same time that Special Agent Guardavaccaro and Special Agent O'Neil were heading to the Embers property to investigate matters, Anthony and Morgan were on their way back into Sky Haven from the hotel where they had stayed overnight. As Morgan's dad patiently waited to meet her at The Caboose bar, the couple (is it too early to call them that?) stopped at Morgan's house first to drop off her cat and belongings. Anthony was careful when entering Morgan's home, efficiently clearing every room in military/marine fashion, mindful of blind spots, and carefully opening closet doors and the doors to the upstairs rooms. Armed with Randy's 12-gauge pump, he cleared every room, including the basement; and only when it was deemed safe did he let Morgan come in.

Naturally, Morgan was digging the thorough sweep and sensed her heart beating faster than usual a couple of times while feeling warm all over as she watched Anthony take charge and put so much effort into making her house safe. But since time was of the essence, she could not focus on those feelings, and she quickly ran into the house to put her belongings away while doing her best to clean up the vodka bottles and hide the TV with the smashed screen. Once everything was set at her house, Morgan and Anthony left in a hurry to go and meet her father at The Caboose bar.

But as fate would have it, in their haste, they never saw the man in the ugly doo-doo-brown pickup truck, who watched them the entire time from around the corner.

Later that night

At approximately 9:00 PM, Anthony was still sitting in his truck in the dark, outside of Morgan's house, as Morgan and her father were enjoying a pizza inside. He knew they were having pizza because he saw a young pimply-faced kid come to the door and bring it. Upon receiving a $10 tip, the kid pumped his fist in the air as he walked back to his patchy 1979 AMC Pacer with a giant Amarilla Pizza sign on top. Anthony laughed to himself momentarily because the sign on top of the car was almost as big as the car itself. The kid pulled out of Morgan's driveway while blaring Ricky Martin's "Livin' La Vida Loca" and enthusiastically sang the refrain, only stopping briefly as he drove by Anthony's car, when he quickly turned down the volume. He nodded at A. J., trying to look cool, as if he hadn't been correctly singing every word of the popular song moments before.

Some thirty minutes went by, and not seeing anything out of the ordinary at the house, Anthony gave himself a good upper-body stretch, trying to fight off the boredom. He fell back into thinking about the magical twenty-four hours he had with Morgan at the hotel, wondering how that experience could have been so unforgettable when nothing physical even happened between the two of them. No kissing, no hugging, nothing. They even slept in two different beds, but somehow it was the best time he had ever had with a woman in his entire life. This daydreaming accounted for another thirty minutes or so, and seeing that the time on his car's radio said 10:05 PM, he got out of the vehicle and decided to give himself another stretch.

"Ohhhhh!" he exclaimed as his shoulder blades came close to touching and a small crack released the tension held there. He mumbled, "Na na na na na, livin' la vida loca. Push and turn and pull…" (He didn't know the words.) "Livin' la vida loca."

Giving up on singing the song, he decided to walk closer to the house just to stretch his legs a little. A closer look didn't reveal anything suspicious, so he made his way back to his truck and got back in. Turning on the radio, he settled on a political-talk channel and propped his face on his right hand while his elbow rested on the center console.

Inside Morgan's house, Joe Carter and his daughter had just finished an entire Yellow Pizza and were talking over a slice of cheesecake acquired from the same establishment as the pizza.

A. TRICERATOPS

Joe was a rather heavyset man with a receding hairline and kind eyes, which were magnified by his eyeglasses. Their thin metal frames hung on his face by his big ears and rested on the end of his nose. A well-groomed mustache and goatee formed a symmetrical rectangle around his mouth, framing his thin lips and nearly flawless teeth whenever he smiled. Not having seen Morgan in a good year and a half, he felt very good about doing a bit of catching up with his daughter.

Joe Carter: I noticed you dipped your pizza crust in blue cheese, Morgan. Is that the new thing now?

Morgan: "Oh, haha, yea, no. I learned it yesterday from a friend, while we were at the... horseback...riding.

Morgan rolled her eyes, realizing how stupid that sounded.

There was a confused look on Joe's face.

Morgan: They serve...pizza as you...wait...

Joe: Uh-huh.

Morgan: So anyway, Dad, how are things back home?

Joe: Your cousin Tammy ran away from home for four hours and then came back because her phone was out of minutes. Tell me more about this friend of yours that you went...horseback riding with."

Joe smiled while nudging Morgan with his elbow.

Morgan: Daaad!

Morgan blushed.

Joe: What? I have not seen you get red in the face like that when talking about someone since... Markus Van Bergmire.

Morgan: Whattt? Mark Bergmire, Dad? From third grade? Marky Big Bird?

Joe: Haha! Yea, well, you were in love with him, kiddo. You would write little poems about him and draw his name on all your notebooks in school.

Morgan: Ohhh emmm geee, Dad, I totally remember that! He had the coolest tree house in the whole neighborhood, but no girls were ever allowed in it. Erika Holiday and I threw devil's food cake at him and his friends for not letting us join their stupid tree-house club one summer.

Joe: I remember that. And big Bill Bundy came to the door because his overweight son, Roger, fell out of the tree house, trying to catch a slice of the cake. Now that I think about it, it was wrong of me to call him a greedy fatso for trying to catch that cake.

Morgan: Hahahahahahaha!
Joe: Hahahahahahaha!

They both finished laughing and exhaled. Joe looked at his daughter lovingly, and with a very serious tone, he said, "I love you, kiddo."

Morgan smiled a sad smile.

Morgan: I love you too, Dad.

He pet her on the head and immediately ruined the sweet moment with "Sooo who's this new boyfriend of yours? Tell me!"

Morgan: Daaad!

Morgan laughed, embarrassed.

Joe: Is he anybody I know?
Morgan: No, he's…

Morgan looked at the floor and allowed the feelings she had for Anthony to completely overtake her, causing her to smile uncontrollably.

Morgan: He's… [She looked at her dad.] He's [with a convincing, authoritative tone] *so great*, Dad!

Joe smiled understandingly.

Morgan: This has never happened to me before, but I think I'm in love with him.

Morgan looked at her dad with sparkly eyes caused by incoming tears.

Joe: Aw, Morgan. I'm happy for you, blondie.

Morgan broke into full-blown tears at hearing the word *blondie*. At that instant, hearing her dad use that word, the same word that Anthony called her, validated her feelings for A. J. in a strange little way; and even though her father had never met Anthony, hearing *blondie* made Morgan almost feel like her dad gave her his approval to be with him. All these thoughts and feelings flashed through Morgan in an instant and caused her to break down in tears.

Joe: It's okay, kiddo. What is his name?
Morgan: His name—

"His name is Anthony," said Deek Embers while limping out of Morgan's kitchen, where he'd been hiding, a bloody rag tied around his head and a .38 special snub-nosed revolver in his hand.

CHAPTER 16

Embers Mansion

Approximately twenty-four hours prior, four men standing in the grotesquely filthy kitchen of the Embers mansion, surrounded by thick cigarette smoke, were having a profanity-laced conversation.

Deek Embers: I can't believe that @#% store owner had the guts to save that stupid @#% and shoot me! Me, Deacon Embers! ME! [He pounded his fist on the table.] I want him, that Hollywood @#%, and their families *dead*! I WANT THEM ALL DEAD!

Deek threw a whisky bottle against the wall, shattering it and triggering several dogs to start barking in the basement.

Elmer Embers: Oh, you're real tough now, with nothing but a wall in front of your face! Where was this venom when that boy punked you and these two retards in front of that @#% in the cemetery?

Deek became visibly enraged and furiously floated across the floor into his uncle's face. Elmer didn't even flinch but instead tucked a snub-nosed revolver under Deek's chin to greet his quick arrival. Their noses were so close they almost touched.

"Eeeasy now, li'l girl. Did you forget your place?" muttered Elmer through his dirty clenched teeth as his right thumb cocked the hammer of the revolver with a swift click. He pierced Deek's skull with his beady, ferocious little eyes. The old man was much skinnier and shorter than Deek, but he had *zero* fear of his nephew.

Deek realized his mistake and tried to back off, but Elmer was not the kind of man who took challenges lightly. As Deek slowly backed away, Elmer walked with him, maintaining the same proximity they had when their noses almost touched. He asserted his dominance over his nephew by sticking his left thumb in the bandaged-up hole in Deek's cheek, courtesy of Anthony Tricerra.

"Uggghhh!" Deek let out a muffled cry but didn't dare lift a finger against his tiny uncle.

Mirroring a twisted version of a parent who was grabbing their child by the ear after the child broke the neighbor's window with a baseball, the old man, who had to reach up to Deacon because Deek towered over him, dug his thumb even deeper into the gunshot wound in his nephew's face.

"Aaargh!" Deek finally let out a painful scream as the blood seeped through the bandage on his cheek and stained Elmer's thumb.

His uncle finally let go and slapped Deek as hard as he could with his other hand, which had just been liberated of the revolver. The revolved now sat quietly in his waistband right above his scrawny buttocks.

Elmer (screaming): I left you idiots in charge up here, and this is what you give me? You do know that if methheads or any other kind of fiend smells weakness on you fairies, the whole Embers's name and business operation is in danger?
Deek: I know that, I never—
Elmer: Shut the @#% up, boy!

All three Embers brothers stood quietly, looking at the floor, because they were afraid of looking at one another or Elmer.

Elmer paced slowly and in silence around the smelly, dirty kitchen. Several times his steps had a crunchy tone to them as he inadvertently stepped on a dead cockroach, a tiny shard of crystal meth, and a smaller dead cockroach. He poured himself a shot of whisky into a dirty shot glass, pounded it, and decided to soften up his tone.

Elmer: I raised you boys after your daddy got locked up and sent to that mental institution, when your tramp mother left him to raise the three of you by himself. I taught you about life, the meth game, and how to handle business. I don't remember teaching you how to be fairies. Did I teach you to be li'l fairies?

The three Embers boys (in unison): No, sir!

Elmer: What?

The three Embers boys (louder): No, SIR!

Elmer: Well, all right, then.

Elmer downed another shot and stared at the wall for a few seconds quietly until a smile draped across his pale, White-trash face.

Elmer: Now here's how we're gonna handle this. I saw that @#% and his little Hollywood girlfriend no more than five, six hours ago in the bar. They are probably together at one of their houses, trying to figure out what to do *right now*. We go visit them tonight, snatch them both up, bring them here, and lock them up in the basement with the others. We'll torture and interrogate him first since he shot you boys, then kill him in front of her to terrify and demoralize her. In the morning, I'll call Cisco in Pittsburgh to round up the troops and dispatch them to wherever Anthony tells us his family lives during his tormenturous [he made up this word] interrogation. We get rid of his body in the mine after he squeals on his people, which they *always* do, and then we let Cisco 'n' them take care of the rest of his family.

The three Embers boys looked up with renewed hope in the future.

Elmer: That'll give you two perverts [he pointed to the twins] plenty of time to do whatever you want with that li'l girlfriend of his before we torture her too and find out where *her* family lives, then send Cisco there and have him film their deaths. And then we show her the footage when he comes back.

The Embers brothers' faces lit up with delight, and they looked at one another, smiling.

Elmer: We keep her locked up for a few more days so the reality of things really sets in, and then we... take her to the mine. [Elmer smiled.] Then we spread the word about it all over town through junkies and put fear in the townsfolk like we used to do in the old days.

The three brothers gasped, in awe of their uncle's diabolical "brilliance."

Elmer: And *that* is how you make an example of your enemies, boys!

Deek, Jethro, and Reggie burst out in cheers and enthusiastic yeahs, very excited about their uncle's plan. The old man grabbed three more dirty shot glasses from the sink, poured whisky in all four of them, and said, "But first we drink!"

More cheers erupted.

The four men standing around the kitchen table downed their shots of whiskey and slammed the shot glasses on the table.

Elmer: You know…I didn't hear a "Thank you, Uncle Elmer" from any of you boys yet. And considering that I just—

Elmer would have finished the rest of his sentence had most of his head not disintegrated into bloody mozzarella and splashed against the kitchen wall with a deafening *boom*. The three Embers boys screamed in unison.

"Don't yous @#% move!" a deep voice with a slight Italian accent commanded the three remaining Embers boys as Elmer's virtually headless body hit the floor hard.

In severe shock, the Embers brothers couldn't move if they wanted to.

From the darkness of the night, three well-armed, well-dressed men walked into the room through the back kitchen door, which no longer had a pane of glass in it.

All three of the well-dressed men had short dark hair, and man no. 1 (the first one to speak) only had hair on the sides of his large head as his receding hairline went almost all the way back to where his neck connected to the back of his skull. He easily weighed at least three hundred pounds, but his weight did not seem to be a hurdle in finding top-of-the-line Armani suits that fit him. Wearing black leather gloves and black leather Ambrogio dress shoes, he waddled into the dirty kitchen and opened his mouth, which was situated above three or four chins. A deep, raspy voice came out of his fat face.

Man no. 1: That was a helluva plan Old Man Winter had, ey, Vito?

Man no. 2: It sure was, Anthony [not Tricerra; it was a different Anthony].

Vito was much thinner than man no. 1 and possibly a bit younger as well, putting him somewhere in his late thirties. He had a full head of short black hair that had been carefully slicked back and was held firmly in place by good-smelling hair gel. He was also wearing a top-of-the-line Giorgio Armani suit and expensive black leather dress shoes, but he was not wearing leather gloves. Instead, his gloves were made of green latex. His facial complexion was rough and bumpy, and his eyebrows were thick and black.

Man no. 3 remained quiet but kept a smoking 12-gauge shotgun fixed on the remaining Embers boys. He was not wearing an expensive suit but a thin black Adidas tracksuit with a white wifebeater undershirt and comfortable sneakers. Short black hair combed to the side and held in place with hair spray sat on top of his head while a black goatee surrounded his mouth. His gloves were also made of green latex, and his fierce eyes implied that all he needed was the slightest excuse to perpetrate violence. He was by far in the best shape out of all three men as his well-defined pectoral muscles peeked out from the top of the wifebeater.

Man no. 1: Too bad for yous [he pointed to the Embers brothers with his pointer finger and pinky] that the general store owner's got important friends!
Man no. 2: G'ahead, have a seat at the table. Yous are making me nervous.

The three Embers boys stepped over their uncle's lifeless body, which was gushing blood all over the floor from the little bit of head that remained above his neck. They each took a seat at the table, which was splattered with tiny fragments of Elmer's skull and brain.

Deek was the first one who mustered up enough nerve to squeeze out a sentence through the shock.

Deek: Who…are you?
Man no. 1: Who, me? I'm Sammy Davis Jr.

Man no. 1 and man no. 2 laughed. Man no. 3 did nothing but stare at the Embers brothers with a ferocious look on his face and keep the 12-gauge pointed in their direction.

Man no. 2: We heard that there were a few hillbillies up here who were…dangerous.

Man no. 1 and man no. 2 laughed again.

Deek: Why…are you…here?

Man no. 1 stopped laughing. Man no. 2 continued to laugh as man no. 1 responded to Deek's question.

Man no. 1: Because *you* @#% with the wrong guy, my friend!
Deek: Anthony Tricerra.
Man no. 2: Bingo! Now all of yous stand up niiice and slow, and we're gonna take a little walk. C'mon, let's go!

All six men exited the mansion, and through the darkness, they headed over to the meth lab. As they entered it, man no. 3 gave man no. 2 some thick sailing rope and he then ordered the twins to have a seat on the floor in the middle of the lab, where he tied them up with a sturdy knot. He then ordered Deek to have a seat in the only chair that was inside the lab, next to the twins, and he tied him up as well with the same technique he used on the other two.

Without anybody telling him to, man no. 3 handed his 12-gauge to man no. 1 and left the meth lab, only to return a minute later with their headless uncle. He tossed him onto the floor, spat on him, and then left the lab again. This time he was gone for twenty minutes, and when he returned, he had a bucket of red water with him and several bloody rags. He threw the rags on the ground next to the twins, and when Jethro asked, "What are you gonna do with us?" man no. 3 cursed in Italian and spat on them.

Man no. 1: The kitchen is clean? No trace of the uncle?

Man no. 3 nodded and spat on the floor again in disgust.

Man no. 2 went over to the various containers in the meth lab, searching for something. Man no. 3 left the lab the third time and, after ten minutes, returned with a large metal can of gasoline. Man no. 2 was heard mumbling to himself as he looked at all the containers in the lab, "Hydrochloric aciiid... hydrogen peroxiiide...ah, here we go, *diethyl*." Man no. 3 went over to him and gave him a hand with the large container labeled Diethyl Ether, and they brought it to the center of the lab and put it down next to the twins and Deek.

Man no. 1: We gotta wrap this up. The sun is starting to come up.

Man no. 2 splashed gasoline all over the contents of the meth lab including the 3 Embers boys and paid close attention to soaking in gasoline the fifty-gallon drum that was full of ether. As he did that, man no. 1 handed the 12-gauge back to man no. 3 and then left the lab. He returned in about ten minutes with a car. He turned the car around so that it was facing away from the meth lab and then went back inside. There, man no. 2 was almost done with the gasoline, and when he was completely finished pouring it over the contents of the lab, the three men headed for the door.

On their way out, Jethro begged them, "Please, don't kill us, please!"

Man no. 3 kicked him in the face, instantly breaking his nose, while cursing at him. Man no. 1 and man no. 2 walked out of the lab while man no. 3 remained behind. When he heard two car doors slam shut, he took out a matchbook, removed a match, struck it, and tossed it at the floor of the meth lab. He then turned around, slammed the door of the lab behind him, ran to the car, and got in. It took off screeching its tires and kicking up a cloud of dry dust.

The moment that the meth lab's door slammed shut, Deek stood up with the chair strapped to him, jumped straight up in the air, and landed on his back, breaking the flimsy wooden chair into pieces. With only seconds to spare, he removed the loose ropes from around his body, threw them onto the fiery floor, and ran toward the closest window. Behind him he could hear the twins, who were screaming in agony while engulfed in flames and were begging him to come back and save them. Deek ignored them, dove through the window, and landed on the dirt outside. He got up and hit about fifteen good strides of running before a massive, deafening blast picked him up and tossed him nearly thirty feet forward into some old bales of hay left over from when the property was a farm. He immediately rolled around on the ground to extinguish the flames that were covering the back of his head, his back, and the backs of his legs.

As adrenaline had completely taken over his body, he couldn't feel any pain; and being the sociopath he was, he still remained calculated even after everything that had just happened. With the meth-lab fire raging on, he made a beeline to the mansion, half of which was now missing while the remaining half was on fire. He covered his nose and mouth with the crook of his elbow, ran through the flames in the living room, and headed straight for the basement, where he knew two women were locked up. He unchained the four dogs that were tied up in the basement; and they took off, running up the stairs and through the burning house, reaching the outside, where they disappeared in the distance. Deacon didn't unchain them out of some humane concern for the animals; he did it because he was a calculated sociopath who knew that having four dogs chained up in a basement could appear to the police like the dogs might have been there to *guard* something. And with Elmer and his brothers gone, the sheriff would have no fear in investigating or arresting Deek in the future.

He pressed the stone to open the back wall of the basement; flipped the lever/switch; ran inside; got a snub-nosed revolver, a flashlight, and a key from the first room with the bunk beds in it; and then opened room number one, which had a dirty, bloody, nineteen-year-old girl in it. He unlocked her shackles, told her, "Get the hell out of here," and pushed her down the long corridor toward Black Rock Mine before closing the door to room number one, which automatically locked on closing. He then did the same with a twenty-two-year-old girl that was in room number two but gave her the flashlight and then fired a couple of shots into a huge rock in the ceiling to scare the girls away and make sure they didn't try to come back that way. The girls had absolutely no desire to come back, and they both ran, frantically screaming down the corridor, toward the mine.

Deek then turned around, flipped the light switch off on his way out, closed the fake wall behind him, and ran back up the steps that led to the living room. Once again he ran through the blaze, and within seconds he found himself in the front yard of the house.

Concerned that the three men could return at any moment, he decided that the best thing to do was run into the woods, where he could lose them if they did return.

He ran past the smoldering wreckage of what was left of the meth lab, but when he was about fifty feet from it, the second explosion went off, sending more debris and shrapnel outward in every direction. One piece of such shrapnel was a jagged shard of sheet metal that came buzzing through the air and embedded itself into Deek's calf muscle.

"Aaaagh @#%!"

A. TRICERATOPS

He pulled it out while screaming in excruciating pain, then threw it spitefully on the ground and continued to limp-run toward the tree line, bleeding the whole way. Once he was in the woods, he continued to hobble for about a quarter mile when he realized he needed to stop the bleeding. He sat down on a fallen tree trunk, ripped a sleeve off his shirt, and created a tourniquet above his calf with it. He then ripped off his other sleeve and used it to clean the wound. Worried that the three Italian men might come after him and find it if he left it there, he tied the bloody shirt sleeve that he cleaned his wound with around his head, got up, and continued moving.

He then remembered that he left his doo-doo-brown truck at the marsh the day before. He checked the pockets of his dirty jeans and was relieved to find his car keys. Making his way through the woods toward the marsh, which was only roughly 0.2 miles from the Embers mansion, he had only one thing on his mind: *revenge.* Deek swore he would make Anthony and Morgan pay if it was the last thing he did.

Reaching the muddy marsh and finding his truck on the stretch of dry land where he always parked it, Deek paused for a moment to look at all the commotion that was happening in the distance, at his mansion. Red-and-blue lights were everywhere. He got in his truck, started the engine, and drove away from the marsh, seeing a helicopter hovering over the mansion in his rearview mirror.

His first destination after leaving the marshland was not one that you would easily guess. Deek headed to Randy the bartender's house first before anything else. On arriving there, he exited the truck, walked up the porch steps, and knocked on Randy's door. When Randy's wife opened the door, he struck her in the face with the handle of his pistol immediately and pushed her out of the way. She screamed and fell into the credenza, knocking it over.

Deek wasted no time. He hobbled into Randy's kitchen, where he was eating breakfast with his daughter; cocked back the hammer of the revolver; and put it right up against Randy's daughter's head. Six-year-old little Emma started crying at the sight of the dirty, bloody man.

Randy: Wait, wait, wait, wait—
Deek: I'm only gonna ask you *one* time, Randy! I know you know where *everyone* in this town lives. WHERE DOES THAT HOLLYWOOD @#% LIVE?

Randy, having no choice, told Deek exactly where Morgan's house was. Deek decocked the hammer of his revolver and took the gun away from six-year-old Emma's temple. He put it in Randy's eye instead while pulling the back of his hair downward to make his face look at the ceiling.

Deek (ten inches from Randy's face): Now you listen to *me*, Randy. If you tell *anyone* I was here, *espe-*

cially Hollywood or her boyfriend, I *will* come back and kill your wife and daughter in front of you and let you live with the guilt of their deaths. You understand me?

Randy (trembling): I understand. I won't tell anyone.

Deek took the pistol out of Randy's eye, slapped him in the head with his free hand, and furiously limped back toward the front door of the house. Regina, Randy's wife, had just gotten back on her feet and was trying to nurse her bleeding nose when Deek (on his way out of the house) grabbed her by the face. She screamed as he shoved her back down on top of the tipped-over credenza before he stormed out the wide-open door.

He got back in his truck, drove over to Morgan's house, parked around the corner where he could still see the house, and waited. And waited. Aaand waited.

Finally he hit pay dirt. Morgan and Anthony pulled up to her house, and Morgan stood outside as he cleared the house quickly but efficiently while armed with a Mossberg pump-action 12-gauge. Deek then watched Morgan and Anthony run in for a few minutes and then run back out in a hurry with no luggage, which, in Deek's mind, meant they were coming back. They then got in Anthony's truck and left.

Deek started his truck and drove it into a parking lot two blocks away. He then limp-jogged back to Morgan's house in his shredded and burnt clothing; used his switchblade to push back the bolt of her back door, disabling the latch from keeping the door closed; walked into the house; snuck into Morgan's pantry; closed door; and waited. Within ten minutes of Deek being in the pantry, Morgan returned to her house with her father.

CHAPTER 17

Payback

Deek slithered out from Morgan's pantry, having heard voices in the living room, and eavesdropped on the Carters.

Joe Carter: Sooo who's this new boyfriend of yours? Tell me!
Morgan: Daaad!

Morgan laughed, embarrassed.

Joe: Is he anybody I know?
Morgan: No, he's… He's *so great*, Dad! This has never happened to me before, but I think I'm in love with him.
Joe: Aw, Morgan. I'm so happy for you, blondie.

Morgan started crying.

Joe: It's okay, kiddo. What's his name?
Morgan: His name—
Deek: His name is Anthony.

Deek limped into the living room with the revolver pointed at Morgan and her dad.

Morgan looked up and felt the kind of pure dread and fear that she had only felt one other time in her life—the moment when she thought she was going to die in Johnathan Harvey Embers's mausoleum. The sheer terror that overtook her body choked the one word she could quietly exclaim and made it have two syllables, which it doesn't have.

Morgan: *Nn-o!*

Goosebumps covered both her arms.

Deek smiled the most evil smile anyone had ever seen directly at Morgan.

Morgan: *No!* It can't be…
Joe: What the hell is this? Who are you? What do you want?

Deek sat on the fancy armchair directly across from the couch where Morgan and her dad were sitting, took Morgan's cigarette pack from the living room table, pulled out a cigarette, and lit it.

Deek: Good evening, sir. My name is Deacon, and I only want one thing. *Payback!*

Deek looked at Morgan, who knew there was no way out of this, and then laughed while making wide eyes at her.

*****

Outside Morgan's house, Anthony sat in his car, swamped in boredom, while listening to political-talk radio. He was completely unaware of the events going on inside the house. After a good bit of time went by and he could longer stand the mind-numbingly boring pontification coming out of his truck's speakers, he texted Morgan around 11:00 PM, "All good?"

*****

Morgan's cell phone vibrated, and its screen lit up, signifying an incoming text. She reached for the phone, but Deek stopped her.

Deek: No, no!

Morgan froze with the phone in her hand.

Deek: I'll take *that*.

He took her phone and read Anthony's text, which prompted him to laugh.

Deek: We're all good in here, right?

He laughed again and texted "All good" back to Anthony.

*****

Approximately twenty minutes had passed since Deek first crawled out from Morgan's pantry, and in those twenty minutes, he had been quite busy.

Morgan's father was now tied up to the armchair in the middle of the living room. His mouth was gagged with a balled-up pair of socks, his face was beaten and bloody, and his left ear had been cut off. Morgan was on the floor in front of him, crying, and her tears made the black area underneath her eye look shiny.

Deek: Because of *you*, all the family I have in this world is dead. Well, tonight I'm going to give you a taste of what that feels like, and *then...* we're gonna take a little ride because there's something I want you to see.

Morgan (begging through tears): "*Please!* It's not his fault. He has nothing to do with any of this! He's innocent! Please! *Please!*

She tried to get up, but Deek hit her with the back of his hand so hard that she did a 180-degree spin and bashed her head against the short-legged living room table as she fell.

Deek: I told you to stay clear of that window! Anthony is not going to see you and get you out if this jam, @#%!

Morgan looked up at Deek while on her back, on the floor, and heard a muffled version of his words as she saw three Deek Emberses hovering over her in a blur.

Morgan (rubbing the small incision on the right side of her head, getting blood on her fingers but not knowing it): Oww!
Deek: Don't you pass out, Hollywood! I want you to see what I do to your pops!

Morgan tried her hardest to focus her eyes and ears on Deek, but she found herself fading in and out. She had a concussion. Deek saw that Morgan was struggling to stay conscious.

Deek: Dammit! I really wanted you to see this while fully conscious! [He shrugged.] Oh well. Just remember, Hollywood, this is *all your fault*!

Deek plunged the largest kitchen knife found in Morgan's kitchen into Joe Carter's chest as he let out a horrifying muffled scream.
Morgan reached her hand toward her father and cried, "Daddy!" before becoming unconscious.

Deek (in a very annoyed tone): Of course, Joe, she's
    gonna miss the best part.

Joe said something that could not be understood because of the gag.

Deek left the kitchen knife in Joe's chest. He
removed the gag from his mouth, held up the severed
ear in front of his (Deek's) face, and spoke into it,
"Speak up, Joe. I can't *ear* ya!" He then threw the ear
in his face as Joe started talking. The ear bounced off
Mr. Carter's face and hit the floor, and Deek stepped
on it as he came closer to hear Joe's words. Deek
pushed the back of his own ear forward with his
pointer finger in a mocking fashion, as if he wanted
to hear Joe better, while squatting in front of him.

Joe Carter (struggling to speak): Please, man, let
    Morgan go. You got your revenge. Just kill me
    and let her go! *Please!*

Joe spat out blood.

Deek: No can do, Joseph. But you can take com-
    fort in knowing that she will not be sexually
    assaulted before she dies. I don't…swing that
    way.

Deek tapped Joe's nose with the tip of his
pointer finger and made a kissing noise at him. He
then stood up and began squirting lighter fluid all
over the living room while spinning in circles and

humming the melody to Justin Timberlake's "What Goes Around...Comes Around."

Deek (full-blown singing with a surprisingly fantastic male singing voice): What goes around, goes around, goes around, comes all the way back around, yeah!

Outside, Anthony was sitting in his truck as rain was now pouring down on the entire street, making the cars that were under streetlights sparkle. The pattering of raindrops hitting car rooftops overshadowed all other sounds on the street. A. J. was listening to 104.5 while humming along to "What Goes Around...Comes Around" by Justin Timberlake.

As the song concluded, Anthony looked up and saw flames coming from inside Morgan's house. He immediately jumped out of the truck, sprinted down the street with his Mossberg in his right hand, kicked open the front door with two swift kicks, and discovered the gruesome scene of Morgan's father tied to a chair in the middle of the living room, covered in blood, with a large kitchen knife sticking out of his chest. Flames roared all around him. His head was slumped forward, and at first Anthony thought Joe was dead.

After clearing the entire house in less than a minute while shouting, "Morgan, Morgan!" A. J. noticed the back door of the house was wide open. He looked through it and into the empty backyard, then came back into the burning living room and kneeled in front of Joe Carter, who lifted his head while mumbling his last words: "FamiSafe app. Morgan. Hurry!" Joe passed from this world into the next while tied to the luxurious armchair in his daughter's inferno of a living room. Anthony reached into Joe's pocket and took out his cell phone, understanding his cryptic words.

Originally, on arriving in Sky Haven, Joe installed his favorite family-tracking cell phone app, FamiSafe, on his phone. He hadn't used it in many years, but because he wanted to surprise his daughter with his visit, he reinstalled the app so he could ping her phone and see where she was. He had a semi-elaborate plan of showing up wherever she was and nonchalantly sitting next to her until she noticed him, and then they would both have a good laugh. Realizing that Morgan was out of the tracking radius of the app, Joe gave up on his plan and just called her to let her know he was in Sky Haven. He did not, however, remove the app from his phone. Morgan's cell phone, which was sitting snuggly inside Deek's pocket, could reveal his and Morgan's location.

Anthony checked Joe's nonexistent pulse, then pulled the knife out of his chest and cut him loose with it. He then dropped the knife, which bounced under the couch, and did his best to try to pick up Joe in an attempt to take his body outside. However, by this point, the blaze was in a full frenzy of flames, and the thick black smoke started making Anthony feel dizzy. Also, Mr. Carter was a rather heavyset man, so the combination of the heavy smoke and Joe

Carter's weight caused Anthony to collapse on the floor with Joe.

With burning timbers now falling left and right and smoke choking him, Anthony had no choice but to leave Joe (whom he without a doubt knew was dead), pick up his shotgun, and stumble through the front door of Morgan's house to safety while hacking up a lung. The second his back foot crossed the threshold of the door way, the entire ceiling came crashing down behind Anthony, the second floor of the house becoming the first floor. The back-draft type of hot wind caused by this collapse shoved Anthony down the steps of the porch and set the back of his clothes on fire. He rolled around in the front yard, extinguishing the flames from his jeans and hoodie.

Functioning on adrenaline alone, he stood up with bloodshot eyes from inhaling smoke, grabbed his shotgun, opened the FamiSafe app on Joe's phone, and ran as fast as he could through the rain to his truck while coughing and vomiting. Several neighbors saw him leave the scene of the burning and collapsing house and called the police to report it.

After throwing the shotgun in the truck through the window, he got in, started the engine, and screeched the tires while peeling out of the parking spot. He did not care that the neighbors were watching him as he clipped the car in front of him while leaving the scene because at that moment, all he cared about was getting to Morgan.

A. TRICERATOPS

With his bloodshot eyes glued to Joe Carter's phone, which was showing a blue dot marked "Blondie" moving east on Route 437, he raced like Mario Andretti himself down the mostly empty streets. The blue dot suddenly stopped. A very confused Anthony coughed, then mumbled, "Why did he take her to the Embers mansion?" He slammed on the gas pedal.

CHAPTER 18

Black Rock Mine

A few hours prior, Frank Guardavaccaro and his partner, Frank O'Neil, had discovered the Emberses' horrifying secret in their basement. Knowing that the only safe way to go further into the mine would be with FBI backup, they decided to call it in, report their findings, request for backup, and wait for it at their motel so as to not arouse the suspicion of Deputy Harris.

Before leaving the Embers mansion to return to the motel, they spoke with Cameron Harris, who still knew nothing about the secret wall in the basement, and told him to call them if he saw *anything* out of the ordinary on the property as he had been stationed there for security night duty by Sheriff Bouchard.

Frank G. and Frank O. did not, at this time, anticipate the missing Embers brother to ever return to the scene of his family's heinous crimes, and they assumed he was somewhere like Guadalajara or Mexico City by now.

Frank Guardavaccaro placed a direct call to Pasquale Siphos Ricketts before going back to the motel, and their conversation went a little something like this:

Frank: There's a big ol' mess down here, PSR. These hillbillies had direct access to the mine. And who knows how long this has been going on for or what the hell is actually down there at this very moment? I don't even want to talk about the countless girls' photos we saw. These monsters have been kidnapping, torturing, and killing young girls for years, Pasquale! My guess is they were disposing of the bodies in the mine. This is bad, PSR. *Real* bad. I'm gonna need a forensics team and a full containment team down here ASAP... What?... Yes, PSR, I would bet there are probably hundreds of human remains down in that mine. This is way worse than what we ever expected. Now we know what Eli was doing in that house all those years... When?... Okay, then. Frank and I will sit tight and wait for the forensics and containment teams to get here in the morning. Okay. Goodbye.

Guardavaccaro hung up the phone, got in the car, and drove off toward the motel with Frank O.

Frank O'Neil: Who in tarnation is Eli, Frank?

Frank Guardavaccaro took out a cigarette, lit it, took a drag, and hung his arm out the window, feeling the cool night air against his skin as he drove with the other hand.

Frank G.: Eli Embers was Johnathan Embers' son, kid. After his dad escaped from the mine, only to die two days later, he went crazy. He became convinced that his dad was still alive. He even tried to go to the mausoleum at the Sky Haven cemetery and dig up his body a couple of times. But the FBI had put a tail on him, and federal agents stopped him before he could get inside the mausoleum. He was then warned that if he didn't stop, he would be indicted on federal charges and spend the rest of his life in prison.

Frank O'Neil: Poor kid. What did he do then?

Frank G.: He sold all his belongings and bought that run-down old mansion from an old farmer who had no family and one foot in the grave. He must've paid $19 for that place in the '50s. The FBI watched the house, but the file logs say he almost never came out of there. After ten years of barricading himself in the mansion and only coming out once a month to get food and supplies, the FBI eased up his tail duty and eventually cut him loose altogether. I guess we know *now* why he bought a property that is only 0.3 miles from the mine and what he was doing in there all that time.

Frank O.: Yea. Digging.

Frank G.: Bingo, Potter. Eli then had a son named Elmer and another son named Marshall, and he left him the house when he died. Marshall was Deek, Jethro, and Reggie's father, but he went crazy too and had to be institutionalized. Mental illness has a long history in that family, Potter. Hell, no sane man can do what those freaks were doing in that house. I don't wish death on anybody, but I'll tell you what, kid. The world is a better place without the Embers boys, that's for sure.

Frank O.: Amen to that.

The two federal agents continued driving in silence in the peaceful Sky Haven night, on a lonely road that had no traffic, while heading back to their flea-infested motel room. Suddenly headlights were seen coming toward them. Another car approached from the direction they were heading toward, going in the direction they had come from. When the car got closer, it drifted into their lane, and the two federal agents were startled by the headlights coming directly toward them. Frank G. lay into the horn, yelling obscenities, and the other driver corrected his driving trajectory back into his own lane but not before forcing Frank G. slightly off the road. As Frank G. slammed on the breaks, the black Cadillac came to a stop, kicking up a giant cloud of dry dust on the shoulder of the road.

Guardavaccaro stuck his head out the window and yelled, "You idiot!"

He couldn't make out the license plate. All he could see was that it was an ugly doo-doo-brown pickup truck as it disappeared into the night.

Reaching their motel shortly after the vehicular scare, the two exhausted federal agents each lay down on his own bed, fully clothed, with their black lacquered shoes still on, and turned the TV on to unwind.

*****

Back at the Embers mansion, Deputy Harris was watching YouTube videos on his phone, trying to combat the boredom. He was in the middle of a video in which some rebels handed a monkey an AK-47 (and he started firing it at their feet as they ran away) when all of a sudden, car headlights approached. When the vehicle got close enough to identify, Harris recognized Deek's truck. He immediately called Agent O'Neil's cell phone while sitting in his police cruiser.

O'Neil: O'Neil.

Harris: It's Deputy Harris. I think Deek Embers just pulled up.

O'Neil: On our way. Don't let him leave.

Frank O'Neil hung up.

Harris got out of his cruiser and said, "Hey, Deek, is that you, man? Everybody's been looking for you all day. Where the heck have you—"

A 0.38 special bullet separated a large chunk of young Deputy's Harris's brain from his skull, and he dropped to the ground. Morgan, who had been conscious since Deek swerved to avoid hitting a Cadillac on the road a few minutes back, screamed and received a slap from Deek.

Deek: Now, now, none of that. You're gonna wake the neighbors.

Figuring he would come back later to dispose of the deputy's body, Deek forcefully pushed her toward the mansion without letting go of her arm. They made their way through the charred living room of his now extremely humble abode, and he directed her to the basement. After opening the false wall at the back of the filthy room, he flipped the light switch and shoved her through as she cried, brokenhearted about losing her father and afraid of losing her own life next.

Deek: There's something that you have just *got* to see!

Morgan's crying intensified, knowing there was very little chance that she would come out of this place alive.

Deek (displaying his fantastic singing skills again): You told me you love me. Why did you leave me all alone? [He pushed Morgan further down the corridor toward Black Rock Mine.] Now you tell me you need me when you call me on the phone. Girl, I refuse. You must have me confused with some other guy. The bridges were burned. Now it's your turn to cry. [He shoved her again as she continued to cry.] Cry me a river. Cry me a river. Cry me a river. Cry me a river. Yeah, yeah.

Outside the mansion, Anthony pulled into the dirt driveway a few minutes later and got out of his truck, holding the shotgun and a flashlight. He put the flashlight's beam on Deputy Harris's dead body and then started frantically searching inside the cursed, crispy mansion—or at least what was left of it after the meth-lab explosion and fire.

Unable to find anyone upstairs and after almost falling through the weakened floor a couple of times, he paced erratically through the downstairs of the house and found the steps to the basement. In the basement, he ran into another dead end because Deek had closed the secret door behind him, and Anthony had no idea it even existed. The FamiSafe app signal was now gone as well.

He started to feel hopeless and panicked as he turned in every direction of the disgusting base-ment, unsure of what to do next. Seconds turned to minutes, and his breathing became more and more erratic. Clips of Morgan smiling at him started flash-ing in his head as fear started to overtake him. He remembered when she spat Mountain Dew all over him because he made her laugh in the hotel room, and he smiled but then kicked a rusty bucket in frustrated anger because he couldn't help her. He saw in his mind her eyes looking him up and down in his car as she called him townie. He had a flashback of the first time she walked into his general store, which had been closed for days now, and tears started to form in his eyes. "Where is she?"

He was now hyperventilating, and his heart felt like it was going to burst out of his chest when suddenly he stopped dead in his tracks and said, "Father, please forgive me of my sins, which are many. I am not worthy of Your help, but I desperately need it. Please show me what to do. In the name of the Father, the Son, and the Holy Spirit."

Two car doors slammed shut somewhere outside. Anthony heard them, and then shortly after, he heard footsteps coming from above, in the living room of the mansion. The footsteps got closer as they started coming down the basement steps along with beams from two flashlights. Anthony turned off his flashlight and took cover behind a shelf that was full of bicycle parts and a bunch of other junk. He heard two men whispering to each other.

Frank G.: Embers is going to pay for killing that deputy! He was just a kid.

Frank O. (looking at his phone): The plate on the other truck came back to a Tricerra...Anthony James. Convicted felon. You think Deek Embers has an accomplice with him?

Frank G.: I'm not sure, kid. But my instinct tells me
that Deek Embers has a lot more enemies than
friends.

They opened the secret door, and on seeing that
the lights were already on, they went in after Deek
with their pistols drawn.

Anthony's eyes widened, and he whispered,
"Thank you!" as he looked up to the sky. He then
followed after Frank G. and Frank O. cautiously.
He stood at the entrance to the corridor and looked
down it toward the federal agents, who didn't see
him since he was doing his best to stay hidden. After
about a hundred feet, the corridor veered right, and
the federal agents disappeared around the corner.

Anthony ran to that point, peeked around the
corner, and saw the federal agents walking down steep
stone steps for about fifty feet and then disappearing
around another corner. He followed them again and
then again and again and again in the same manner, constantly descending lower and lower into the
Earth via steep stone steps that extended at least fifty
feet per section. The federal agents reached a massive
underground area where they took cover behind a
large boulder after hearing voices nearby.

The spacious area was at a depth of about four
hundred feet beneath the mansion, and massive
boulders surrounded all sides, but the ceiling was
much higher than the ceiling in the corridor. It was
a natural underground cavern that Eli Embers must
have stumbled on while digging all those years ago.

A. TRICERATOPS

It resembled some sort of gargantuan chamber that only Indiana Jones or Nathan Drake would ever come across. Countless LED lights illuminated it, and in the middle of the chamber was a huge hole in the ground about thirty feet in diameter, with a makeshift elevator hanging above it. The elevator was really just a big, sturdy metal cage with a flat metal floor that was held up by several thick chains. A long metal lever sprouted up from the ground near the edge of the huge hole. It looked like it controlled the lowering and raising of the elevator.

The bodies of two young girls, the skin of which were covered in dirt as well as dried blood, lay on the cold ground near the big hole, in a pool of their own blood. No doubt they were the two young girls that Deek had "released" into the mine previously and, after stumbling across them in the chamber, shot in cold blood so they wouldn't interfere with his plans.

He had known they would never find a way out of the mine when he originally "released" them, and he hoped they would just fall to their deaths through the thirty-foot hole in the middle of the chamber. But since they did not, he couldn't risk either one of them getting in his way now, so he "put them out of their misery."

That was one thing about Deek. He had a rage inside him that never stopped. He never felt anything besides rage and hate. And he thought that everyone else in the world was the same way, so when he killed people, he viewed it as setting them free from the torment he himself felt every hour of every day. One might argue that in a demented kind of way, he was trying to help people by killing them, but one would lose that argument based on one fact alone. Deek truly enjoyed and took pleasure in "setting people free," and he often became aroused while doing it. Make no mistake, Deacon Embers was an irredeemable psychopath deserving of nothing good.

Morgan, who was hysterically crying at this point, was standing inside the metal cage that was suspended above the large hole in the ground, and Deek was about to pull the lever to lower her into the abyss below when Frank Guardavaccaro yelled, "Freeze, Embers!"

Deek turned around and, with disbelief and fury in his eyes, fired two shots at the federal agents, who took cover.

Anthony could not contain himself, and he ran right past the federal agents toward Deek while shooting and pumping his 12-gauge three times in a row as he screamed, "Die!" He missed the target because of the instability of his weapon, and the shotgun pellets hit the ground near Deacon as Anthony ran toward him.

Deek recognized that Anthony had no concern for his own safety anymore, and he pulled the lever that controlled the elevator, which started to descend slowly. Immediately after pulling the lever, Deek jumped from the edge of the huge hole into the metal cage with Morgan, got behind her, and put the revolver to her head while antagonizing Anthony by saying, "Easy, Capone! Wouldn't want to kill an Oscar winner by mistake now, would ya?" He laughed maniacally. His laughter echoed throughout the entire cavern, making it seem even more sinister, as the cage lowered into the abyss below.

Deek (shouting while looking up at Anthony again from the descending elevator): BTW…anybody touches that lever, and we all get to see what the inside of Morgan's head looks like before the cage even makes it back up to the ledge!

Frank Guardavaccaro, after seeing and hearing the entire exchange between Deek and Anthony, yelled to A. J., "Hey, you, freeze and drop the shotgun!"

Anthony looked back at the federal agents, then turned around and looked down into the massive hole as the elevator slowly descended into the faraway pit. Knowing he didn't have much of a choice at this point, he murmured to himself, "This is a *very* bad idea, Ant!" and then jumped from the ledge where he was standing into the cavern and landed on top of the elevator, shaking it something fierce. He didn't land on his feet but flat on his stomach, injuring his arm while dropping the shotgun into the abyss.

Deek's eyes opened really wide as he was shocked by the act of foolish bravery, but on seeing that Anthony was now unarmed and lying on top of the metal cage, he smiled and pointed the revolver at him, then squeezed the trigger. But before the gun went off, Morgan yelled, "*No!*" and kicked

Deek's hand, forcing the bullet widely to the left. The revolver then twirled into the abyss below as well, never to be seen again.

Deek: You @#%!

He hit her in the face, and she tumbled backward out of the elevator. Only at the last second did she grab the metal edge of its floor. Hanging on for dear life, she screamed while looking down at the ground below.

Deek took his switchblade out of his dirty, burnt jeans and pressed the button that instantly released the blade with a click. He then stepped forward to stick it into Morgan's hand when Anthony swung into the elevator feetfirst from above and kicked Deek into the back of the cage. He let out a yell as his back slammed against the metal. Since the elevator was not big enough to comfortably fit three people, there was almost no room for the two men to fight, but that didn't stop them.

Almost instantly Anthony grabbed both of Deek's arms, attempting to prevent him (with all his might) from pushing the switchblade into his eye while Frank G. and Frank O. watched helplessly from above, yelling indecipherable commands in the distance.

Morgan dangled from the edge of the cage as it was still descending while the two men were locked in a tense display of force that Anthony, who had injured his arm on landing on the elevator, maintained for a good while, but then he started losing. His injured arm could not withstand Deek's strength, and slowly the blade inched closer to his eye. Anthony knew he was going to lose his eye, and he accepted it. But then he kneed Deek directly in the groin as hard as he could, making him miss his eye but instead slice A. J.'s cheek open.

Deek groaned and took a step back, but he did not drop the knife. Anthony ignored his cheek laceration, which was gushing blood down his chin and neck; and he turned around, pretending to try to pull Morgan up. When Deek saw his exposed back, he stepped forward to thrust the switchblade into it, walking right into Anthony's trap. Having anticipated this move, A. J. slid out of the way at the last second and tripped Deek, causing him to go right over the edge of the elevator—but not before he grabbed Anthony's arm and Morgan's hair on his way down. All three of them fell fifteen feet and hit the bottom of the deep pit with a disorganized thud and crunch. They all groaned in pain, but they were alive.

The elevator slammed against the ground next to them, marking the end of its 150-foot journey from above.

CHAPTER 19

The Anomaly

Deek, Anthony, and Morgan lay on the ground at the bottom of the cavern, inside a circle of manmade light that shined down from 150 feet above. Beyond the circle of light was darkness in every direction, darkness that became more and more black the further you looked into it.

All three of them were groaning in pain after having fallen fifteen feet and landing on dry, hardened earth that held no buffer. Well...almost no buffer. More on that shortly. The walls of the cavern were unforgivingly steep, and neither man nor beast could have climbed them to get out. The only way to reach the top was to use the makeshift elevator, but there was no lever at the bottom of the cavern, so it certainly seemed as if whoever built it had no intention of using it to descend to the bottom of this place. So what was its purpose, then, since the elevator could only be operated from the top?

Rolling over and grunting in pain, Morgan lay on something hard and uneven that was roughly the length of a human arm. She reached underneath her back and pulled it out, only to realize that it *was* the skeletal remains of a human arm. She screamed and dropped it on the ground next to her, where several more skeletal remains lay.

At this moment, both she and Anthony realized that the bottom of the cavern was full of hundreds, maybe thousands, of skulls and countless human bones, some more intact than others. Entire rib cages, femurs, and pelvic bones as well as a plethora of skulls of all different shapes and sizes lay sprawled out all over the ground. The crunch sound that rang out when Deek hit the ground had been made by a human skull that he crushed by landing on it.

Morgan and Anthony exclaimed in unison, "*Oh…my—*" but never finished the sentence because Deek interrupted them as he slowly stood up.

Deek: Yea, yea, spare me, Mr. and Mrs. Morality!
Morgan (looking around in disbelief): You monster! How long have you animals been dumping bodies here?

Deek laughed and responded, "You think this is all just from me and my brothers? Haha! Oh, no, honey. Three generations of Embers have created *this* marvel."

Anthony: You're *sick*!

Deek limped over to the edge of the circle of unnatural light shining from above, reached six inches beyond it and into the darkness, and picked something off the ground. His hand returned to the light with Anthony's shotgun in it, and he turned around to face them, his back to the darkness.

Deek: Game over, folks. It's been fun, but this is where this story ends.

Anthony put his hands up.

Anthony: "Wait. Deek, you don't have to do this!"

He pushed Morgan behind himself to shield her.

Deek: I mean, you're right. I don't *have* to do this, but I would absolutely *love* to. Remember in the cemetery when I told you I would kill you as you lay there with your little ski mask on? Well, that day has come, @#%! I'm going to end you here in this cavern, in front of *her* [he pointed to Morgan], and then I'm going to use her as a hostage to get out of here. Then the feds will find pieces of her in three different counties, strung along the highway like trash.

Morgan started crying as Anthony shielded her with his body from the anticipated trajectory of the shotgun blast. Deek pumped a fresh round into the chamber of the 12-gauge, ejecting the old round,

while humming the tune of "What Goes Around…
Comes Around" by Justin Timberlake.

A subtle creaking sound that was foreign to the
human ear came from directly behind Deek, just
beyond the light. He made a scared face, but before
he had a chance to turn around, a powerful high-
pitched scream of an almost unbearable frequency
filled every inch of the cavern, causing even Special
Agent Guardavaccaro and Special Agent O'Neil, who
were 150 feet above, to cover their ears.

The unearthly, high-pitched sound was immediately followed by a jagged black crystal shard entering Deek's back and exiting through his chest. He
screamed and clenched the trigger of the shotgun,
causing it to go off before he was lifted three feet off
the ground. The 12-gauge bird shot hit Anthony
in the abdomen, sending him flying backward into
the metal elevator that was directly behind him. He
knocked Morgan, who was also directly behind him,
down, but she was not hit by any of the pellets from
the shotgun blast. Deek's entire body hovered three
feet above the ground, with the black shard in his
chest, for a moment, and then he disappeared backward into the darkness as he dropped the shotgun.
His screams continued for a few more seconds, but
they stopped as a loud crack rang out. Three seconds
later, his decapitated head rolled out of the darkness
and into the circle of light and stopped in front of
Morgan. She ran into the elevator and started screaming in terror, "Pull us up! Pull us uuup!"

Frank Guardavaccaro barely heard her command echoing from the bottom of the pit and pulled the lever in front of him, causing the metal cage to slowly start moving back up the cavern.

Morgan continued screaming from inside the elevator while looking into the darkness with terror and anticipation as the creaking sound, which was unfamiliar to human ears, continued. Anthony was still conscious too, and he was also watching the darkness with sheer horror on his face as blood seeped out of his stomach and onto the elevator floor. He could not move as he lay on the bottom of the cage, and he knew that if the anomaly charged forward, he would not be able to protect Morgan this time. *Please, God, save Morgan!* was all he kept repeating in his mind. That was his only concern, not the fact that he had sustained a likely fatal injury.

As the metal cage slowly ascended, the anomaly stuck its head out for a moment from beyond the darkness, revealing an enormous scaly black head that resembled that of a triceratops dinosaur but with only one jagged black crystal horn on its face. The black crystal horn was covered in blood, and so were the creature's two rows of razor-sharp black crystal teeth. Its catlike pupils blinked vertically once before the anomaly disappeared back into the darkness.

Morgan screamed again at the sight of the creature and fainted in the cage, slamming her head hard against the metal floor. The impact immediately reopened the cut she sustained while hitting her head on her living room table. Anthony stayed conscious for about halfway through the ascent, but his vision faded to black before they reached the top. Blood was covering the entire elevator floor when it reached the federal agents.

CHAPTER 20

Intensive Care

Morgan opened her eyes and discovered that she was inside a hospital room. She had a massive headache and was hooked up to machines that were monitoring her vital signs. She tried to figure out what was happening or how she got there but found herself struggling to remember.

"Hello? Anybody?" she cried out.

A very good-looking Black nurse rushed into the room, followed by two men dressed in nice suits and black lacquered shoes.

Nurse: It's okay, honey. I'm here.

Morgan: What's going on? What happened? Why am I here?

Nurse: Honey, you've suffered very serious head trauma twice within a few hours, and you were brought to Sky Haven Memorial Hospital by these men.

The nurse pointed to Frank Guardavaccaro and Frank O'Neil.

Morgan touched the stitches on the side of her head and exclaimed, "*Owww!*"

Nurse: Easy, honey. We had to stitch you up. Don't touch it, okay? We gon' make sure you—
Frank G. (interrupting the nurse): Ms. Carter, what is the last thing you remember?

"*Excuse* me? No, nuh-uh! You are *not* about to interrogate this girl in this condition, *okay*? I don't care *who* you are!" exclaimed nurse Rasheeda Jenkins.

Nurse Jenkins was a very good-looking older woman who was a widow, having lost her husband, Cecil, in Iraq in 2005. Ever since her devastating loss, she had been known not to take lip from anyone and was certainly not afraid of anyone or of speaking her mind.

Frank G.: Ma'am, I'm gonna need you to step out of the room.
Nurse: What you say?
Frank O.: I'm sorry, Nurse Jenkins. *Please* give us a few minutes with Morgan. We won't be long, I promise.

Nurse Jenkins looked at young Agent O'Neil for a moment, then softened up her demeanor. She rolled her eyes and walked out of the room while talking to herself, saying, "I *know* he ain't talkin' to *me* like that, talkin' 'bout I need to leave the room. Nuh-uh! I don't have time to play with no feds today.

That poor girl lost her father, she *all kinds* of injured, and he wanna be in there, asking her questions she probably won't know the answers to because she has a concussion. Dumbass feds always wanna be all up in somebody's business…" She continued talking as she walked further down the hall, but the further she got from the special agents, the harder it was for them to hear what she was saying. The last thing Frank G. and Frank O. heard was "And I'll tell you another thing," but they could not make out the rest.

Frank O.: Was that really necessary, Frank?

Frank G. looked at Frank O. with an expression that said, "I know you're right, but I'm too old and stubborn to admit it."

Frank G.: "Ms. Carter, I am Special Agent Guardavaccaro from the FBI, and this is Special Agent O'Neil.

Frank O. waved in a goofy, excited manner as he was a bit starstruck, but he straightened up when Frank G. looked at him sternly.

Frank G.: Please tell me. What is the last thing you remember about last night?

"I…I…" After a few seconds of reflection, she donned a serious look on her face and yelled, "I remember that Deek Embers killed my father in cold blood! Where is he? Did you arrest that murderous piece of @#%?"

Frank G.: Is that the last thing you remember, Ms. Carter?

Morgan (still yelling): YES, IT IS THE LAST THING I REMEMBER! ISN'T IT ENOUGH? IS HE IN CUSTODY? WHERE IS HE?

Frank G. and Frank O. looked at each other.

Frank O.: Ms. Carter…Deek Embers is dead.

Frank G.: "He tried to kill you in your house last night after killing your father, but Anthony Tricerra saved your life by getting in the way of the shotgun blast. We were able to take Deek out immediately after, but unfortunately, we could not save your house from burning down.

Frank O'Neil looked at his partner, then at Morgan.

Morgan: Anthony! Where is he? Is he okay?

Frank G.: I'm afraid not, miss. Anthony is in the hospital room next to yours, but it's not looking good. He sustained a 12-gauge gunshot wound to the abdomen.

Morgan burst into tears. "*What?*"

Frank O.: Frank, can I talk to you outside for a
minute?

The two federal agents stepped out into the
hallway, leaving Morgan to cry by herself in the room
for no more than one minute.

Frank G.: Listen, kid. I will explain everything to
you, but for now, you're gonna have to trust me
and let me take the lead on this.

Frank O., knowing that his partner was a good,
honest man, paused for two seconds, then responded,
"Okay, Frank."
They went back into Morgan's room, and she
immediately burst out with "I need to see Anthony!"

Frank G.: That might be possible, Ms. Carter. Let
me go and speak with the doctor, and I will be
right back.

Frank G. exited the room, leaving Frank O. in
there with Morgan, as the young FBI agent was doing
his best to keep her calm and console her for the loss
of her father. Guardavaccaro then went over to the
reception desk of the particular hospital wing they
were in and asked to speak to Dr. Eric Hamilton,
who was then paged over the intercom system and
showed up after a few minutes.
Dr. Hamilton was of about average height
and had a full-grown reddish-brown beard and

thick framed glasses. His short, reddish-brown hair was parted to one side, and it looked as if it very rarely cooperated with the good doctor. He was an extremely smart forty-three-year-old man who was very good at his job and simply did not have time for childish behavior, immature jokes, or any kind of horseplay in his hospital wing.

Frank G: Hey, Doc. I just need to ask you a few questions. How is the Tricerra boy doing?

Doctor Hamilton: Well, Agent Guardavaccaro, he's extremely lucky that you guys brought him in when you did. He would have bled out and died if you had gotten here ten minutes later. Also, because he was shot from about twenty feet away and not point-blank, his body did not receive the full concentration of the pellets. The bird shot had already spread out some before hitting him, which really helped matters. Furthermore, it seems that the shooter's arm was moving upward and slightly to the left when he pulled the trigger, so most of the pellets, which were already few in numbers to begin with, hit his right rib cage instead of his abdomen. If they were buckshot, he would have died on the spot. But because the pellets were bird shot, which are smaller in size than buckshot, it looks like he's going to be okay. Now…he *will* still need to go through physical rehabilitation for a few months and then take it easy for a long time after. But he's going to live, and I expect he will make a full recovery. That includes regaining full function of his legs and motor skills and full use of all his body parts.

Frank G.: That's great news, Doc! What about Morgan Carter?

Dr. Hamilton: Ah, her story is a little bit different. Let me show you the MRIs we did on her brain. [He took MRI photos out of a folder he had tucked under his arm.] You see how there is a small dark spot over this area? Well, that is one of Morgan's temporal lobes. This particular one is located on the right side of her cranium. Something struck this area of her brain once and then again a few hours later. That first hit was bad enough to give her a concussion, but when the second trauma happened, the CT scans show that it bruised her hippocampus, causing something called retrograde amnesia. This particular type of amnesia is selective, meaning that it only applies to a time that took place right before the injury, but it doesn't affect memory that is from days, weeks, months, or years ago. Morgan might even remember certain things from last night but has probably forgotten how she sustained the second injury and what took place right before that event.

Frank G.: I see. Can Morgan ever regain the ability to recall these memories?

Dr. Hamilton: Yes, she can. But *only* if there is either a constant verbal reminder of these events, like someone who was there describing them to her in detail, or if there is some kind of audio or visual icon or aid that is powerful enough to trigger her brain to recall them.

Frank G.: I see. Okay, Doc, thanks for the info. You've been very helpful.

Dr. Hamilton: Sure thing.

Special Agent Guardavaccaro took his leave from Dr. Hamilton and headed to Anthony's room. He knocked on the door twice and walked in. Nurse Jenkins was in there with Anthony, adjusting his hospital pillows to a position that would change his posture and put less pressure on his rib injuries. Seeing Special Agent Guardavaccaro walk in, she exclaimed, "Ohhh, no!" while quickly waving her finger back and forth to symbolize *no*.

Frank G.: Nurse Jenkins, before you say anything, I would just like to apologize for earlier. I was out of line. I just always seem to get flustered around beautiful women, and then I say something rude or something stupid...

Nurse Jenkins: Or both!

Frank G. dropped his head.

Frank G.: Yes, sometimes both.

Frank G. smiled at the nurse with the guilty smile of a little boy.

Nurse Jenkins: Mmm-hmm, don't think you can get on my good side now just because you cute!

Nurse Jenkins walked out of the room, leaving Frank in there with Anthony.

Frank was flattered and stuck his head out the door to watch the beautiful nurse walk away. She never turned around, but she let him know, "I saw that!" Frank retracted his head back into the room quickly and closed the door.

About ten minutes went by; and Frank opened the door, exited the room, and then went into Morgan's room next door, leaving a tearful and visibly very upset Anthony in his room by himself.

Frank G.: Ms. Carter, you can see Anthony now.

Morgan had been bawling her eyes out the entire time that Frank G. was gone despite Frank O.'s best efforts to calm her down. She immediately ripped off all the wires that were attached to her to monitor her vital signs (as both special agents yelled, "Easy!"), jumped out of bed, and rushed into Anthony's room, where she saw him with a stitched-up cheek, a black eye, a bandaged-up torso, and in tears. She became upset on seeing his appearance and began crying even harder.

Frank G. and Frank O. walked into the room right behind Morgan. She came closer to his bed, and he took her hand in his, then began speaking.

A. TRICERATOPS

Anthony: Morgan...do you remember the day that you came into my general store for the first time?

Morgan nodded and continued to cry.

Anthony: Well, when you walked in, I could tell that you were trouble. And after speaking no more than a few sentences to you in my store, I could tell that you were a spoiled brat and that you blamed the whole world for your problems.

Morgan nodded again in agreement and continued to cry.

Anthony: *But*...when I looked into your eyes, I saw the most beautiful person I had ever seen in my life. Not just your face, which has, no doubt, once belonged to a celestial being of some kind, but your soul, Morgan. I saw the real you in your eyes. The kindness that you tried to hide from me by being rude to me that day, it was all in there, and I saw it. And once I looked into your eyes and saw the *real* you, I fell in love with you on the spot.

Morgan's crying intensified.

Anthony: Morgan, I have been madly in love with you ever since that day, and I will always love you from now until eternity here or anywhere else. And regardless how you feel about me, I just want to thank you for letting me experience such a true love with another human because not only have I never had that, but I also never thought such a thing existed. [He coughed.] *No matter* what happens, Morgan, remember who you really are and how you made me feel. [He coughed again.]

Morgan (through unrelenting tears): I love you too! I've never felt this way before either, and it was the last thing I told my dad before he died.

Anthony coughed and was visibly struggling to stay conscious.

Anthony: Remember, Morgan, God will always be there with you. No matter what. [He started really laboring to get out his words.] God will *always* be with you!

Anthony, who had been holding Morgan's hand this entire time, turned her hand over and placed her grandmother's brooch in it. Her eyes widened to almost inhuman sizes, and she covered her mouth with her hand as tears gushed down her face more intensely than they had been before that moment. She tried to speak, but she couldn't.

The brooch, having been through so much while sitting in Anthony's pocket the last few days, was now missing one of the five small blue sapphire stones, but that did not diminish Morgan's amazement on seeing it.

Anthony: I love you, Morgan!

He fell back on his hospital bed, and his heart monitor flatlined. Three nurses and Doctor Hamilton rushed in while a fourth and fifth nurse pushed Morgan out of the room, having to use their full force against her because she refused to leave. She screamed, "*No!*" at the top of her lungs and clawed at the nurses. She was only effectively restrained when Nurse Jenkins put her arms around her, and all four of them crumbled to the floor.

Morgan was crying the hardest she had ever cried in her entire life as she lay on her side and screamed "*No!*" while Nurse Jenkins pet her head and repeated, "It's okay. It's okay." She continued to scream and cry until something came over her to make her stop screaming, and in her mind, she said the following heartfelt prayer: "Dear God, I know I deserve nothing from You. I know I am a murderer and that I have lived my life foully ever since I left Texas. I am not worthy of Your love *or* to ask for anything from You, but, Lord, I have nowhere else to turn. Please save Anthony, and I will give You my life like I did when I was little. In the name of the Father, the Son, and the Holy Spirit. Amen."

The entire hospital wing was buzzing at this point as nurses ran to and fro and other patients were sticking their heads out of their rooms to see what all the commotion was about.

Inside Anthony's hospital room, Doctor Hamilton was repeatedly using a defibrillator and yelling, "Clear!" with no success. The dreadful sound of the flatlining heart monitor wasn't going anywhere as ten seconds turned into five minutes in the blink of an eye.

During all the commotion, the two special agents migrated to one corner in the back of the room to allow the hospital staff to work on Anthony. Frank O'Neil looked over at Frank Guardavaccaro, who didn't think anybody was watching him, and he saw Frank G. throw an empty syringe into the trash can next to him.

Fifteen minutes later, after repeated attempts to revive Anthony, Dr. Hamilton stopped using the defibrillator, shook his head, and said, "I'm calling it. Time of death is 9:37 AM." He then walked out of Anthony's room and into Morgan's room next door, where she was lying on her hospital bed, being consoled by three nurses. Dr. Hamilton said with a quivering voice, "I'm sorry, Ms. Carter. We did all we could. Anthony has passed away."

CHAPTER 21

Who Is Frank Guardavaccaro?

In Anthony's room, immediately after Dr. Hamilton called his time of death, Frank O'Neil looked over at Frank Guardavaccaro with anger and suspicion in his eyes while nurses were fussing about, making preparations to move the dead body.

Frank O.: We need to talk outside. Now!

Frank G. made a surprised face, completely unaware of the fact that O'Neil had spotted him as he disposed of the syringe while Dr. Hamilton was trying to revive Anthony Tricerra.

The two federal agents walked down the hall of the hospital wing (O'Neil was ahead of Guardavaccaro) and entered an elevator. O'Neil pressed the button for the lobby. He stood there in silence with anger draped all over his face, put one hand on his hip as he stared at the elevator door, and started tapping his foot impatiently but didn't respond to Frank G., who was standing behind him, asking, "What's this about, Frank?"

The elevator reached the lobby. The doors opened, and Frank O. walked out quickly, heading for the sliding glass doors located at the entrance of the hospital, while Frank G. walked several feet behind him, trying to engage his partner again: "Frank! Where you going? Frank?"

Frank Guardavaccaro reached the parking lot of Sky Haven Memorial Hospital, where O'Neil sat in the passenger seat of the black Cadillac and made a quick, cold motion to Frank G. to get in. On doing so, Guardavaccaro made a final attempt to find out what was going on: "What has gotten into you, Frank? Why did you bring me out here, kid? What is so—"

Frank O. (cutting off his partner with a cold, angry tone): Anything you wanna tell me, Frank?

Agent O'Neil put his hand inside his suit jacket and unsnapped the button of the leather strap that held his pistol in place inside its leather holster.

Agent Guardavaccaro heard the leather strap unbutton and deciphered the seriousness on his partner's face. He looked at O'Neil, remained quiet for a few seconds, and then said confidently, "Easy, kid." Frank G took out a cigarette from the pack sitting on the dashboard of the Cadillac, lit it, rolled the window down, and said, "Remind me again, kid... What security clearance does a second-year rookie have?"

Frank O.: That's irrelevant. I'm giving you one chance to come clean, Frank. I saw you!

Frank G.: You don't know your ass from your elbow, kid.

Frank O.: Last chance, Frank. How could you do that to an unarmed man posing no immediate threat? You took an oath! Who even *are* you, Frank?

Frank G.: Kid, I'm only gonna tell you this once. [He turned to him.] *Stand. Down!*

Four seconds of extremely tense silence passed as the two agents stared each other down, followed by O'Neil drawing his Glock 17 and pointing it at his partner.

Frank O.: You are under arrest for the murder of Anthony Tricerra! You have the right to remain silent. Anything you say will be used against you in a court of law—

Frank G. (shaking his head while dropping his lit cigarette out the window): Oh, for crying out loud!

Frank O.: You have the right to an attorney—

Frank G., using a lightning-fast technique, hit the gun being held in his partner's left hand with his own right hand, pinning the pistol and O'Neil's arm against the headrest of Frank G.'s seat. With his left fist, Guardavaccaro struck O'Neil twice in the chest. O'Neil cried out in pain and pulled the trigger of his pistol. The bullet blew out the driver's side window, temporarily deafening Frank G. in his right ear. Guardavaccaro screamed, "Aaah!" and grabbed O'Neil by the throat, pinning him up against the passenger's side window in an attempt to subdue him. Frank O., using his free right hand, pulled the handle on the passenger door, opening it, and spring-boarded himself with his legs off the brick wall that was Guardavaccaro. He fell out of the car backward as he dropped his Glock pistol on the seat. O'Neil then quickly jumped to his feet and ran away from the black Cadillac while Guardavaccaro took out his own pistol and took aim at his partner, putting his back in the crosshairs of his 0.45 caliber, 1911-model pistol.

Frank G. held the crosshairs on Frank O.'s back for a good three seconds but did not pull the trigger. Only after a couple more seconds did Frank O. remember his training and start zigzagging as he ran away from the Cadillac, but Frank G. had already lowered his weapon. Getting around the corner of the hospital, Frank O. managed to flag down a yellow taxicab, jumped in the back seat, and screamed, "DRIVE!"

The taxicab's driver said, "Where to?" but O'Neil's ankle-carry .357 Magnum revolver got parked an inch from his face as Frank O. repeated, "DRIVE NOW!"

Back in the Cadillac, Guardavaccaro put his 1911 pistol back in its holster, under his left arm, and took out his cell phone. After a few frustrating seconds during which he swiped the screen up and down, trying to remember how to unlock the phone, he finally dialed Pasquale Siphos Ricketts's personal number; and when he picked up, Frank said, "We have a problem, PSR. A big one."

*****

As the yellow taxi was speeding down Bridge Street, Special Agent O'Neil put his .357 Magnum revolver back in its ankle holster and said to the taxi driver, "Okay, listen. Calm down, okay? I'm sorry about sticking the gun in your face. I'm not gonna hurt you. I'm a federal agent." He showed him his FBI documentation. "I just need to get as far away from the hospital as possible right now."

The driver believed him and calmed down. The taxi then adopted more of a cruising speed instead of a racing speed as it made several turns on different streets to avoid being followed.

Frank O'Neil put his face in his hands, trying to process what had just happened. He had known Frank Guardavaccaro for two years, and nothing about his behavior during that time had ever indicated that he was in any way dishonest, let alone a murderer.

O'Neil was in shock and unsure what to do. He rolled down the window and asked the cabdriver for a cigarette. He obliged. Frank had never smoked before, so the first few drags were quite jarring. But he powered through them *and* the tears they caused him as the ultimate goal of calming his nerves was what was on his mind. With a trembling hand, he took out his cell phone and dialed Siphos Ricketts. This conversation ensued:

O'Neil: Frank Guardavaccaro has lost it, sir! He killed Anthony Tricerra with some kind of lethal injection at Sky Haven Memorial Hospital. I tried to place him under arrest, but he assaulted me, and I barely escaped with my life! I need backup to bring him in… Wait… What? What do you mean, stand down?… You want *me* to come in? For what?… No, we can talk about it right now over the phone… Why are you…"

Realizing that something was not right, Frank O'Neil stopped talking, and he hung up. A thousand thoughts ran through his brain. *How could Ricketts give Guardavaccaro a pass for murder? Is he in on it? And if so, why? How long has this been going on? Has Guardavaccaro murdered anyone else? I thought Frank was a stand-up guy. How could I have been such a horrible judge of character? Are they going to come after* me *now?*

I can't believe this is happening! was the last thought he had before he threw his cell phone out of the window of the moving taxicab.

CHAPTER 22

Alone

I think it's important to acknowledge at this point in time that things had taken a really crazy turn, and we need to regroup for a moment.

So far, all the Embers boys were dead; Morgan's father, Joe Carter, was dead; and the male protagonist of our story, Morgan's love interest, Anthony Tricerra, was dead as well. We don't 100 percent know Guardavaccaro's motive for killing him; but if I had to guess, I'd say that after speaking with Dr. Hamilton, Frank Guardavaccaro viewed killing Tricerra to be the quickest, most effective way to keep the events at Black Rock Mine a secret.

With Morgan Carter suffering from retrograde amnesia and Anthony dead (and with nobody else to remind Morgan of what had happened in the cavern below the Embers mansion), the secret was effectively contained.

The murder committed by Special Agent Guardavaccaro, however, was beyond shocking, I know. It might have even made you stop chomping on your Cool Ranch Doritos momentarily while angrily thinking of insults you'd like to throw at your humble narrator. Smh. Look, sir/ma'am, that's life. It isn't always pleasant or fair. But if you keep reading, I might find a way to redeem myself in your eyes with the rest of the story despite it missing the main protagonist. Let's keep going, shall we?

Okay, so young Deputy Harris had also been needlessly killed along with hundreds, maybe thousands, of young girls who were tragically murdered by the Embers family, spanning over fifty or sixty years (give or take).

Now, not only was the lead investigator on the Black Rock Mine case a murderer as well, but also, he operated with impunity as Pasquale Siphos Ricketts (FBI director) had sided with him when alerted of his crimes by rookie special agent Frank O'Neil. Upon realizing this and fearing for his life, O'Neil had gone into hiding for three months, which was exactly how much time had passed between Anthony's death and the current moment.

O'Neil, fully aware of the FBI's methods of tracking people, had avoided using his credit cards and his cell phone (which he tossed from the cab) during that time, but he had remained in Sky Haven for three reasons. Here are those reasons, not in any specific chronological order of importance:

Reason number one: Ever since his encounter with Morgan Carter in her hospital room, he could not help but develop some sort of feelings for her, which he could not seem to shake.

Reason number two: He wanted to bring Guardavaccaro and Ricketts to justice, and therefore, he was determined to surveil his ex-partner, who remained in Sky Haven.

But I don't want to get ahead of myself. After escaping from the hospital parking lot with his life, O'Neil had the taxi driver immediately take him to his and Guardavaccaro's motel room, where he had some cash and other belongings.

Agent O'Neil, being the sharp kid he was, always brought a few thousand dollars in cash with him when departing for missions that required being in the field for longer than twenty-four hours. Why? Because you "never know when you'll need cash," he would say. And apparently, *this* was one of those instances.

Granted that usually, Frank G. and Frank O. used the money to pay informants and snitches to gain important information, but there was no doubt that O'Neil thought the money would be useful to him in this situation too as he went rogue from the FBI for what O'Neil considered to be a necessary but only temporary period.

After grabbing his money and belongings, he staked out the motel room from the taxi (by paying the taxi driver extra to stick around) until Guardavaccaro returned to it. To O'Neil's surprise, not only did Frank G. not leave Sky Haven; but also, he never even changed motel rooms, remaining at the flea circus called the Adelaide Motel.

A. TRICERATOPS

"He must have unfinished business here in town," O'Neil told himself, vowing to stick around and tail Guardavaccaro. Finding out exactly what Frank G. was up to could certainly be a good way of building an airtight case against him.

Later Frank O. would find an abandoned house in town to set up as a base of operations; and using only cash, he would purchase a burner phone, a used laptop, inexpensive audio surveillance equipment, and a beater car to follow Guardavaccaro around with. Finding a maroon 1993 Buick Century on a used-car lot for $43 (not the real price), Frank O. was determined to follow Frank G. around, see what he was up to, compile evidence against him, and bring him to justice.

His crush on Morgan Carter would not have been enough for him to give up his career in the FBI, but seeing Guardavaccaro murder an innocent man, a man who was virtuous enough to risk his life to save someone else's (especially someone as beautiful as Morgan), was an atrocity in O'Neil's eyes. Momentarily giving up his career to bring down a dirty federal agent *and* a corrupt FBI director seemed quite the noble pursuit to the idealist in him even if he had to do it alone.

Frank O. thought that sooner or later, he'd be able to get enough conclusive dirt on his old partner and present it to someone who was over Ricketts's head, perhaps someone at the DOJ, and be a hero for bringing them both to justice.

But there I go, getting ahead of myself again.

On stalking Guardavaccaro from the cab that day, Frank saw that his ex-partner went straight to the Sky Haven police department after leaving the motel, which made O'Neil wonder if Sheriff Bouchard was in on whatever Guardavaccaro was up to. But so far, Frank O. could not piece anything together apart from the motive I guesstimated at the beginning of this chapter. He also had a suspicion that Frank G. went to the sheriff to muddy the water about O'Neil and cut off any form of assistance or allies Frank O. might find in town if he had decided to stick around.

That didn't matter to O'Neil, though, because he was determined to blow the whistle on this entire matter. Covert operations to keep the mine a secret were one thing, but cold-blooded murder was *not* something the young agent had signed up for. And since O'Neil was a "Boy Scout" who was absolutely free of corruption, he definitely viewed himself as the perfect agent to take down Guardavaccaro and his enabler, Pasquale Siphos Ricketts.

The only thing that O'Neil was worried about, however, was the fact that Frank G. was in possession of his Glock service pistol (because he dropped it in his car), which Guardavaccaro could use to commit other murders and then frame O'Neil for them later if he wanted to. This was the third reason Frank O. decided to stick to his old partner like glue. He wasn't going anywhere until he had enough evidence to put

Guardavaccaro and Ricketts behind bars and clear his own name if they decided to frame him.

*****

On the day of Anthony's death, FBI forensic and containment teams arrived in Sky Haven, as requested by Guardavaccaro, to seal up the entrance to Black Rock Mine, which was located below the Embers mansion. After being made aware of the danger posed by the anomaly at the bottom of the cavern, the forensic team only worked on the large area known as the underground chamber, the ascending steps, the corridor, and the six rooms with shackles and radiators in them. Even without being able to investigate the remains at the bottom of the cavern, the forensic team still found enough DNA evidence that matched with countless missing persons reports, therefore solving numerous abduction cases dating back several decades.

Sealing up the Embers mansion's entrance to Black Rock Mine all but guaranteed that Morgan Carter would never remember the events that happened there. Under the guise of sealing away the Embers mansion because of dangerous underground natural-gas deposits, which supposedly aided—if not flat-out *caused*—the meth-lab explosion, the FBI Meta Division successfully covered up all records of the anomaly's existence once again. And with the only other entrance in and out of the mine permanently sealed, based on the FBI Meta Division's calculation, the creature would starve to death in time, which was a much safer and quieter way to get rid of it once and for all, as opposed to blowing up the mine, for example, which risked underground tremors, earthquakes, and other seismic activity that could draw unnecessary attention to Black Rock Mine. Not to mention run the risk of the massive explosions causing the Earth to open up somewhere, letting the creature out. It was also debated whether sending FBI agents into the caverns below the mansion in order to destroy the "monster" was feasible, but it was quickly vetoed by Siphos Ricketts, who viewed it as too great of a risk with regard to the loss of life, time, and resources. He knew that chasing the creature in the damp, dark tunnels five hundred feet below the Earth (on its own turf) would be an astronomical and extremely dangerous feat, so sealing the mine was ultimately what was decided on. And quite frankly, every Meta agent breathed a sigh of relief when the decision came down from Siphos Ricketts.

So then, once again, all was quiet and peaceful in Sky Haven, maybe even more peaceful than before since the world was now free of all Embers.

And speaking of peaceful, something strange happened to Morgan Carter as well. After Anthony's death, she stopped drinking and became a member of the small, nondenominational church around the corner from her old house, attending every Sunday service and Wednesday-night Bible study.

Since Morgan never bought home insurance for her house, she took a huge loss when it burned down, but her father had left his house in Texas to her in his will. Upon selling it, the Keller Williams real estate company in Jefferson, Texas, sent Morgan her share of the money a few weeks later, which she used to buy another house in Sky Haven. After resettling in the new house, she also vowed to change and get herself right with God.

She assumed that Anthony's death must have been her "punishment" for killing Carla Romano in her drunk-driving accident, and she accepted this "punishment" as just.

She then humbled herself to the point of finally asking God for forgiveness for Carla's death. She was honest with herself and with God and truly broke down before Him while asking for forgiveness in a way she never had before. After doing so, she found peace in her heart and was finally able to let go of the overwhelming guilt that was destroying her. She even stopped drinking and started attending weekly services at the nondenominational Christian church in Sky Haven. She liked it there, and the congregation fully accepted her despite knowing she was the famous Hollywood actress who once killed someone in a drunk-driving accident. A couple of months later, she was even asked to join the worship team because it was a Pentecostal-leaning nondenominational church, which, if you know anything about churches, meant they jammed *hard* up in there, boi!

Yes, strangely enough, after Anthony's death, Morgan stopped being bitter at the world, and she even stopped hating herself. She became a much different person, and even though she missed Anthony every single day and wished God had answered her prayer differently in regard to him, she did not hold resentment in her heart toward anyone, including herself or even the Embers.

She attended Anthony's funeral a few days after he passed away in hopes of seeing him one last time, but his parents had asked for his body to be cremated instead of buried and for the ashes to be sent back to Philadelphia. Also, Anthony's parents did not attend the funeral, which Morgan figured was because it would have been too painful for them to travel to Sky Haven, the place where their son was killed. Having never met them and not knowing how to get in contact with them, Morgan had no way or reason to call and ask them why they did not attend. And being of a completely different mentality after Anthony's passing, Morgan had a far more laid-back, "live and let live" demeanor, so she respected the Tricerras' reasons for not attending.

She did see Agent Guardavaccaro at the funeral and thanked him for attending as well as Randy the bartender and a few others from town.

She did not see Agent O'Neil, but Frank G. assured her that if he hadn't been reassigned to a case in Belize, he would have been there.

O'Neil, who had bugged Frank's suit with one of his many tiny audio surveillance gadgets, heard the whopper of a lie and cursed his old partner out in his mind at the time while observing the verbal exchange between him and Morgan from a small wooded area across the street. After Anthony's death, Guardavaccaro was unable to make a move in Sky Haven without O'Neil shadowing him.

Morgan Carter was learning to accept that Anthony was gone, but she also knew that she would have to learn to be alone because even though she had made peace between herself and God as well as herself and drunken Morgan Carter, she missed Anthony more than she had ever thought it was possible to miss a human being. She also swore she would never let another man into her heart again. Despite their short-lived relationship, their connection was one that most people could live an entire lifetime and never find. In fact, if you were to ask Morgan, the figure would be closer to ten lifetimes.

Morgan knew that despite being very young still, she would never find someone like Anthony again or perhaps even be able to accept a substitute who might come in at a distant second. Part of her heart died with Anthony, and because it was gone, she would never be able to give that part to anyone else in the future. She wasn't angry about it or bitter, but she missed him more than words could explain. She would often daydream about waking up one day to find out it was only a nightmare and that Anthony was still alive, but the sad reality of his death always returned like an unwelcomed cruel sobriety, crushing her heart all over again.

Leaving church one afternoon after dropping off some canned goods for the food drive, Morgan went home, grabbed her mail from the mailbox, went inside, and fed Pepp some wet food (the fat calico cat did not like dry food).

Pepp had escaped from the fire in Morgan's house by running out the wide-open back door; and Morgan had one day found her running around the back porch of her new house, which was only a block away, after purposely leaving her cell phone outside as it played "La Cucaracha" continuously for eight minutes.

Morgan put down the bag of groceries she had picked up earlier from the Sky Haven market (which, BTW, did not contain any vodka but did have some cold cuts) on her kitchen table and took a good, long look at her grandmother's brooch, which she kept in the center of the kitchen table. It was a great reminder of everything good that had ever been in her life and also a good motivator to stay on the straight and narrow path in the future.

She went through the envelopes that had come in the mail one by one, tossing all the useless stuff aside until she came across a small cream-colored envelope with no return address. She opened it and was surprised to see nothing in it. She held the envelope upside down, and a very small blue stone fell onto the kitchen table, bounced a few times, and landed next to her grandmother's brooch. At that moment, Morgan realized that the small blue stone was the actual missing blue sapphire from her grandmother's brooch.

CHAPTER 23

Hope

All the blood in Morgan's body rushed to her head. She dropped the remaining mail onto the floor and felt the seat of the kitchen chair hit her backside as it stopped her fall when her legs gave out. Her hand, shaking like that of an alcoholic's during their first day of sobriety, reached for the small blue sapphire and picked it up.

Morgan: How? *How?* And who?

As she asked herself these questions, her mind raced in thirty-eight directions at once, trying to make sense of what she was looking at. *Somebody is playing a prank!* she thought but then realized the impossibility of that notion. Only two people had ever had the brooch in their possession in Sky Haven, and one of them was dead—only she and Anthony.

"*How is this possible?*" she repeated to herself. Morgan looked at the envelope the sapphire came in, but there was nothing but her name and address written in cursive handwriting and no return address.

This had to be some sort of prank. But nobody else knew about the brooch; and even if by some strange happenstance someone else did know about this, why would they send her the sapphire now with no return address so she could thank them? It really made no sense. How would a stranger even get ahold of the tiny stone? It would have to be deliberate, right? Nobody would just find it somewhere on the ground, assume it belonged to Morgan Carter, and then mail it to her. That would be asinine.

"Okay, hold on, Morgan. Think about this rationally," she told herself. "Who all knew about this brooch in the entire world?" She counted on her fingers, saying, "Grandma, Mom, Dad, Anthony, and me. And everyone else but me is dead. *How is this happening right now?*" She tried over and over to come up with a logical explanation, but she just simply couldn't. All her logical speculations hit one dead end after another. There was absolutely no feasible explanation that encompassed someone who didn't know her finding it and knowing where to send it. Morgan just could not wrap her head around this. And then the most insane thought came flying across her mind: *What if Anthony is alive?*

She immediately started to hyperventilate as her face became bright red, and her heart beat with the intensity of the ATF pounding on David Koresh's door. "Easy, Morgan." She tried to calm herself. "There has to be a far more reasonable explanation. You saw him die. Do *not* let your imagination run wild and get your hopes up for something that is impossible." But the thought of Anthony being alive caused her entire body to break out in goose-bumps and every fiber of her being to be warm and adrenaline-charged.

She continued trying to figure out how it would be possible for Anthony to still be alive, but she could not come up with a single scenario.

Morgan regained some of her strength, then got up from the kitchen table with the envelope in her hand. She grabbed her car keys and headed for the door. Her cell phone was going off, and the name Gabby was displayed on the screen. But Morgan didn't hear "La Cucaracha" despite the phone being in her hand, nor did she notice Pepp running in circles around her living room as she closed the front door behind her, abruptly cutting off the sound of a flower vase crashing on the floor.

Meanwhile, at the Adelaide Motel

Frank Guardavaccaro was sitting on the edge of the bed, polishing his already way-too-clean, way-too-shiny black shoes. His cell phone rang. Frank picked it up and greeted Pasquale Siphos Ricketts. This conversation followed:

Frank G.: No, no sign of O'Neil yet. My instinct tells me he's still in town, though. That kid is way too hardheaded to let this go… Right… Exactly… Who? Oh, Morgan Carter… I've been keeping an eye on her, and our mole at the post office has been screening all her mail. So far, nothing out of the ordinary. An envelope without a return address did come for her this morning, but there was nothing in it except a little blue rock she probably ordered from Amazon or something. Women… [He laughed.] Yea, without anybody to tell her what happened below the Embers mansion, her selective amnesia will remain unchanged, so we're good… Yup, everything seems to be okay, but you know what? There is *one* loose end, that has had me worried for years. Johnny Embers… Yes, I know we've talked about this, but having that option so many years ago was stupid, PSR. Cremation is the only sure way to keep this thing from getting out… Yea, I know, Pasquale, but… Yes, I know… No, I'm *not* being paranoid… Okay, fine. Whatever, PSR… Okay, I'll talk to you later. Bye.

Frank G. hung up the phone, put on his shoes, left the motel room, and drove away in the black Cadillac.

Across the street, O'Neil, who had bugged Guardavaccaro's motel room, heard this entire conversation while he sat in his crappy Buick, eating soggy french fries and smoking menthol cigarettes. Satisfied, he spat the soggy fries out of his mouth through the window and sat up, exclaiming, "Gotcha!"

*****

Morgan Carter, who was now flying through the Sky Haven streets with the most vacant look on her face, could not hear the song on the radio of her car or her cell phone's ringtone because she had only one thing on her mind. She pulled up in front of Anthony's house and got out of the car, leaving her driver's side door wide open. Now, when I say she pulled up in front of Anthony's house, I literally mean *in front*. Her car was diagonally parked on his lawn, with the headlights pointing at his living room window.

In some sort of trance in which nothing on the planet mattered except for whatever mission she was trying to accomplish, Morgan tried to open the front door but found it to be locked. She walked around back and found his back door locked as well. She punched and broke the small window of the back door with no hesitation, and with a bloody hand, she reached in and unlocked the door from the inside. Leaving the door wide open, she walked into his living room and started going through all the shelves on the north wall. She opened book after book, and after not finding what she was looking for, she tossed them over her shoulder. Finally, she found a book titled *Winnetou*, opened it, and found a piece of paper inside it. Most likely, it had been used by

Anthony as a bookmark. Morgan held up the piece of paper, which had Anthony's notes on *Winnetou* on it, next to the envelope she received earlier that day and was shocked to discover that the handwriting on both items was identical.

*****

Agent O'Neil followed Agent Guardavaccaro for a few minutes, and on realizing he had staked himself out outside Morgan Carter's house as usual, he decided to leave him be and investigate his new lead instead.

Approximately ten minutes later, after stopping at the G&A hardware store to pick up an axe, he pulled up next to the Sky Haven cemetery. He was lucky to have been able to purchase the axe since it was getting very close to 8:00 PM, which was closing time for Mr. and Mrs. G&A.

After hopping out of his less than luxurious Buick, which was absolutely phenomenal on gas mileage, Agent O'Neil turned on his flashlight and headed toward the Embers mausoleum while whistling the theme to *Unsolved Mysteries*, completely unaware of the fact that Frank Guardavaccaro had followed him there and was watching him from his black Cadillac.

*****

Morgan Carter was now driving home from Anthony's house after finding out that the envelope she had received earlier that day containing a small blue sapphire had handwriting on it that was identical to Anthony's. She was in shock and completely torn between believing that Anthony was alive and that someone was playing a cruel joke on her. Her mind was overwhelmed, and her tears were soaking her soft white skin as she drove back to her house in the dark. One million possibilities were swarming through her head, but among them was not *one* viable option for how Anthony could still logically be alive.

She didn't even realize that she reached for the dial on her radio and turned it. It was probably just something she did instinctually, but after three full turns, the dial landed on 104.5 and was left there. A song wound down, and the radio DJ spoke as another song's intro started. Morgan continued to ponder the state of things as the new song played through the first verse without Morgan paying any attention to it. Suddenly every strand of fine blonde hair on the back of Morgan's neck stood up as the singer on the radio reached the song's prechorus.

You told me you love me.
Why did you leave me all alone?

Images flashed in Morgan's mind of Deek shoving her through a corridor.

A. TRICERATOPS

Now you tell me you need me
When you call me on the phone.

Images flashed in Morgan's mind of her and
Deek walking down steep underground steps.

Girl, I refuse. You must have me
confused with some other guy.
    The bridges were burned.
Now it's your turn to cry.

Images flashed in Morgan's mind of Deek
shooting two young girls in front of her in some kind
of underground chamber.

Morgan's grip on her steering wheel tightened,
and her eyes become as wide as they could possibly
be. She inadvertently stepped on the gas as her memories took her to another place. The song's chorus
penetrated her eardrums, and she screamed, seeing
herself being lowered into a cavern while she was
standing in a metal cage.

Cry me a river, cry me a river, cry
me a river, cry me a river, yeah,
yeah!

Suddenly Morgan remembered Anthony and
Deek fighting in the cage as the two special agents
were shouting commands from a distance above. She
then remembered falling from the elevator as well as
Anthony being shot only moments later. She almost

lost consciousness but fought hard to stay lucid as the song was still blaring on the radio. She yanked the wheel hard to the left to turn onto her street, but she overshot the turn and hit Mrs. Lintbottom's trash cans. She sent them flying down the street before straightening out the car and pulling into her own driveway, which was ninety feet from Mrs. Lintbottom's house. She exited the car, leaving the driver's door open, and stumbled into her own house.

Special Agent Frank Guardavaccaro saw everything from three parking spaces down the street, having just returned from the cemetery, and assumed she had fallen off the wagon.

At this exact time, Frank O'Neil reached Johnathan Harvey Embers's mausoleum, unbothered by Guardavaccaro, who left immediately after spotting him in the cemetery. He easily entered it since the lock had been broken some time ago by one of the Embers twins. He pointed his flashlight at a stone slab on the wall of the mausoleum that had JHE written on it. A few swift hits with the axe shattered the thin slab, revealing an ornate mahogany coffin behind it. Agent O'Neil reached inside the stone slot, grabbed the casket handle that was closest to him, and pulled as hard as he could, ejecting the coffin out of the slot halfway. He stood for a moment, trying to catch his breath, having been surprised by how heavy the old mahogany casket was, and then braced himself before opening the casket's lid.

Frank O'Neil: You have *got* to be kidding me!

He quickly slammed the casket's lid shut and pushed it back inside the stone slot. He grabbed his axe and flashlight and headed back to his car through the dark cemetery while shaking his head.

Morgan's house

Morgan was sitting on her couch, the TV on, unaware that Agent Guardavaccaro was parked outside, on her street. Her memories of the night her father died had returned; however, they had stopped right after Anthony was shot in the cavern. She was now flipping through the channels without knowing that she was doing it, deep in thought.

Morgan (to herself): I remember that Deek Embers shot Anthony when we were in that...place. Guardavaccaro lied about where Anthony was killed. Why would he do that? I mean, he died saving me either way, so why does it matter if it was at my house or in some dungeon? Why would he not want me to know what really happened? Who sent the blue sapphire? Why does Anthony's handwriting match the writing on the envelope? I saw him get shot in the stomach with a 12-gauge and then die in the hospital, so how could he possibly be alive? I mean...I saw it with my own eyes! But why would Guardavaccaro try to cover up where he died?

Suddenly she stopped flipping through the channels and paused the screen of her TV, a feature that all Dish Network customers knew about. Her eyes became the size of Agent O'Neil's and Agent Guardavaccaro's steering wheels. She dropped the remote, started shaking, let out a bloodcurdling three-second-long scream, and fainted on her couch.

The paused image on her TV screen was a Discovery Channel 3D rendering of a triceratops dinosaur's head.

CHAPTER 24

Johnathan Harvey Embers

The following morning, Morgan woke up on her couch; and on seeing the image that remained paused on her TV while she slept, she fully regained her memories from the night her father was killed. She remembered the anomaly, the cavern beneath Embers mansion, the multitude of human remains, Deek's death—everything.

The fact that Guardavaccaro lied about where Anthony was killed made perfect sense to her now. The FBI agent wanted to keep the creature's existence a secret at all costs. But who sent her the blue sapphire, and was it even possible for Anthony to still be alive? Morgan saw him get shot in the abdomen with a 12-gauge, and then she saw him die in the hospital with her own eyes. Dr. Hamilton did everything he could to revive him for roughly twenty minutes. Anthony being alive was a physical *impossibility*.

Suddenly her cell phone started vibrating, signifying an incoming call from a phone number she had never seen before. She had placed the phone on vibrate after discovering the broken flower vase from

Pepp's speed run the night before. She picked up the phone, and a voice that she thought she had heard before said three words before hanging up the call: "Johnathan Harvey Embers."

She thought about the strange call for a few moments. She then picked up her car keys, fed Pepp her wet cat food, and left the house. She entered her car without realizing that her driver's side door had been shut by someone (otherwise, her battery would have died), and she started the engine. Three seconds later, she was driving down state route 940 as a black Cadillac pulled out of a parking space on the very same street to follow her.

Morgan turned left at the end of her street, passing by Amarilla Pizza, where a man was standing next to the pay phone located in front of the store while reading a newspaper, which was blocking the entire top half of his body. As Morgan and Special Agent Guardavaccaro (who was following her) passed by, the man lowered the newspaper, revealing that he was Frank O'Neil, who then immediately jumped in his Buick, which was parked in front of the pizza shop. Not only had he called Morgan from the pay phone out front of Amarilla Pizza and given her the clue "Johnathan Harvey Embers," but he had also devised a very cunning plan that involved using Morgan as bait to entrap and catch Guardavaccaro trying to commit murder.

Unaware that his former partner had seen him in the cemetery, O'Neil thought, *Morgan isn't stupid. She will understand the clue I gave her and go to the mausoleum to investigate. And since Guardavaccaro is surveilling her, he will follow her to the cemetery. When he sees where she is headed, he will try to kill her since the last thing he wants is for her to see what's in that mausoleum. I will stop him, save her life, and then arrest him. She will not only consider me a hero for saving her life, but I will then have a witness who will be willing to testify against Frank in court for attempted murder. Guardavaccaro will then squeal on Siphos Ricketts to receive a reduced sentence, and I will be an instant FBI legend with a new and very beautiful blonde girlfriend.*

Solid plan, right? On paper…

O'Neil was not only very ambitious but also very smart and, most importantly, a man of conscience and virtue, which was why the more he thought about his "brilliant plan," the more he started having second thoughts as he followed Frank toward the cemetery. The dangers of reality started to set in.

As the graveyard drew closer and closer, O'Neil, still only a rookie FBI agent, began having doubts that were really riling up his conscience. *What if I don't get to Morgan in time, and he kills her?* That nagging thought kept getting louder and louder in his mind while recognizable landmarks passed by outside as he made his way to the cemetery.

So many unpredictable factors could make things go in a way he had not foreseen once all three of them were in the graveyard.

"The slightest miscalculation, and not only will I not have a witness that could put Guardavaccaro away, but also, I will be responsible for Morgan's death." O'Neil paused to think. "And what if he kills her with *my* gun and then frames me for the murder?" He paused again while a little bit of fear started creeping in. "Too many things can go wrong. This isn't a foolproof plan. Not to mention that luring Frank to the mausoleum with Morgan is easy, but is it really the right thing to do?" O'Neil wondered if his ambition had blinded him into putting an innocent girl's life in danger. "This isn't the movies, Frank. What have you done? You're an FBI agent, not Lex Luthor running diabolical schemes!" He paused yet again. "And Guardavaccaro is a very experienced and cunning veteran FBI agent. You're gonna get yourself and that girl killed in that cemetery if he catches on before you want him to!" O'Neil took a long pause, then exhaled. "I have *got* to stop this while there is still time! But how am I going to stop it now that everything is in motion?"

Truth be told, his plan really *was* great on paper, but O'Neil was right. Even the slightest error in executing it, and Morgan, an innocent civilian and his only potential witness against Frank G., would be toast, not to mention that Guardavaccaro could frame him for her murder or potentially take his life as well if things went *completely* south.

"I have to stop this!" he repeated to himself; and then, panicking, he took out his cellphone and dialed Morgan's number, which he had gotten from a simple Whitepages search. He had previously avoided using his phone to contact her directly because he knew the FBI was most likely monitoring her calls, but this was a legitimate life-and-death emergency. He would just have to dump this phone and get another burner later. It was ringing. "C'mooon, pick up, pick up!" said Frank O'Neil out loud to no one.

Morgan: Hello?
O'Neil: You are being followed!

The dial tone sounded.

Morgan hung up the phone and looked in her rearview mirror, where she spotted Guardavaccaro's black Cadillac.

If these events had taken place *before* she received the blue sapphire in the mail, she would have probably done the sensible thing and *not* gone ahead with the plan to go to the mausoleum, but she didn't care about Guardavaccaro anymore. All she cared about was getting to the truth. Besides, in her mind, Guardavaccaro was a liar who had no say in whether she investigated matters for herself, especially after smiling in her face at Anthony's funeral while *knowing* he was lying about how Anthony died.

She slammed the gas pedal down and lost all concerns over red lights and stop signs as the only thing on her mind was getting to the cemetery before Guardavaccaro.

Seeing her speed up and drive so recklessly, Frank G. deduced that she had made him; and he, too, sped up to try and catch her.

"Ah, *crap*!" exclaimed O'Neil out loud to himself while realizing what was happening. "She's not going to abort the plan of going to the cemetery! And now Frank might think she's running from him because her amnesia has worn off. Well, you really screwed *this* one up, O'Neil! Frank Guardavaccaro is definitely not gonna stop now. He's gonna catch her, arrest her, and then take her somewhere and shoot her, probably with *my* gun, to make sure the secret about the anomaly doesn't get out! I have to do something!"

Realizing that catching Frank G.'s brand-new Cadillac with his ancient Buick was probably not going to happen, the brilliant idea of taking a short-cut and cutting him off before Frank G. reached the cemetery sprung up in his mind. Screeching tires, he turned left on Chemung Street and gunned it all the way to Berwick Street, where he turned right. Speeding up toward the intersection at Berwick and Lehigh, he put his seat belt on and clenched his teeth. He saw the red light facing him ahead, which meant that Morgan would have a green light at the Lehigh-Berwick intersection. Sure enough, Morgan flew through the intersection one second later, followed by Guardavaccaro, who would be caught completely off guard as an old crappy Buick plowed into the side of his Cadillac with a deafening bang. The impact instantly dented his driver's side door inward, crushing his left leg before setting off his airbag and blowing out all the Cadillac's windows.

The two cars formed a big metal T as the Buick slid forward another fifteen feet while pushing the Cadillac through and out of the intersection.

Operating on pure adrenaline after the collision, O'Neil, who had his seat belt on and had braced himself for the impact, jumped out of his car once both vehicles came to a full stop, ran around the side of his Buick with his .357 Magnum in hand, opened Guardavaccaro's door, and stuck the gun in his face, yelling, "Don't move, Frank!"

Guardavaccaro, whose face was cut in three places from the broken glass and had a bloody nose from the air bag and a broken leg, was not exactly in any condition to resist.

O'Neil: We're gonna take a little walk now, Frank!
Guardavaccaro: Where are we goin', kid? [He spat out blood.] The abandoned house on Church Street, where you've been staying the last three months?

*****

Morgan saw the accident in her rearview mirror, but she did not stop. Hell-bent on reaching the cemetery to get to the truth, she had no concern for herself or anybody else. A few minutes later, after reaching the massive graveyard, she bolted out of her car like a bat out of hell and kept full stride the entire time she ran toward the enclosed grave. She could hear her own breathing and her heartbeat in her head, but nobody was going to stop her from reaching the mausoleum.

She ignored the traumatic memories of the surroundings that were trying to snake their way into her psyche once she arrived at the tomb next to the pond and quickly swung the metal gates open. She ran down the steps and, after missing a step, fell facefirst on the ground, scraping her elbow, but she didn't feel a thing. She then stood up and frantically looked all over the mausoleum. After finding the hole in the stone slab that O'Neil had dug the night before, she looked inside it and saw the mahogany casket, undisturbed, untouched, and exactly where Frank O. had left it.

Normally, she might not have had the strength to pull it out by herself; but as she was yanking the handle closest to her with both hands, she kept seeing images in her mind of Anthony smiling at her and calling her blondie. The coffin budged a little bit toward her as it scraped the large stone it was sitting on. Morgan burst into tears as she imagined Anthony pretending to ride a horse in the hotel room as she was on the phone with her dad, and the heavy coffin scraped a little bit closer to her again. Finally, remembering how she laughed at the injuries on his face in The Caboose, unaware that he had sustained them while saving her life, she screamed and pulled harder than she had pulled anything in her entire life, causing the coffin to slide halfway out of its slot in the wall. Morgan's grip on the handle slipped as the coffin slid out, and she fell backward onto the ground again, scraping her other elbow this time.

Dark-red blood ran down her arm as she stood up and looked at the casket. Her breathing resembled that of an elephant with emphysema. She slowly moved closer as she tried to slow down her breathing and heart rate to avoid passing out. She put both hands on the lid of the casket, exhaled, closed her eyes, and opened it. One second later, she opened her eyes and looked down—empty. The coffin was empty. Instantly all the pieces in her mind clicked together, and for the first time since she had received the blue sapphire in the mail, *everything* made sense.

Morgan Carter: The FBI faked their deaths.

CHAPTER 25

The House on Church Street

An empty black Cadillac sat in the intersection at Berwick Street and Lehigh Street with its badly dented driver's side door wide open. Shattered glass was sprinkled all around the car as it did not have one window intact. A crowd had gathered around it but parted to make way for Sheriff Charles Bouchard's cruiser, which was approaching the scene. Shortly after, the cruiser of newly minted Deputy Daniel Espinoza pulled up behind Charlie Bumper. He, too, exited his car and came over to inspect the black Cadillac.

Sheriff Bouchard: A one-car accident with no driver. Nice. [He spat on the ground.] Run the plate for me, will you, Danny?"
Deputy Espinoza: Sure thing, Sheriff.

Danny Espinoza was a young man in his mid- to late twenties, with a clean-shaven face and very short black hair. His tanned complexion was consistent with his Mayan and Guatemalan ancestors, and he was about six feet tall with a thin build. He had a pleasant face with dark-brown eyes and an unusually thin nose on it. Also, he had very nice teeth, having worn braces when he was little, which seemed to have really paid off in his adult years. Espinoza was an honest, diligent, and conscientious deputy, very eager to impress the sheriff and climb the law enforcement ladder.

The deputy ran the Cadillac's plate from his cruiser's computer, then came back to the sheriff, shaking his head.

Espinoza: No hits.
Sheriff Bouchard: Exactly as I thought. Feds. [He shook his head and sighed.] O'Neil must have finally caught up to Guardavaccaro.

Espinoza nodded. Sheriff Bouchard lit a cigarette and addressed the crowd. "Did anybody see the crash?"

"I did, Sheriff!" answered an obese man with a bald head and large beard. He was wearing a Legend of Zelda T-shirt that was at least two sizes too small.

Sheriff Bouchard exhaled as if he was annoyed.

Sheriff Bouchard: Okay, Kenny, what happened?

Kenny went to speak, but the sheriff cut him off with "JUST WHAT YOU SAW, KENNY! No speculation or conspiracies please!"

Kenny: But, Sheriff, it had to be the CIA, man! The young guy took the old guy out of the car at gunpoint, and they both got into a banged-up maroon Buick and went down Berwick, that way. [He pointed down the street.] I'm tellin' you, Sheriff, it has to be about some classified alien stuff, man. The old guy was wearing a black suit and—

Sheriff Bouchard: Thanks, Kenny.

He walked away from the scene with Deputy Espinoza as Kenny continued talking about his theories, which became more and more "out there."

Sheriff Bouchard: "Do me a favor, Danny...pull surveillance video from that coffee shop at the corner down there and find out which way the Buick went from there. Then do the same for any other shop that has cameras pointing out into the street, in a four-block radius."

Espinoza: "You got it, Mr. Bouchard."

Sheriff Bouchard: "Call me Charlie, kid."

Kenny was still heard rambling as the words *Roswell* and *Area 54* came into play at least once.

Thirty minutes later in an abandoned, boarded-up house on Church Street where a banged-up Buick was parked in its alleyway, covered by a blue tarp with medium-sized holes in it

Frank Guardavaccaro sat on a chair in the middle of a room that was badly lit by a single light bulb, which was hanging from the ceiling above him. It had a small round metal shade hanging over it, and it swung ever so slightly back and forth above Guardavaccaro. Frank O'Neil sat outside the circle of light that was shining down from the light bulb, on a dusty, ripped-up couch that was left behind by the previous owners of the house. The room didn't have much in it apart from the couch, the chair, and a small table in one of the dark corners of the room, a laptop on top on it. Tiny slivers of light came from random holes and cracks in the boards that were covering the windows from the outside. Chinese takeout boxes were spread out all over the floor around the table. A sleeping bag covered the couch that O'Neil was sitting on, and a pillow sat on top of it on one side. Both special agents sat quietly in the dimly lit room until Guardavaccaro broke the silence.

Frank G.: "*Ugh… Ohhh!*"

He fell forward to his knees, with his hands zip-tied behind his back, giving another growl as he put pressure on his broken leg. Then he looked in O'Neil's direction and fell forward on his stomach with his eyes closed.

O'Neil stared at him from the couch while holding an empty syringe. He stood up, walked over to Guardavaccaro, and checked his nonexistent pulse, after which he looked at his watch.

Exactly thirty minutes prior to these events, Frank G. and Frank O. had found themselves in a tense, slow-paced verbal exchange that started with O'Neil welcoming Guardavaccaro to his humble abode.

Thirty minutes ago

O'Neil: It ain't much, but it's been home for the last three months. By the way, Frank, how *did* you know I've been staying here?

Guardavaccaro (while sitting in the chair in the middle of the poorly lit room with his hands zip-tied behind his back): I know a lot more than you think, kid.

O'Neil paused.

O'Neil: I bet you do, Frank. I bet you do.

Guardavaccaro: Lemme guess, kid… This is an interrogation? [He laughed.] Is that why you're filming this with that cell phone on the table, next to the laptop?

O'Neil: Nothing gets by you, Frank! Except *me*!

O'Neil laughed.

Guardavaccaro joined O'Neil in laugher but for different reasons.

Guardavaccaro: Yea, you're a regular J. R. Ewing, kid. Making anonymous tips from pay phones and pulling everybody's strings behind the scenes, huh?

O'Neil stopped laughing and made a serious face.

O'Neil: What?

Guardavaccaro laughed again.

Guardavaccaro: This ain't the movies, kid. Nobody stands next to a pay phone, reading the newspaper, unless they're trying to blend in.

O'Neil made a confused face and was also a little embarrassed.

Guardavaccaro: By the way...did you find what you were looking for in Johnny Embers's mausoleum?

O'Neil quickly got out of his chair and walked into the light shining down from the light bulb above Guardavaccaro's head.

O'Neil: How do you know I went there?

Guardavaccaro: I followed you, kid.

O'Neil was starting to get angry. "What are you talking about!" he exclaimed.

Guardavaccaro: Kid, you didn't find it even remotely strange that I never changed motel rooms after our fight at the hospital? I wanted to make it easy for you to find me so you would come and talk to me.

Truth be told, O'Neil found the fact that Guardavaccaro did not change motel rooms very strange all along. He responded, trying to commandeer the conversation away from Frank G. and regain control over it, "You didn't change motel rooms because you knew I would follow you and find your new location anyway! Nice try, Frank, but you're not going to manipulate me like some mark."

Guardavaccaro: Kid, if I wanted to harm you, you would already be dead.
O'Neil: Well now. Is that so, Frank? Care to explain how you would have pulled that one off?
Guardavaccaro: At the hospital. When you ran away. FBI training tells the agent to zigzag when running from an assailant with a firearm. You ran straight for the first few seconds. Adrenaline, no doubt, clouded your judgment. And having never been in that situation before, your instinct to get away as fast as possible took over.

But then you remembered your training a few seconds later, and you zigzagged as you fled the parking lot. I could have shot you dead for three whole seconds, kid.

O'Neil knew this was all true. He remained silent.

Guardavaccaro: Not to mention that I've known that you've been here for three months. I could have killed you in your sleep at any time.

O'Neil: That's not true! I have a perimeter set up, and I would have heard you come in.

Guardavaccaro: And did I ever *try* to come in?

O'Neil knew Frank was right again. He looked at the floor for about five seconds, then looked up and smiled.

O'Neil: Okay, Frank. Okay. You're very convincing, I'll give you that. And okay, I'll bite. Why didn't you kill me or even try to come after me when you had the chance?

Guardavaccaro: For the same reason I lied to Siphos Ricketts about not knowing where you were, kid. You bugged my motel room, right? So you heard that conversation too, *right?* I knew you were listening, and I purposely gave you the Johnny Embers clue so you'd investigate and realize I'm not a killer once you saw the empty coffin. I wanted you to come and talk to me all along, kid. [He paused.] And there is a reason for that too.

O'Neil's jaw dropped, but he somehow still managed to ask a question.

O'Neil: And…that reason is?

Guardavaccaro: I never told you this before, and I should have. [He paused while fighting back tears.] I never had any children, but…*you* are like a son to me, Frank. I could never hurt you, kid.

O'Neil teared up but tried to keep his composure. His voice trembled as he replied, "That doesn't change the fact that you're a murderer, Frank! You killed Tricerra in cold blood! I saw you!"

Guardavaccaro: Tricerra? You mean the same kid that I saved from that thing in the mine when I pulled him and his girlfriend out? Why would I save him, only to kill him later?

O'Neil: Because if *you* hadn't pulled the lever to bring up that elevator in the mine, *I would have*! You knew that and needed a more covert opportunity to kill them. But when you learned that Morgan couldn't remember the creature in the mine, you thought, "Okay, she can live, but Tricerra still has to die to keep this a secret"!

Guardavaccaro laughed and looked down.

Guardavaccaro: In the two years you've known me, have I ever murdered anyone in cold blood? Or even done *anything* to suggest I am that kind of person, capable of such a thing? You're a good judge of character, kid. Am I that guy? [He got angry and started shouting.] *Am I?*

A single tear rolled down Guardavaccaro's cheek. O'Neil turned his back to Frank G. and grabbed his own hair with both hands. He knew that what Frank was saying was true but was also afraid that Frank, who was an expert in psychology, could be conning him. Unsure of what to do, he paused to think for a minute.

O'Neil: Okay, Frank. I will admit I don't know why you let me live when you could have killed me at the hospital, and I don't know why you lied to Siphos Ricketts about knowing my whereabouts or why you never came after me here at this house. I don't understand why Johnathan Embers's body is missing from the mausoleum in the Sky Haven cemetery, and I don't know how I could have misread your character so badly even though you are a cold-blooded murderer. I *don't know* the answers to those questions. So...I will give you an opportunity to explain everything. No more games. No more BS, Frank. *What is going on?* Make it all make sense!

Guardavaccaro: Kid, what did I tell you while we were sitting in my car in the parking lot at Sky Haven Memorial Hospital?

O'Neil: What?

Guardavaccaro: You are a second-year rookie FBI agent. Your security clearance is level 2. You need at least a five-year security clearance to know the information that you are asking me for, kid.

O'Neil smiled while shaking his head.

O'Neil: How convenient, Frank.

Guardavaccaro: Kid, listen to me for one second. [He looked him dead in the eyes.] Turn off the cell phone camera.

O'Neil: Not a chance, Frank.

Guardavaccaro (snarling through his clenched teeth: *Just. Do it!*

O'Neil was taken back and a little frightened by Frank's demeanor. "Okay, geez!" he replied and stopped the cell phone camera from recording further.

Guardavaccaro: Come here!

O'Neil walked over to Guardavaccaro and stood in front of him.

Guardavaccaro: "I cannot legally tell you what you want to know without facing the risk of being court-martialed for revealing classified information. *But*…it would be different if, let's say, my life was in danger.

Guardavaccaro looked into Frank O.'s eyes and winked.

O'Neil thought for a couple of seconds, then understood and went back to the table in the corner of the room to turn the cell phone camera back on.

O'Neil took out his pistol and pointed it at Guardavaccaro.

O'Neil: I'm only going to ask you one more time, Frank! Why is Johnathan Embers's coffin empty, and what happened to Anthony Tricerra?

Guardavaccaro: Okay, kid, take it easy. I'll tell you. Just don't kill me. There is something in my jacket pocket. Reach in and take it out.

Having already frisked Guardavaccaro for weapons, O'Neil knew he would not find a knife, a pistol, a Taser, or anything of the sort in Frank's jacket pocket, so he reached in and took out two small glass vials and a very small plastic syringe that would have been hard to feel during frisking. One glass vial was marked GX14, and the other GX14A.

O'Neil: What is this, Frank?

Guardavaccaro: It's what I stuck Tricerra with in the hospital. And it's what you're gonna stick *me* with after I bring you up to a level 5 security clearance.

CHAPTER 26

Intensive Care Revisited

At this point in time, you probably have at least one or two theories about what is going on, right? And if not, then you just want some straightforward *answers*, not more cliff-hangers and time-line jumps, right? Heh-heh, I *bet* you do. Well, okay. I am going to tell you *exactly* what is going on *right now*. And the best way to do so is to do a time-line jump 😊 to approximately twelve minutes before Anthony died in his hospital room. Before his conversation with Morgan (during which he gave her back her grandmother's brooch), Anthony had a private conversation with Special Agent Guardavaccaro for about ten minutes in his hospital room, a conversation that left him very upset and tearful, if you recall. It was a conversation that we did not know the contents of—until now.

Twelve minutes before Anthony's death

Special Agent Guardavaccaro stuck his head out of the hospital room door to watch Rasheeda Jenkins walk away.

Nurse Jenkins: I saw that!

Frank retracted his head back into the room quickly and closed the door.

Anthony: Special Agent Guardavaccaro, they told me what you did for Morgan and me by bringing us here and saving my life. Saving both our lives. I want to thank you and—
Frank: Well, don't thank me just yet, kid. I have some good news, bad news, and even worse news for you.

Anthony formed a bewildered look on his face.

Frank: I'm gonna give it to you straight, kid. The good news is you're going to be fine. Your injuries will heal, and you will not have any permanent damage of any kind.
Anthony: Oh, thank God.
Frank: Also, Morgan is perfectly fine, with the exception of something called retrograde amnesia, which she will probably have for the rest of her life.
Anthony: What is that?
Frank: She just can't remember anything from last night after Deek killed her father. But don't worry, I told her you saved her life, and you're a hero, kid. However, I cannot tell her about anything that went on in that mine. Plus, and here's

where the bad news is going to start coming in, we're going to have to fake your death.

Anthony: *What?*

Frank: I'm sorry, kid, but that is the way it has to be. Here is the reality of things. By the way, I'm gonna talk fast, so try and keep up. You saw that creature, and so did Morgan. At this point in time, all those who have ever seen it are dead except for my partner, me, you, and Ms. Carter. Now, Morgan cannot remember anything, but if she could, we would have to fake her death and relocate her as well, just like the FBI did to Johnny Embers and Emitt Clydesdale in the 1950s. It was done to make sure they wouldn't spread the word of what they saw to other Sky Haven residents and inspire them to go looking for the creature in the mine. Hell, if three generations of Embers hadn't fed that damn thing, it would've been dead by now, and we wouldn't even be having this conversation. [He shook his head.] You see, kid, the FBI division that I work for specializes in investigating and keeping occult, paranormal, or otherworldly events secret. If Mr. and Mrs. John Q public knew half the stuff that is out there, the world would be pure chaos, kid. Anyway, the only way that Morgan will remember what happened in that mine is if something or some*one*, *you*, reminds her. So, and here's the worst news of all, not only are we going to have to fake your death and relocate you, but also, you can never see her again, kid. I'm sorry.

Anthony, whose jaw had hit the floor approximately four times during Special Agent Guardavaccaro's speech, suddenly changed his demeanor to furious and confidently replied, "No! That's never going to happen. I won't go along with it!"

Frank: Right. So I thought you might say that, and let me assure you that you *will* go along with this plan.
Anthony: Oh yea? How are you going to make me?

Frank pulled out a large kitchen knife that was inside a Ziploc bag in his suit-jacket pocket.

Frank: I recovered this knife from the ashy rubble that was Morgan's house. It was underneath what was left of her living room couch. It is the weapon that took Joe Carter's life and...it has *your* fingerprints all over it. Sure, it has Deek's prints on it as well. But he's dead, and you're not, which means...if you don't go along with this relocation plan, I'm going to charge you with killing Joe Carter. You *will* be convicted of first-degree murder and sentenced to life in prison, and you will never see Morgan again anyway.

Anthony was shocked and terrified. He managed to mumble, "I didn't...kill...anyone..."

Frank: Yea, well, half a dozen neighbors who saw you fleeing the burning house with a shotgun in your hand say otherwise, kid.

Anthony felt panic grip every molecule of his body. Agent Guardavaccaro turned his back to him and continued to talk as he looked out the hospital room window.

Frank: I truly am sorry to do this to you, kid. For what it's worth, I think you're a good kid. And I know you care for that girl. I saw how you risked your life to save her in that mine. It was very brave, and you have my respect. Please believe me when I tell you that I get no pleasure from doing this to you. But I took an oath, and I have a job to do.

Anthony, who had an IQ of 153, shut down the feelings of panic and allowed his brain to scan for possibilities rooted in logic, which might otherwise be drowned out by emotion at critical times such as this. "Just keep him talking," he told himself as he started thinking in terms of chess and started seeing ten moves ahead.

Anthony: I dunno what to say, Special Agent. I mean…how would something like faking my death even work?

As soon as the last word in his sentence left his lips and Frank started speaking again, Anthony reached over to his jeans, which were hanging on the back of the chair next to his hospital bed, and took out Morgan's grandmother's brooch from his pocket as well as a small Swiss Army knife. After unfolding the most basic blade of the Swiss Army knife, he immediately began trying to scoop one of the five small blue sapphire stones out of the brooch.

Special Agent Guardavaccaro, still standing with his back turned to Anthony, was not aware of what he was doing; but he continues speaking, wanting to answer Anthony's question.

Frank: Well, it's quite simple, really. [He took two glass vials out of his pocket, one marked GX14 and the other marked GX14A.] About five years ago, the Meta Division of the FBI started recruiting the brightest scientists, physicists, and molecular biologists the world had to offer in order to better equip our agents in the fight against…unnatural or otherworldly forces.

Anthony succeeded in removing the small blue sapphire from the brooch, and he swallowed it as Frank continued speaking.

Frank: Well, about three years ago, those brilliant minds came up with a serum called GX14. What it does is this. Once injected into a human subject, it takes approximately two minutes for ten milligrams of GX14 to infiltrate the bloodstream. Once it is in the bloodstream, it causes the human heart to slow down so much that it is virtually undetectable by ECG or EKG machines or, really, *any* digital heart monitor. In other words, your heart will beat so slowly and so faintly that nobody will be able to feel your pulse, not even a machine. Neat, right? At that incredibly slow pace, your heart will only pump enough blood through your body to keep you from dying or having permanent brain damage, but to the world, you will seem dead as a doornail. Once the doctors do their song and dance of trying to "revive you," which will be unsuccessful as long as GX14 is in your system, I will order an extraction team to come to the hospital, disguised as personnel from the coroner's office. And once we are in the extraction van together, I will administer ten milligrams of the GX14 antidote. [He turned around to show Anthony the vial marked GX14A.] Within two minutes, you'll be as good as new.

Anthony—who had finished removing the sapphire out of the brooch, swallowed it, and put everything back in his pants pocket—was now watching Frank speak to him face-to-face.

Anthony: That's insane. You know that, right? I mean…is that even safe? And where will I go? And what about my mom and dad?

Frank: Way ahead of you, kid. You will be given a new name and relocated to a quaint li'l town called Tonopah, Nevada. Population? Roughly 2,300. We will give you $250 thousand to start over, and yes, kid, the GX14 procedure is safe. In fact, before I agreed to carry the serum with me in the field, I had them test it on me. I refuse to inject anybody with anything I would be scared to take myself. It is perfectly safe. As for your folks, well… I'm sorry, kid. More bad news. You can't ever contact them again either. Otherwise, the whole plan falls apart. They will be told that you drowned in Arrowhead Lake in Mount Pocono and that your body was never recovered. Everyone who knows you in Sky Haven will be told you were cremated after dying in the hospital. No more empty coffins. It leaves loose ends, and it is a liability.

Anthony: You can't do this. My parents will be devastated!

Frank: I'm sorry, kid. I really am, but there's nothing else I can do. This is the way it has to be.

Anthony looked at the floor for about ten seconds and then looked up at Frank with tears in his eyes.

Anthony: I guess I have no choice. But you have to let me say goodbye to Morgan at least.

Frank: Okay, kid. After I stick you with the serum, you will have about two minutes before it takes effect. I will let you say goodbye to Ms. Carter, but remember, if you tell her about *any* of this, when you regain consciousness, you will be arrested for first-degree murder and tried. And, kid, you *will* do life in prison without the possibility of parole because of your previous conviction. Same goes for if you call, text, or email her after your relocation or write her letters to tell her the truth. And, BTW, her incoming mail will be monitored as well as her phone and email. And I *will* be standing here the whole time you speak to Ms. Carter as well. Don't do anything stupid, kid.

Anthony agreed. Guardavaccaro administered the GX14 shot to Tricerra, who then took the brooch out of the pocket of his jeans again as Frank headed next door. Less than five seconds later, Morgan walked into his room, followed by Guardavaccaro and O'Neil, who closely supervised the proceedings.

On seeing his demeanor, Morgan burst into tears. Anthony took her hand and began saying goodbye.

CHAPTER 27

Level 5 Security Clearance

Back in the abandoned house on Church Street, in the tiny town of Sky Haven, Special Agent Guardavaccaro lay on the dirty wooden floor, unconscious, with his hands zip-tied behind his back as the light bulb with the small metal shade swung back and forth ever so slightly above him.

Frank O'Neil, having been brought up to speed by his old partner about *everything*, including GX14 and Anthony Tricerra being alive in Tonopah, Nevada, was sitting on the dusty, torn-up couch in "his" living room. On hearing Frank G.'s fantastic story about secret serums that made the human heartbeat undetectable to monitors, he scoffed and even laughed in Frank G.'s face once or twice during the epic tale. Naturally, he did not believe any of it and was certain that Frank was trying to con him. I mean, let's face it. If it *was* a con, it was both a really good one and a terrible one at the same time—really good because only a very creative mind would be able to come up with something like that and put as much detail into such a lie 😌 and terrible because…I mean, c'mon, really? Only a doofus would believe something like that. And Special Agent O'Neil was far from a gullible doofus.

So anticipating that Frank O'Neil would not believe him, Guardavaccaro dared his old partner to stick him with ten milligrams of the serum, check his pulse/heartbeat, and then, after twenty to thirty minutes pass, stick him with ten milligrams of the antidote and see his glorious revival.

At first, O'Neil had reservations because if this little experiment failed, he would be guilty of murdering an FBI agent, which was *not* a road he wanted to go down; but after Guardavaccaro assured him there was nothing to worry about, he gave it more thought and told himself it was going to be fine since Frank G. was not exactly the suicidal type, not to mention that Guardavaccaro setting O'Neil up by killing *himself* would most certainly be the most idiotic way to take somebody down. Besides, it was never going to work anyway, right? Frank G. would probably just pass out at most, but his pulse would still be detectable, proving his entire story to be false. So in the worst-case scenario, O'Neil had Guardavaccaro on video admitting to killing Tricerra via lethal injection.

Once O'Neil administered the first ten-milligram injection and Guardavaccaro hit the deck like a sack of bricks, Frank O. walked over to him and checked his pulse, which was nonexistent. "Did I just kill Frank Guardavaccaro?" he asked himself and defecated a bit of the ol' proverbial brick while looking at his watch. Sitting back on the couch nervously, he told himself he would administer ten milligrams of the antidote to GX14 in about twenty or thirty minutes, which was about how long Guardavaccaro had claimed passed between him sticking Anthony with the serum and then reviving him. "Man, this better work!" said O'Neil nervously to himself.

As Frank O. waited to complete the experiment in the badly lit room, Sky Haven PD had watched all the security-cam surveillance footage from shops in a four-block radius and came to the conclusion that O'Neil had kidnapped Guardavaccaro and taken him to a house somewhere on Church Street. Combing the street, Sheriff Bouchard and two of his deputies were getting closer and closer to house number 115, which was where O'Neil was playing solitaire on his laptop while Guardavaccaro lay on the floor, possibly dead.

Closing in on the house, Charlie Bumper spotted the blue tarp covering the Buick; and on looking through the holes in the tarp, he noticed the smashed-up maroon sedan. "Bingo!" he said to himself and gave his deputies the signal to surround the house.

In doing so, a couple of them came too close to O'Neil's proximity sensors, which alerted him that someone had breached the perimeter. On checking his laptop for the real-time surveillance footage and seeing Sky Haven PD surrounding the house, he exclaimed, "*Crap!*"

About twenty-five minutes had passed since he had stuck Guardavaccaro with the serum, and he figured plenty of time had gone by to test the GX14 theory.

Frank O. (to himself): I better administer that antidote before Sky Haven PD comes in and catches me in here with him like this!

Sheriff Bouchard: Frank O'Neil, we know you're in there. If Frank Guardavaccaro is still alive, release him and surrender yourself! There is nowhere to go. The house is surrounded.

O'Neil stuck Guardavaccaro with the antidote and immediately checked his pulse—nothing. "Oh no!" he told himself, letting out another piece of the proverbial brick. "C'mon, Frank, wake up!" He checked his pulse again—still nothing. O'Neil started pounding on Guardavaccaro's chest when two Sky Haven PD deputies burst through the front and back doors, screaming, "HANDS UP! GET YOUR HANDS UP NOW!"

Frank O. put his hands up, and Sheriff Bouchard, who immediately followed behind the deputy who kicked open the front door, put O'Neil facedown on the floor and handcuffed his hands behind his back.

"You don't understand," said O'Neil.

Deputy Espinoza checked Guardavaccaro's pulse and then said, "He's dead, Charlie!"

O'Neil: He's not dead!

Sheriff Bouchard: You are under arrest for the murder of Frank Guardavaccaro!
O'Neil: HE'S NOT DEAD!

Sheriff Bouchard picked Frank O'Neil up off
the ground by his handcuffed arms and started walking him outside while telling him his Miranda rights
when he suddenly heard both deputies scream in unison. Turning around, he discovered Guardavaccaro
lying on his back with his eyes open, looking at the
lightbulb swaying ever so gently from the ceiling.

Frank Guardavaccaro: Hey, Frank, how *did* you get
electricity in here anyway?

Ten minutes later

Frank G. and Frank O. were both sitting on
the front steps at 115 Church Street as they caught
an earful from Sheriff Bouchard, who was shouting
and gesticulating frantically. Among many colorful
phrases and words he was using were "causing trouble ever since you came into my town," "I don't have
time for stupid fed games," and "to hell with the both
of yous!"

Frank G: Sorry, Sheriff!
Frank O: Sorry, Sheriff!

Charlie Bumper stopped yelling eventually and
exhaled, *very* annoyed.

Charlie Bumper: Billy, give jackass number one here a ride to the hospital to get his leg and face looked at, please!

Deputy William "Billy" Corruthers: Sure thing, Charlie.

Guardavaccaro got up with the deputy's help and got into the back of his cruiser, where he took out his phone and made a phone call.

O'Neil sat on the steps for a few more seconds, smoking a menthol cigarette in silence, then he put it out and got up to follow Guardavaccaro.

Sheriff Bouchard: Where the hell do you think *you're* goin'?

O'Neil: We have to do a conference call with our FBI director ASAP, Sheriff. I've been AWOL for three months, and he needs to be briefed right away.

Sheriff Bouchard: And when you're finished, what are the chances I can get you boys to get the hell outa my town?

O'Neil smiled at him, turned around, and got in the back of Bill Corruthers's cruiser, where Guardavaccaro was.

On entering, he heard Frank G. say, "PSR, the way I see it, we have two options. Either court-martial him or promote the kid to a level 5 clearance... Right... Yup... Okay."

Frank Guardavaccaro hung up the phone and looked at O'Neil.

Frank G.: Congrats, kid. You've just been promoted.

CHAPTER 28

Tonopah

It certainly is great to finally see Special Agents Frank G. and Frank O. back together again and to learn that Guardavaccaro is not a murderer, yea? Not to mention finding out that Anthony Tricerra is...*alive!* Wow! How 'bout that, huh? GX14? Relocation to Tonopah, Nevada? Crazy stuff, right? And all this time, you were crying over spilled milk that hadn't even actually been spilled. SMH. Told ya I'd redeem the story, y'doubting doofus. ☺

Now then. Let's think about this logically. While the two federal agents were at odds, Frank O'Neil tried to use Morgan Carter to entrap Frank Guardavaccaro by sending her to the cemetery, knowing that Frank G. would follow. But on realizing the danger (which actually never existed) of such a plan, Frank O. backed out at the last minute and stopped his ex-partner (at the time) from reaching the graveyard.

Morgan still went there, though, right? And what repercussions did *that* have? Well...Morgan now knew about Johnny Embers's coffin being empty, and she strongly suspected that the FBI not only faked *his* death but also probably faked Anthony's death as well, especially after receiving the envelope with the sapphire in it, the same envelope that had Anthony's handwriting on it. Geez. Almost sounds like a bad *The Twilight Zone* episode or something, doesn't it?

So since Frank O. was the one responsible for Morgan finding out about Johnny Embers, he now had a choice: rejoin the ranks of the FBI and stonewall Ms. Carter as if she was wrong to think Anthony was alive, or continue helping her get to the truth. The funny thing about stonewalling Ms. Carter is the fact that it would actually benefit him personally in several ways: (1) convincing Morgan that Anthony really was dead would potentially increase his chances of being with her *if* she could effectively move on from Tricerra on accepting he was gone, (2) it would get him back on Siphos Ricketts's good side after going rogue for three months, and (3) it would also justify his brand-new promotion, which he *certainly* could not afford to spit in the face of. Decisions, decisions.

Well, at least he had time to think about it all while he sat in the waiting room of Sky Haven Memorial Hospital as Frank Guardavaccaro was getting his broken leg cast and his face stitched up.

Frank O'Neil (to himself): This is a tough choice. Frank had my back the entire time I thought he was a killer. He even lied to Siphos Ricketts to protect me. And he knew I bugged his motel

256

room and still gave me the clue about Johnathan Embers so I would discover the truth and come back and talk to him. He risked a court-martial for that, and he really is like a father to me. I just *can't* double-cross him for Morgan.

Morgan Carter (standing four feet from Frank O'Neil): Please, Dr. Hamilton, was there anything out of the ordinary about that day? Anything at all?

Dr. Hamilton: I'm sorry, Ms. Carter, I don't recall anything strange from that day. Except…

Morgan: Yes?

Dr. Hamilton paused while deep in thought.

Dr. Hamilton: Well…I didn't think much of it at the time, but the two guys from the coroner's office showed up about ten minutes after Mr. Tricerra passed away. They usually take hours, sometimes even days, to show up while we keep the bodies frozen in the hospital morgue. In fact, it wasn't even the usual guys, Markus and Alexei, who took the body. It was two guys I've never seen before.

Morgan stayed silent.

Dr. Hamilton: Sorry, Ms. Carter, but that's all I got. Hope that helps.

Dr. Hamilton walked away while Morgan stood there with a suspicious look on her face, pondering the possibilities. She looked like she was trying to burn a hole in the hospital floor with her suspicious gaze.

O'Neil: Ms. Carter?

Morgan snapped out of her stare and turned around.

Morgan: Oh, Agent O'Neil! Wh-what are you doing here? Are you back from Belize?

Frank O'Neil made the mistake of making eye contact with her and immediately felt waves of warmth all over his body as his heart rate sped up.

O'Neil: I... Belize...

That was all he managed to get out. An awkward three-second pause took place.

Morgan: What?
O'Neil: No, I, uh... I mean...

Morgan looked at him questioningly.

O'Neil: There's a...

Morgan was still waiting for a response.

O'Neil snapped out of it.

O'Neil: Ms. Carter, listen to me very carefully.

Morgan made a confused and worried face.

O'Neil: You must listen very carefully and do as I say. Within a day or two, Special Agent Guardavaccaro and I will call you and ask you to meet us so we can ask you a few questions. You must accept without any fear, reservations, or hint of concern. Do you understand?

Morgan: But he...

O'Neil: Upon meeting us, we will ask you a few questions about your amnesia and memory. You *must* tell us there is no change in either. Got it?

Morgan: But what about—

O'Neil (raising his voice): *Ms. Carter!* You don't know *anything* more about the night your father died other than what you already told us at the hospital the next day! And you certainly don't know anything about Johnathan...Harvey... Embers...

Morgan recognized his voice as the same voice from the strange phone call that tipped her off about the contents of the mausoleum. She gasped and covered her mouth with her hand. O'Neil winked at her and walked away as she continued to stand there in shock.

A few seconds later, O'Neil entered Guardavaccaro's hospital room and made small talk with his partner about his cast while sporting a guilty smile.

O'Neil: Can I sign it?
Guardavaccaro: What are you, twelve?
O'Neil: C'mon, Frank. Lemme sign it.
Guardavaccaro: It's not gonna happen, kid.
O'Neil: Cranky ol' man.

O'Neil gave out a forced laugh and pointed to Frank G. while Nurse Jenkins, who was helping him put his pants back on, nodded her head with an expression that said, "You've got *that* right."

Morgan finally came to her senses in the hospital hallway, tried to snap herself out of whatever she was feeling, turned around, and walked out of the front door of the hospital without Frank Guardavaccaro ever knowing she was there. She understood her assignment despite not being able to see the full picture at that exact moment.

The next day, around 11:00 AM, Morgan's cell phone rang; and upon picking it up, she found out that Special Agent Guardavaccaro of the FBI would like to know if she was available to answer a few questions.

Morgan: Sure! I'm doing laundry at the laundromat across the street from Antonio's, but I want to get some coffee anyway, so I can meet you in the diner if you'd like.

Guardavaccaro: That will be fine, Ms. Carter. Meet
   you there in fifteen minutes.
Morgan (cheerfully): See you then!

Confused by her cheerful demeanor only
one day after she had fled from him in her car,
Guardavaccaro looked at O'Neil and said, "This
broad is up to something."

O'Neil played stupid, as if he knew nothing.

Fifteen minutes later, the federal agents walked
into Antonio's, where Morgan was sitting at a table
with a cup of coffee in front of her.

Morgan: Heeey, guys, it's great to see you again.
   Agent O'Neil, how was Belize?
O'Neil: Oh…yeah. [He looked at Guardavaccaro,
   then back at Morgan.] I, uh…caught a parasite
   and had to come back for treatment. I'm doing
   much better now, thanks.

Guardavaccaro looked at him as if Frank O. had
just told her that he was Santa Claus, and then he sat
down. He did not see the quick glances that O'Neil
and Morgan exchanged, which resembled two people
having this conversation:

Morgan: What?
O'Neil: I dunno. You caught me off guard. Sorry.
Guardavaccaro: Ms. Carter, would you care to tell
   me *why* you ran from me yesterday, recklessly
   speeding and running through red lights?

Morgan: What? I didn't run from you, Agent Guardavaccaro. [She laughed.] I didn't even know you were behind me. My cat swallowed a marble yesterday, and I was trying to make it to the vet before they closed because I thought she might choke to death. Wait...were you following me? Why were you following me?

Guardavaccaro (didn't buy it): Ms. Carter, did you go anywhere else yesterday besides the vet?

Morgan looked at O'Neil, who nodded, and then she responded, "Yes."

Guardavaccaro: And where would *that* be?

Morgan looked at O'Neil again, who nodded at her again.

Morgan: I...went to the Sky Haven cemetery.

Guardavaccaro (a little surprised by her honesty): And why did you do that, Ms. Carter?

Morgan: Well...

Guardavaccaro: Yes?

Morgan looked at O'Neil on the third occasion, and he nodded for the final time.

Morgan: Some freak pranked my phone and said, "Johnathan Harvey Embers."

Guardavaccaro: What about Johnny Embers?

Morgan: I dunno. That's why I went to the cemetery. To see.

Guardavaccaro: See what?

Morgan: See why someone would call me to seemingly direct me there.

Guardavaccaro: Why did you think it was the caller's intent to direct you to Johnathan Embers's mausoleum? Just because he said his name?

Morgan (growing tired of Guardavaccaro's tone): Listen, Special Agent, I'm not a rocket surgeon, but that's what I got out of it, okay? [She used *rocket surgeon* on purpose to play stupid.]

Guardavaccaro (moving his line of questioning along): Fair enough. And?

Morgan looked at O'Neil one final time, and he shook his head no.

Morgan: And nothing. Some vandal had broken the stone slab covering his coffin. I tried to pull the coffin out and open it, but it was way too heavy, so I just got creeped out and left. I figured some kid was just playing a stupid prank on the ol' "ditzy blonde actress" in an attempt to impress his friends or something, and I got the heck out of there.

Guardavaccaro: You…

Morgan: Got the heck out of there. Hey, what is this about, Agent Guardavaccaro? Why did you ask me here to question me about this?

Guardavaccaro (softening up his tone): Ms. Carter, I apologize. I do not wish to be insensitive. You have lost a great deal in a short period of time and have also sustained serious injury. Please forgive me.

Morgan (acting like she didn't see through Guardavaccaro's ruse): Thank you, Agent Guardavaccaro.

Guardavaccaro: Are you feeling any better, by the way? How is your head? Is your memory any better?

Morgan (having anticipated this to be Guardavaccaro's next line of questioning): Unfortunately, still the same. But...to be completely honest... [She paused, then activated her top-notch, Oscar-worthy acting skills and let one lone tear roll out of her right eye.] I'm kind of glad I don't remember seeing Anthony get killed by that monster Deek Embers. After seeing him kill my dad, I don't know if I could handle having both those memories in my head for the rest of my life.

Morgan made eye contact with Guardavaccaro as tears were gushing out of both her eyes now.

Guardavaccaro was skeptical about her explanations until now, but this brilliant thespian's final display had seemingly convinced the veteran FBI agent.

Guardavaccaro touched her hand.

Guardavaccaro: I'm sorry, dear. I apologize for upsetting you. I won't waste any more of your time.

Guardavaccaro stood up as the waitress came over and put a check on the table.

O'Neil joined him in standing up as the waitress walked away while looking back at the crying Morgan Carter.

Miss Carter reached into her purse with her right hand as she held the $1.59 check in her left hand. O'Neil immediately touched her left hand with his right hand as he reached in his inside jacket pocket with his left hand.

O'Neil: Allow me!

Guardavaccaro turned to look at both of them and saw Morgan freeze with her right hand in her purse. O'Neil took out a $20 bill from the inside pocket of his suit jacket and placed it on the table with Andrew Jackson's face down. He winked at her with his right eye (which Guardavaccaro could not see) and spoke to her for the last time in his life: "Take care of yourself, Morgan. And good luck."

Both federal agents walked out of the diner, one using a cane while hobbling and the other not. They got into Guardavaccaro's Toyota Camry rental and drove away.

Morgan sat at the table, staring at the $20 bill for a full minute, then turned it over, only to discover that five numbers were written on Andrew Jackson's

A. TRICERATOPS

face in blue ink: 89049. She did a quick Google search for "89049 zip code" with her cell phone, and the Google-voice lady said with a robotic tone, "Eight-nine-zero-four-eight, Tonopah, Nevada."

CHAPTER 29

Goldfish

Leaving the diner thirty seconds after hearing the Google lady's robotic voice, Morgan immediately drove over to The Caboose, went inside, and grabbed a seat at the bar. She had not had a single drink or a cigarette in months, and the smoke-filled dive bar made her wonder how she could have ever enjoyed spending countless hours in there, drinking and treating her lungs like Jackie Chan's stunt double (aka Jackie Chan).

Randy the bartender was very happy to see her and gave her a big, warm smile.

Randy: Hey, kiddo! How the heck are ya? Not that I'm not happy to see you, but what are you doing in here?
Morgan: I really need your help, Randy. How is your wife doing?

Randy made a very confused face, and Morgan gave him the "come here" sign with her pointer finger. He leaned in, and she whispered something in his ear as the other patrons in The Caboose watched with envy while incorrectly assuming Randy was the luckiest man alive.

On leaving Antonio's diner, Frank Guardavaccaro drove around the block once, with O'Neil in the passenger seat, and then returned to the diner. He didn't stop, but he did drive by slow enough to get a good look inside the laundromat across the street *and* inside Antonio's, where a bored waitress was playing Candy Crush on her phone since she had no customers.

O'Neil: What's up, Frank?
Guardavaccaro: Doing laundry, my ass.

The two federal agents went back to Morgan's street and parked the car, preparing themselves for another long stakeout.

O'Neil: What is this about, Frank?

Guardavaccaro was silent for a few seconds.

Guardavaccaro: And to think I believed her when she
      turned on the waterworks in the diner. Oh, she's
      good. I can see how she won an Oscar at only
      twenty-two years old.
O'Neil: I'm confused.
Guardavaccaro: Let's just hope we see her again, kid.
O'Neil: Okay? Where else would she go?

Guardavaccaro took out a cigarette from his cigarette pack and lit it up.

O'Neil: Gimme one of those, will ya?
Guardavaccaro: Don't you know smoking is bad for
   you, kid?

O'Neil took out a cigarette from Frank G.'s pack and lit it up too as the two agents sat in the rent-a-car in silence, puffin' Marlboro Reds.

O'Neil: I don't think you're supposed to smoke in
   here, Frank.
Guardavaccaro: Me neither.

Several hours later

Guardavaccaro turned on the radio.
Justin Bieber and Ed Sheeran's "I Don't Care" started playing on 104.5, which was where the last person who rented the Camry left the radio dial.

Guardavaccaro: Hey, you know what, Potter? This
   Beaver kid is pretty good. I like this song.

Guardavaccaro turned up the radio.
O'Neil's eyes got big. He was so shocked that Frank Guardavaccaro knew the song on the radio that he completely overlooked the fact that his partner said *beaver*.

A few seconds later, O'Neil realized the error and burst into laughter, but it was not at calling him Justin Beaver. It was at Frank G. now mumbling, "'Cause I don't care when I'm with my baby, yea. All the bad things disappear. And you're making me feel like maybe I am somebody. I can deal with the bad nights when I'm with my baby, yeah!"

Frank G. and Frank O. were both badly singing, "'Cause I don't care as long as you just hold me near. You can take me anywhere. Yeah, you're making me feel like I'm loved by somebody. I can deal with the bad nights when I'm with my baby, yeah!"

They both let out a healthy, long-needed laugh that released almost all the tension and worry in the car. This was only the third time O'Neil had seen Frank G. laugh in the two years of knowing him. Suddenly the veteran special agent said, "Look alive," as he abruptly turned the radio off after spotting Morgan's car's headlights coming down the dark street.

Frank G.: Looks like we will see her again after all.

Morgan drove by the two FBI agents and pulled into her driveway. She got out of her car, unlocked her front door, and went into the house. Her living room light came on.

Frank G.: I really thought she was gone, kid.

O'Neil played stupid.

O'Neil: Gone where, Frank? She just—
Guardavaccaro: Hello, what's this?

A teal Honda Civic sedan pulled into Morgan's driveway and turned off its engine. An unknown woman got out. She was wearing an absurd long black raincoat that resembled a trench coat you would see in a noir detective film, a bright-red wig, and dark shades (at night) while a black Patty Hearst hat was sitting slanted on her head. From the bottom of the trench coat stuck out two shapely calves wrapped in bell-bottom jeans that resolved in white platform shoes with what looked like goldfish in the heels.

The federal agents looked at each other, and both said, "What in the hell?"

The woman walked up Morgan's steps and knocked on her door, and as the door opened, Morgan greeted her with "Thank you so much for coming." She then closed the door as the two women went into Morgan's house.

Guardavaccaro: This thing just gets weirder and weirder.

Approximately twenty minutes later, the woman in the red wig, black sunglasses, and absurd trench coat strutted her bell-bottomed calves out of Morgan's house as her goldfish-filled platform shoes click-clacked down Ms. Carter's steps. She was carrying a suitcase and a small pet carrier. After putting the suitcase in the back seat and the pet carrier on the floor of the passenger seat, she got in the car, backed out, and then left, driving in the opposite direction of where the federal agents were parked.

Guardavaccaro: Why would she give away her cat? She loves that cat. This makes no sense, kid.

Morgan's silhouette was seen through her living room window as she went over to her couch and sat down. For the next three hours, there was not a single movement in the house as Morgan was presumably watching The Lord of the Rings or some other really long movie. Two more hours passed, and still no motion in the house. The federal agents were utterly dying of boredom at this point.

Frank G. stretched his arms while mumbling, "I don't care as long as you just hold me near. You can take me anywhere." Suddenly he stopped. "You can take me anywhere...," he repeated. "Take me any-where..." He paused, thinking for a second, and sat up in his seat while looking at O'Neil.

Guardavaccaro: No way!

He yanked his car door open and took off like a bat out of hell (a limping bat that held a cane) toward Morgan's house, leaving O'Neil behind, who was asking, "What? Frank? Frank!"

O'Neil got out too and chased after Guardavaccaro, who was now kicking Morgan's door with his good leg. The door swung open, and O'Neil heard a woman's scream from inside.

Guardavaccaro was now inside the house, and O'Neil heard him shout, "Who the hell are *you?*" as he, too, ran into the house, right on Guardavaccaro's heels.

"Don't shoot, don't shoot!" screamed the woman, who was wearing Morgan's clothes while sitting on the couch as she put her hands up. "My name is Regina. I'm Randy the bartender's wife."

O'Neil's eyes became the size of his old Buick's steering wheel, and his jaw dropped, realizing what had happened. Guardavaccaro took his phone out of his pocket, dialed it, and said with an angry, urgent tone, "I need an immediate flight to Nevada!"

CHAPTER 30

Final Act

All right, dear reader. This is it—the final chapter. This is where everything comes together and culminates into an epic conclusion for the ages, a conclusion so memorable that you will just *have* to tell your mom and dad about it tomorrow. Or your boyfriend/girlfriend. Or your buddy Pete, who used to work at the gas station on Main Street before they caught him stealing Virginia Slims for his mom, Tracy-Lynn, and fired him. It's a shame too; he was a good kid. He always had a good heart, but he got in with the wrong crowd in tenth grade and just never got back on the right track. SMH. Fair warning: Pete won't care when you tell him about *The Anomaly*, but he *will* offer to return the JNCO jeans he snagged from you in '96 if you can hook him up with a cigarette (not a Virginia Slims).

Yeees, sir. This finale is gonna tie it all together, my good man (or lady). It's gonna bring all these loose ends into one solid knot of epic cohesiveness.

Either that or I screw it all up and make us *both* look stupid. (I shrug.) Hey, at least we're not Pete, am I right? That kid's a freak.

Okay, so Morgan, having outsmarted the federal agents, had a five-hour head start, but they *were* still hot on her trail to Nevada, where she had fled because she believed that was where Anthony was.

Special Agent O'Neil, having a soft spot in his heart for Morgan and being a good egg, had put aside his personal feelings for her, and he just wanted her to be happy. Sure, he took an oath and had a job to do, but he had never seen two people go through so much for each other. And he knew that if they would just be allowed to be together, they wouldn't care about Black Rock Mine or even speak about it ever again. In his mind, Morgan and Anthony spreading the word about their classified escapades was just not a realistic liability. He truly believed that slapping the two of them with a gag order, or a…gag clause or… You know what I'm talking about, right? That contract that says you can't talk about something, or you will be brought under the penalty of legal prosecution? Well, Special Agent O'Neil believed it would be enough to make them keep their mouths shut forever.

Besides, Anthony didn't want to go to prison for the first-degree murder of Joe Carter, and Morgan didn't want to lose Anthony. So neither one of them would squeal about the mine.

"Just let the kids be together already! What's the big deal?" you might say.

Well, I'll tell you what the big deal is, y'bleed-ing-heart doof! It's called *the rule of law*. This is the real world, not some figment of your (or my) imag-ination. 😊

Frank Guardavaccaro knew exactly how serious this highly classified matter was, and he was prepared to do whatever he legally could to split up the reck-less lovebirds and follow protocol. Furthermore, he was not going to lie to Siphos Ricketts again, nor was he about to be bested by a couple of kids (three kids if you count O'Neil). The day he allowed some snot-nosed youngsters to get the best of him would be the day he retired.

But you know what? Wait a minute… Why are we assuming that Anthony was really alive? Just because Frank Guardavaccaro told some silly story about GX14? Okay, so the serum worked, but what if Frank was lying anyway? What if he really was a mur-derer? We don't know for sure he was not, do we? For all we know, he could be the most cunning FBI agent in history, and he could have really killed Tricerra. I mean, wouldn't killing him be easier since Morgan had amnesia at the time? With Tricerra dead, the job was done, right? I'm sorry, but as far as I'm concerned, we just don't know the answer to this mystery for sure yet. *You* certainly don't know, considering you're the same guy/gal who let Pete, the Virginia Slims thief, make off with your JNCOs in '96.

After arriving in Nevada and landing at Tonopah Airport, Morgan hailed a cab and asked to be taken downtown. Her cabbie, a polite elderly German man named Dietrich, quickly loaded her suitcase in the trunk and her fat calico in the back seat of his cab, and within minutes they were on the road.

Dietrich was in his early fifties and had a very polite and helpful demeanor as well as a great attitude. He was of about an average build and slightly taller than average height; had short blonde hair that was neatly combed to one side, blue eyes, and a blonde mustache; and wore small round glasses, which he always had on the end of his nose despite them being reading glasses. He felt the thin frames made him look more distinguished.

Dietrich was wearing a light-blue collared shirt that day, which peeked out from beneath a dark-blue knitted vest, and black dress pants with black dress shoes. He liked to look clean-cut and professional whenever driving his cab and was a firm believer in treating his customers with courtesy and respect. Sure, the taxi business was not exactly known for being a...rapport-based, repeat-customer type of business, but Dietrich truly believed that if he was courteous and professional enough, he would indeed receive repeat customers.

And he was right. The people of Tonopah liked him and his taxi service so much that some of them would even think up excuses to use his services (e.g., "I need a ride to the airport, D" or "My wife has the car, and I gotta take my kid to soccer practice, D."). There was never a shortage of townsfolk calling Stuttgart Taxi for a ride.

Having been born in the German city and immigrated to the US in the '80s, Dietrich had made a good life for himself and his family here with hard work, professionalism and a side of good German etiquette.

Morgan: How far is downtown Tonopah from the airport?
Dietrich (with a thick German accent): Iss eleven minutes exactly, *fräulein.*
Morgan: Awesome. Say, you wouldn't by any chance know where I might find this man?

Morgan showed Dietrich a picture of her and Anthony taken in the hotel room the day they fled from Elmer Embers and his serial-killer family.

Dietrich: *Nein, fräulein.* Sorry.

Morgan frowned and responded in a faint voice, "Thanks anyway."

Dietrich: He isss yo boyfran?

Morgan looked out the window of the cab, at the dry desert scenery passing by.

Morgan: Yah, he is my boyfran.

She was not sure why she said the word *boyfriend* exactly how Dietrich said it.

Dietrich: Maybeee Ernesto at the Tonopah Station knows heem."

Morgan: Who? Where?

Dietrich: Tonopah Station, also called Ramada Inn. Has restorant und caseeno und museeum iiin basement. My fran Ernesto isss managher. I tek yu to see heem?

Morgan: Yes, please take me to see your friend Ernesto, the Ramada Inn manager. I need to find a motel for the night anyway. Thank you.

Dietrich: *Gern geschehen!* [You're welcome.]

It dawned on Morgan that if she was going to search for Anthony, she had her work cut out for her. She sighed as she continued looking out the window.

On arriving at the Ramada Inn, Morgan told Dietrich to wait for her in the cab. Realizing that the large Ramada Inn might be too high profile and probably one of the first hotels the feds would search if they were following her, she decided to ask around about Anthony and then go to a smaller hotel or motel in order to remain under the radar. Dietrich told Morgan what Ernesto looked like, and she made her way into the majestic hotel, casino, restaurant, and museum.

Tourists, treasure hunters, ghost-town explorers, and all sorts of out of towners of various shapes and sizes were buzzing around the cool, air-conditioned lobby.

Standing behind the service desk was a gorgeous young woman with long red hair and piercing green eyes, wearing a neatly pressed maroon-and-blue uniform with a dark-gray stripe running across the side. Pinned on the right side of her chest was a small brooch of a butterfly, the delicate frame of which was outlined by small but flawless diamonds.

"Hello, do you know where I might find Ernesto? Also, I love your brooch," said Morgan; and the beautiful red-haired woman smiled, thanked her, and then pointed to an area near the bar where Ernesto was instructing two employees on the proper way to water down whiskey without the customer knowing it by taste. Morgan thanked the unusually attractive lady and walked away while thinking, *What is a stunning girl like that doing working at a service desk? Chanel would give her a perfume line like that.* She snapped her fingers on the word *that*, then realized she probably looked crazy to anybody watching her, and she abandoned the thought process.

Morgan: Hi, I'm sorry to interrupt, but are you Ernesto?

Ernesto (with a thick Mexican accent): Yes, ma'am. How can I do for ju?

Ernesto was a short, olive-skinned man with spiky hair that had been carefully shaped around his forehead and sideburns by the barber. His eyebrows had also been carefully waxed, and his facial hair had received the same attention to detail as the rest of the hair on his large head. He was wearing a Rolex watch on his wrist and a buttoned-up black vest over a white collared shirt with black dress pants and black dress shoes. He was chewing spearmint gum, and he smelled like Versace Man cologne.

Morgan: Could you tell me if you have seen this man?

Morgan showed him the picture of Anthony.

Ernesto looked at it for a few seconds and responded, "Maybe, but I cannot be wand hondred percent chure. We get many of de people dis time of year. I'm sorry, miss. If I see, I can call ju."

Morgan thanked the man, left her number with him, and made her way over to the blackjack tables, where she asked a few of the dealers the same question but with no success.

Looking over the small sea of gamblers, Morgan felt the first wave of discouragement. "This is going to be like finding a needle in a haystack," she told herself and headed back out to the cab.

Immediately after leaving the casino floor, Ernesto picked up his cellphone and made a call. "Yes, hello? De woman ju ask about, chee was here, but now chee leaf. Okey. Okey." He hung up.

What Morgan didn't know was that Special Agent Guardavaccaro had cast a dragnet ahead of time, knowing she had a five-hour head start. Every hotel, motel, and inn in town had been alerted of Cordelia Rose's arrival in Tonopah, and the moment she set foot on the property, the managers or owners of these establishments were to call Guardavaccaro directly and report her.

Getting back in the cab, Morgan put her face in her hands and started crying, to the surprise of Dietrich.

At this juncture, I would like for you to know something about Morgan, dear reader, something that you may have picked up on by now but maybe not since, even though it has been there from the beginning, it was only just below the surface. It's something I kept in the dark or at least veiled a little. You may have thought in the back of your mind that Morgan was...not the sharpest knife in the drawer, let's say, yeah? Or perhaps not the brightest bulb in the room, as the saying goes. Well, let me tell you something. If you have found yourself thinking such things about Morgan, then you couldn't be further from the truth because she was actually very, *very* smart, but throughout most of the story, you were led to believe that she was stupid.

You see, Morgan purposely behaved in this manner in order to better assimilate with other Hollywood bobbleheads her age and fit in. As the youngest Hollywood star to ever win an Oscar, Morgan figured she would be hated and envied by a lot of other female stars and starlets, so dumbing herself down seemed like a good way for these girls and women to perhaps view her as someone who was not a threat, which would help her either gain their friendship or at least avoid some of their hatred. The only problem was that after Morgan's accidental vehicular homicide and her fall from Hollywood grace and into a bottle of liquor, she more or less became stuck in the dumb persona she had fabricated, only for the real Morgan to start slowly being awakened again after she met Anthony.

His death was the final act that snapped her out of the trance of false stupidity and back to her regular self. Yes, the beautiful Ms. Carter was quite naturally intelligent, which one could perhaps deduce if he/she paid close attention to the details from some of her previous behavior—for example, when she conned Agent Guardavaccaro during her interview with him (saying *rocket surgeon* in an attempt to seem stupid was actually rather brilliant). Also, being able to understand instantly what Agent O'Neil was doing and that what he had written on the back of the banknote was a zip code took some extended brain capacity, not to mention that she had the presence of mind to instantly understand the silent clue that Anthony had left for her on the envelope in which the blue sapphire came, in the form of his handwriting. Morgan knew right away that she had to compare the handwriting on the envelope with handwriting she could find at Anthony's house in order to get to the bottom of that particular mystery. And Morgan knew exactly what to do after receiving the somewhat vague clue of "Johnathan Harvey Embers" (given to her by Frank O'Neil) and then going to the mausoleum immediately after. You see, dear reader, none of these are the actions of a stupid girl.

So why, then, you might ask, was Morgan so foolish to think that she could easily find Anthony with only a zip code? Well, when Morgan rededicated herself to God, she placed her life in His hands completely, therefore fully trusting Him to show her the way despite only having a zip code to try and find Anthony with. However, on encountering her first dead end at the Ramada Inn, she realized what a difficult task this could potentially be and became discouraged, the same way we all do sometimes, forgetting that God is still in control.

Dietrich: Oh no, *fräulein*, don't cry! You vill find your boyfran. I vill help yu, yah?

Morgan: Thank you, but this is an impossible task. Can you please take me to a small motel where I can stay for the night?

Dietrich: Oh no, iiis not safe for a *fräulein* to stay at smol seedy motel in Tonopah by herself. You come stay with meee und my wife und childrens tonight. You are special guest iiin our home. The home of the Bauer family.

Morgan was quite skeptical about the proposal, but on seeing pictures of Dietrich's wife and three children pinned to the visor of his cab, she reluctantly agreed.

Dietrich picked up his phone and said to his German-speaking American wife (in German), "You're not going to believe this, but 'Alice' is coming to stay with us for the night!" (Dietrich and his wife were big fans of Morgan's movies.)

*****

A few hours later, the feds touched down in Nevada, and they headed straight to the Ramada Inn to investigate, having received a phone call from Ernesto. Looking at all the security cameras—three of which showed Morgan inside the lobby and casino, asking Ernesto and his staff questions—the feds deduced that she was indeed there to ask about Tricerra. Furthermore, security footage showed her getting in a cab and heading east on Erie Street. Unable to make out the cab's license plate, they searched a few more motels on the strip before it got dark but then checked themselves in at the seedy Tonopah Motel, where Guardavaccaro announced they would pay Mr. Vincent Falcone a visit in the morning.

The next morning, as the sun rose over Tonopah, beating back the darkness that lay over its desert landscape like a massive knit blanket of black yarn, Special Agent Guardavaccaro sat on a lawn chair out front of the Tonopah Motel, drinking a hot cup of coffee and smoking his morning cigarette.

Frank O'Neil walked out of their motel room, fixing the tie of his two-piece suit while holding a cup of coffee in his other hand.

O'Neil: Hey, Frank, why do we always have to stay at these shady, low-budget motels?

Guardavaccaro: For two reasons, kid. [He took a sip of his coffee and a drag of his cigarette and continued talking as cigarette smoke exited his mouth with every word he spoke.] Number one, never underestimate the criminal mind. Most of the time, the criminal is of at least average intelligence, and they know to stay clear of big hotels, choosing instead to retire at smaller, hole-in-the-wall flea circuses like this place, because they think they will be harder for us to find. And number two, even if the culprit is not at a budget motel, never underestimate what the other shady guests might know and are willing to tell you for a couple of bucks.

O'Neil: That's pretty good, Frank.

Guardavaccaro: I didn't just put this badge on last week, kid. I've been doing this job for more decades than I care to think about.

O'Neil: Speaking of which, you might wanna upgrade to a new suit besides the standard-issue 1930s one they supplied you with, Frank."

O'Neil smiled and winked at Guardavaccaro, who shook his head, dumped out the little bit of cold coffee left in his cup, and stood up.

The special agents walked toward their black Cadillac rental, and O'Neil said, "Are we going to go see Vincent Falcone now, Frank?"

Guardavaccaro: Not yet, kid. First, we're gonna try something else. Ms. Carter left her number with Ernesto at the Ramada Inn yesterday in case he sees Tricerra. Well, Ernesto is about to see him today and give her a call.

A. TRICERATOPS

O'Neil: Really? Tricerra is going to be at the Ramada
     Inn today?
Guardavaccaro: Nope.

The black Cadillac drove away, kicking up the
dry Nevada dust.

*****

Elsewhere, Morgan woke up in a very comfortable queen-size bed that sat inside a clean and neatly
organized guest room that smelled like freshly sprayed
Febreze, at Dietrich's house. Buried beneath several
soft comforters, Morgan yawned and gave herself a
morning stretch as she looked at the different pictures of German folklore and culture on the wall. A
black-and-white picture of 1919 Stuttgart, which sat
next to a beautiful oil painting of a German *bierhaus*,
caught her eye. She admired its historic charm for
a minute or two and then got out of bed and got
dressed.

Walking down the stairs, she saw Dietrich and
his wife sitting at their kitchen table as a friendly
looking young man was pleading some sort of case
before them: "But, Mom, I don't think she will mind,
please!"

Dietrich: Johann, Cordelia Rose iiis our guest. Do
     not bother her with such tiiingz. Iiit would be
     diiistasteful.
Morgan (walking into the kitchen): Good morning.

Young Johann looked over at Morgan, and his eyes became as big as Mercedes-Benz steering wheels. His mouth opened a little in shock. The young man had a friendly demeanor to him, seeming like the type of kid you might sit next to in study hall and have no reservations about asking for a pencil despite not knowing him particularly well. With blonde hair combed neatly to one side, a fair complexion, chiseled German good looks, blue eyes, and a thin build, he was dressed in a collared polo shirt and black dress pants. It was probably fair to assume that this young Zack Morris lookalike would most likely not have any issues making lady friends at college.

Johann: I…

That was all he managed to get out.

Morgan looked at him and smiled, and then she addressed Dietrich's wife: "Anna, I want to thank you guys again for letting me spend the night here. It was very nice of you."

Anna was a very attractive, very fit, and elegantly dressed woman in her forties, with balayage highlights in her long and flowing brownish hair, manicured French nails, kind brown eyes, and soft facial features that would make any young male grocery store cashier stare a little too long while nervously fixing their own hair.

Anna: Good morning, dear. Oh, please think nothing of it. We are a Christian household, and we do not turn away anybody in need. Not that you're in need, per se, but staying at a motel by yourself can be dangerous for a young girl this day in age. You're much safer here with us.

Johann was still staring at Morgan with wide eyes as if Ludwig van Beethoven was standing before him.

Morgan: I really appreciate that. If it wasn't for Dietrich's gracious offer to stay here, I would have just gone to the Tonopah Motel last night.
Dietrich: Johann, iiit iiiis iiiimpolite to stare. Please stop staring and say hello to Ms. Rose.

Johann closed his slightly open mouth and then made an effort to speak: "Cordelia Rose...I...love... you..."

Dietrich (shaking his head while smiling): Johann!

Morgan laughed and then smiled at Johann. She then extended her hand to him and said, "Hi, Johann. It's very nice to meet you, and please call me Morgan. That's my real name."
Johann shook her hand and then looked at his own hand as if it was no longer a real part of his body.

Anna: Please excuse Johann. He is a big fan of your work, Ms. Rose. He has every poster of yours that was ever made, but I assure you he's just a harmless nineteen-year-old boy with a crush on a Hollywood star.

Johann: Mooom, *stop*!

Morgan: Please call me Morgan, Anna. Cordelia Rose was my stage name, and I don't go by it anymore. My real name is Morgan Carter. By the way, you have a wonderful family. Did I see that you have two other boys? Dietrich keeps their picture in his cab.

Anna: Oh, yes, our other two boys are seven and nine years old, and they are at school. Johann just graduated high school last year, and he's going to Stanford University next year. So until then, he will be hanging around the house, professing his undying love to our female houseguests.

Johann: *Mom!*

Anna smiled and felt a little bit bad about jousting at Johann's expense, so she tried to make it up to him. "Ms. Carter, Johann wanted to ask a big favor of you. He wanted to know if you would autograph his *Alice* poster. If it's not too much trouble, would you be able to sign his poster so he doesn't hold it against Dietrich and me for the rest of our lives?"

Morgan: Absolutely!

Johann's eyes returned to the size of Mercedes-Benz steering wheels. He quickly walked up the stairs, forgetting to invite Morgan to follow him; and after Anna and Dietrich motioned to Morgan to go after

Johann, she headed up the stairs and into his room. The walls of his room were covered with official and unofficial Cordelia Rose posters.

Morgan (noticing a specific poster on Johann's wall that was smaller than the rest): Oh, wow, you have the little poster I had printed of my character from the Scorsese movie. It was the first movie I ever did, and I had a small talking role in it. Did you know that I used that poster—

Johann: In your headshot portfolio and mailed it out to all the big production companies in LA after the movie came out? I know...

Morgan: Wow. I'm impressed, Johann. I haven't seen that little poster in years. You're a true fan. I will sign whatever you'd like, my friend.

Johann's entire face was drowned in happiness as a genuine smile stretched from ear to ear. He quickly opened his closet door, took out a huge cardboard box filled with Cordelia Rose merchandise, and placed it at Morgan's feet with a silly smile on his face. Morgan's eyes got big for a second, and then she looked at Johann and laughed before she said, "You got a Sharpie?"

*****

As Morgan was upstairs, undertaking the enormous but flattering task of autographing all of Johann Bauer's Cordelia Rose posters and merchandise, downstairs Dietrich opened the door after hearing the doorbell and found his across-the-street neighbor, Allan Winter, standing on his doorstep.

Allan was a short-statured chubby man with a small bald head where hair still grew around the sides and back. His large thin glasses rested on his semi-likable face, which had no facial hair. His khaki slacks sat slightly too high on his belly, and his tucked-in baby-blue collared shirt showed signs of a mustard stain that was recently present before someone tried to scrub it out with club soda.

Allan: Good morning, D. Hey, I'm sorry about this, but…my wife sent me over here to ask if you… umm…

Allan paused while scratching the back of his head as he looked down.

Dietrich: Yes, what iiis iiit, Allan?
Allan: Ah, geez, this is so dumb. Well…she says she saw Cordelia Rose getting out of your cab last night and walking into your house.
Dietrich (stunned): What?
Allan: It's stupid, right? I'm sorry. She just wouldn't give up until I came over here to ask you that.

Dietrich found himself in a predicament because being a God-fearing Christian man, he didn't lie, but he also did not want to tell Allan the truth because his wife, Debby, was a well-known neighborhood gossip and local bigmouth. Letting her know about their houseguest would ensure that the entire neighborhood would know before noon.

Dietrich: I uh…

Allan: I told her it was stupid, D. She's been driving me nuts about it all morning and wouldn't stop until I came over here to ask you. She just loves Cordelia Rose. Hell, she's watching us from across the street right now.

Dietrich looked over Allan's shoulder and saw Mrs. Winter propped in her living room window with a look of anticipation on her face as she held a DVD box in her hand marked *To Hell and Back* (Debby Winter's favorite movie). She was a heavyset woman with the kind of hairdo that screamed "Karen," and she was wearing an enormous all yellow dress, which made Dietrich think of several jokes about the sun that he would never say out loud to Allan.

Dietrich: All right, Allan. I'm gonna level with yu, yah? Cordelia Rose iiis iiin my house right now…

Allan: *What?* She's here!

Dietrich: Shhhh, pleeez keep iiit down, Allan!

Allan: Sorry, sorry.

Dietrich: You cannot tell Debbee, though. You know shee vill have the whole neighborhood here iiin an hour if you do. Pleez keep ziis between us. Iiif you doo, I vill ask Cordelia to autografff our copy of *To Hell und Bak*, and I vill geev iiit to yu for Debbee.

Allan: You want me to lie to her, D?

Dietrich thought for a moment.

Dietrich: "How about ziis? I have to go downtown right now to pay a parkiiing tiiicket anyway. You come along with meee so yu don't have to go bak home und tell Debbee anyting just yet. Miiiss Rose vill beee leaving shortly as well because sheee has some business iiin town, but when sheee returns later, I'll ask her to sign our copy of *To Hell und Bak* for yu, yah? Meanwhile, *before* Cordelia returns, yu can call Debbee und tell her Miiiss Rose was here last night but dat sheee left, which vill be true at that moment, yah?

Allan: You know what? That's a pretty good bad idea, D. I need to run a few errands anyway, and I've been meaning to check out that new general store that just opened on Mc Quillan Street downtown. I talked to the owner yesterday as he was putting up the general store's sign out front. He seems like a nice guy. He said they open today.

Dietrich: Okay. Come iiin. I'll get my keez, und vee vill go there.

A few minutes later, after instructing his wife, Anna, not to answer the door if Debby Winter came by, Dietrich and his neighbor were on their way to Mc Quillan Street to have a look at the new general store that just opened there.

Dietrich was planning on stopping at the magistrate's office afterward to pay his parking ticket, during which time Allan could call Debbie (after Morgan had left the house) and tell her Ms. Carter was gone. He knew that Morgan had other business in town anyway and figured she would be out looking for her "boyfran" by then, giving Allan the opportunity to tell Debbie the truth about Morgan being gone (ingenious, if you ask me).

Dietrich had hoped to be the one to drive Ms. Carter around and help her with her task, but Debbie Winter had thrown a monkey wrench into that plan. So Miss Carter could either call a cab from the house or just take Anna's car to search for Anthony. Why would Anna allow that? I will discuss that more in a minute.

After arriving at their destination, Dietrich parked his cab out front, and both men entered the general store. Inside they found a variety of items from canned food items to housewares, collectibles, electronics, DVDs, VHS tapes, video games, tools, clothing, etc. This was a general store and then some.

A good-looking man in his early thirties with long, mostly gray-and-silver hair and a well-groomed salt-and-pepper beard greeted them. "Good morning, gentlemen. Welcome to my store. My name is Vinny. Please take a look around and let me know if you have any questions."

Dietrich and Allan thanked him and began to browse the store. Dietrich, however, kept looking at the man from time to time, unsure where he had seen him before.

*****

Back at Dietrich's house, Morgan had just finished autographing all of Johann's stuff, including all the posters on his walls. She was now taking several pictures, standing with him in his room, so he could prove to all his friends that he really met Cordelia Rose. Just as they were taking the last photo, in which Morgan kissed Johann on the cheek while he made the face of the coolest man on the planet, Morgan's phone rang. She heard glass breaking downstairs as "La Cucaracha" reverberated throughout the entire house. "Oh no!" she exclaimed as she stopped the phone from ringing and then ran downstairs to apologize to Anna for her cat. Anna, while laughing, let her know that the empty broken wineglass was not a big deal, and she refuses to let Morgan pay for it or sweep up the broken shards of glass. Morgan continued to apologize as she answered her phone, which was now ringing again.

Morgan: Hello?
Ernesto: Hello, thees eees Ernesto from de Ramada. The man ju look for, he just check eeen.

Morgan's heart rate suddenly became 185, and she dropped her phone on the floor, cracking the screen. Her face turned red, and she could not hear Anna, who was asking her if she was okay.

Morgan looked at Anna with a deadpan, expressionless look on her face and said, "I need to get to the Ramada Inn immediately."

Anna: Okay. I will call Dietrich to come back.

Morgan: I'm sorry, but it cannot wait. I can call a cab.

Anna: Nonsense. I can't take you because I have something in the oven, but here, take my car. [She gave Morgan her car keys.] You have a valid driver's license, correct?

Morgan: Yes.

Anna: Okay, then, just take my car, and we will see you later. You *are* staying with us while you are in Tonopah, right?

Morgan: Yes. Thank you, Anna. I will not forget this.

Anna: What is your cell number in case there is an emergency and we need to get in contact with you, Ms. Carter?

Morgan: It's 555-057-0507.

Morgan picked her cell phone off the floor, thanked her gracious host again, and walked out of the house through the door that connected the home to the two-car garage as she told Ernesto she would be right over. She got into Anna's red Subaru Outback SUV and drove off, following the GPS directions to the Ramada through the cracks in her cell phone's screen.

Now you might wonder, *What would possess Anna to entrust her car to someone who literally got blacklisted from Hollywood for killing a person in a drunk-driving accident?* Furthermore, how could Morgan legally drive? Not only that, but did Morgan violate her probation by leaving the state of Pennsylvania? Well, you sure are an inquisitive li'l bugger, ain't ya? I assure you there are very simple answers to all your questions, dear reader. Allow me to tackle your concerns by addressing them one at a time, but let's go backward from the last one to the first.

So, then, number one, Morgan had *not* violated probation by leaving the state of Pennsylvania because she had completed most elements of her probation as well as her community service after one year of living in Sky Haven. The only legal stipulation that remained was the one that required her to avoid being arrested for a DUI in the next five years. In fact, Morgan had to avoid *any* arrest for the next five years or face serious jail time.

Number two, on completing her community service and most of her probationary stipulations, Morgan was permitted to renew her driver's license, which she did a couple of weeks before she met Anthony. You have to remember, dear reader, Morgan spent millions on her legal team and was able to get the best attorneys money could buy, which was how she avoided jail time to begin with as well as other stiff legal penalties.

As for the question of why Anna would trust Morgan with her car… There are two simple answers to this quandary as well, the first being that in Dietrich and Anna's home, in the basement, above Dietrich's pool table, there was a sign that was made by Anna by hand. The sign said, "You are not your past mistakes." The reason this resonated so close with Anna was that in her midtwenties, she had a rough go of things as well. Not only did she have a serious drinking problem that led to a fallout with her family after she was caught stealing money from her mother to buy alcohol, but also, it wasn't until she met Dietrich that she turned her life around and became a model citizen and an exceptional mother. I guess it makes sense that the Bauers owned a copy of *To Hell and Back* and were big fans of Morgan's work.

The second reason Anna felt comfortable enough to allow Morgan to use her car was that the night before, Mrs. Bauer and Ms. Carter had an in-depth heart-to-heart talk after finding out they were both devout Christian women. They spoke about their pasts as well as their regrets and their transformations into the people they were now. Morgan shared with Anna about her deep regret of accidentally killing Carla Romano and how she hit rock bottom after the car crash. She then explained how she quit drinking after her father's and Anthony's deaths (without revealing anything about the anomaly, the mine, or the FBI faking Tricerra's death), and Anna shared with Morgan some of her past mistakes as well and her rebirth into the woman she was today.

The two ladies had bonded in only a few hours the way most people cannot even bond in a matter of years, so Anna did not think twice about letting Morgan use her car after everything they had shared the night before. The only subject the two women had not discussed in depth was Anna's other two children besides Johann, which is why Morgan had asked about them earlier that morning.

Anna was under the impression that Morgan was in Tonopah to find an ex-boyfriend she had lost contact with ages before even meeting Anthony Tricerra, and the goodhearted Mrs. Bauer just wanted to help Ms. Carter find some semblance of happiness after all she had lost.

Morgan did not like lying or being devious, but she knew that telling the Bauers about what really happened to Anthony would put them on Guardavaccaro's radar, which would endanger their entire family.

Morgan left all her belongings at the Bauer residence and headed to the Ramada Inn, where the cunning and experienced Special Agent Guardavaccaro had set a trap for her.

Ernesto was to direct her to room 44, where Guardavaccaro would apprehend her and bring her back to FBI headquarters to be given a new identity and then relocated. Frank G. would then relocate Anthony as well and make sure the two of them would never see each other again.

"But why room 44?" you ask. Because it was the only vacant room, of course. Also, you ask too many questions. 😠

Over at the Tonopah general store, Dietrich and Allan had found all the items they wanted to purchase and were standing at the register. Dietrich paid for his items first; and then Allan, who had grabbed more odds and ends than Dietrich, walked closer to the register to be rung up. As Vinny scanned Allan's items, Dietrich kept looking at him, trying to figure out why his face looked so familiar. It was right on the tip of his tongue, but he just couldn't come up with the answer. He would have just dropped it, but for some reason, he felt like it was important. But he did not know why.

*****

Across town, Morgan pulled up in front of the Ramada Inn and double-parked the Subaru there with the flashers on. As she ran inside the massive hotel, a bellboy called to her, "Miss, that spot is ten minute parking only!"

Morgan shouted back at him after she ran past, "I'll be right back!"

She skipped waiting for the elevator, which had a bunch of people waiting in front of it, and headed straight for the stairwell. Ernesto had already told her about room 44 on the phone, so Morgan hustled up the steps, knowing that the fourth floor of the Ramada Inn was where room 44 was. Her breathing intensified as she made it to the third floor, and her anticipation overwhelmed her. "This is it. I'm almost there!"

*****

Back at the general store, Allan had paid for all his items as well, and the two men headed out of the store. Dietrich still could not recall where he knew the general store's owner from.

On reaching the outside, Dietrich saw a bus drive by, on the side of which was an old, ripped-up, and sun-worn advertisement of Cordelia Rose's Chanel perfume line called Old Flame. A light bulb went off in his brain, and he turned around and looked inside the general store. He yelled, "Oh my!" and took out his phone to call his wife.

*****

At the Ramada Inn, Morgan had reached the fourth floor, and she was now completely out of breath. She was no longer running but walking in the direction of room 44 after having run up all four flights of stairs.

*****

Anna answered her phone while standing in her kitchen and petting Morgan's cat, who was very friendly, fat, and soft.

Anna: Hey, hun… Who? Morgan?… No, she left a little while ago… Wait, *what*? You can't be serious!… Okay, okay… I'll give her a call right now.

She hung up the call with her husband and dialed Morgan's number.

*****

Morgan continued to walk down the fourth-floor hallway of the Ramada Inn. She passed room 41, then 42. Her heart rate accelerated despite having just calmed down some after the slow walk down the hallway. As she passed room 43, her cell phone, which was now on silent after Pepp's wineglass debacle earlier, started to vibrate. Morgan didn't recognize the Nevada phone number, and she hit the Ignore button. Three seconds passed, and she was standing in front of room 44. Her heart sounded like Tommy Lee covering the *Jumanji* drum line in an upside-down steel cage. She raised her hand to knock on the door, but before her knuckles connected with the door, her phone vibrated again—same unknown number with the Nevada area code. Morgan went to tap the Ignore button again, but something in the deepest recesses of her psyche told her, *Answer it.*

Ugh! she exclaimed in her mind and took a few steps away from room 44 as she answered the phone.

Morgan (almost whispering): *Hello?*

The frantic voice on the other end of the phone gave her information that was about to save her neck. After a minute of listening while making a shocked face, she said, "Thank you, Anna" and hung up. She turned around, looked at room 44, and said to herself, "You're good, Guardavaccaro. But not good enough!" Looking up to the sky, she quietly mouthed the words *thank you*.

She backed away from the room slowly at first and then turned around and began to run down the hallway with newly found strength.

After jogging back down through the stairwell, she made it to the street out front of the Ramada Inn, got in Anna's car, and drove away while looking in the rearview mirror from time to time to make sure she wasn't being followed.

Completely shaken up by almost being caught by the feds, Morgan decided to go back to the Bauer residence to regroup and plan her next move since in Tonopah, all businesses that were not open twenty-four hours a day closed by 6:00 PM, and Morgan knew that going to the new general store in town would be pointless because it was now 6:37 PM.

After speaking with Mr. and Mrs. Bauer around 7:00 PM, she decided to spend another night at their home, then pack all her stuff in the morning and have Dietrich drive her to the general store on Mc Quillan Street. There, she expected to get some long-awaited answers once and for all.

*****

At the Ramada Inn, approximately six hours had passed; and since Morgan Carter never showed up, Special Agent Guardavaccaro had deduced that she wasn't coming.

Frank G.: Something spooked her, kid. She's not coming now, nor will she come here in the future. We only have one option left at this point.

Frank O.: You mean, stake out Vincent Falcone's place on Mc Quillan Street?

Frank G.: You got it, Potter. Grab your stuff. We're outa here in five minutes.

In case you haven't figured it out yet, dear reader, Vincent "Vinnie" Falcone was Anthony Tricerra. The feds assigned him a new last name and allowed him to choose his own first name before relocating to Tonopah. Wanting to keep his friend Vinnie DeRossi's memory alive, Anthony chose Vincent as his new first name.

After living in Tonopah for about three months (and completing his physical rehabilitation), he had opened up another general store; and on the day of its grand opening, he had been recognized by Dietrich Bauer to be the man that his favorite movie star (whom he just happened to be hosting at his house) had come to Nevada to find.

With this "six degrees of separation" type of discovery, Morgan was now destined to come to the general store in the morning to see for herself if Anthony really was alive. Special Agent Guardavaccaro and

Special Agent O'Neil, however, would stake out his home starting tonight. Oh, and by the way, Anthony—err, uh—Vinnie lived directly above his general store, in a two-bedroom apartment he shared with a small tabby cat named Jackie, which he had nicknamed Mouse.

So in the morning, we are going to find out exactly how all this shakes out. We are getting very close now, dear reader—very close indeed. By tomorrow afternoon, our journey and all its twists, turns, and close calls will reach its conclusion; and I bet you will immediately feel compelled to give your ol' buddy Pete a call, raving about what you've read. Or not. Who knows? But one way or another, we are going to cross the finish line with our heads held high, unlike Pete, who most likely just *is* high.

All right, here we go.

As Morgan lay in the extremely comfortable bed in Mr. and Mrs. Bauer's guest room, she found herself tossing and turning, uneasy with anticipation for the next day.

Dietrich was convinced that the man he saw at the Tonopah general store was the same man in Morgan's cell phone photo. He was so certain that he told Ms. Carter that if he was a gambling man, he'd bet every dollar he and Anna had on the store owner being the same person.

This was certainly reassuring, not to mention very exciting. Morgan felt like every cell in her skin was vibrating at the notion of Anthony being alive. A few times, she thought she could feel her blood traveling through her veins as her heart beat entirely too fast. She kept seeing Anthony smiling at her in her mind. She had never wanted anything to be true in her entire life as much as she wanted this to be true. If Anthony really was alive and had sent her the envelope with the sapphire in it, and she understood his unspoken message and somehow successfully tracked him down, reuniting with him after thinking he was dead for three months, it would truly be a love story for the ages.

Morgan fantasized about how their children would one day listen to this story on cold, snowy winter nights, in front of a calming fire as the flames did a docile, hypnotic dance in the living room fireplace, while everyone sipped hot chocolate and thanked God for all the good in their lives. She might have been getting a little bit ahead of herself with her daydreaming, but Morgan had prayed to find Anthony alive and be reunited with him every single day since she saw Johnny Embers's empty coffin. The thought of being with him meant more to her than every award or million she had ever earned in Hollywood.

Immediately after her father's death, Morgan blamed herself for what Deek Embers did to her dad; but after asking God for forgiveness for Carla Romano's death, she was miraculously able to let go of all guilt, anger, resentment, and hatred of every kind—even hatred of herself and Deacon Embers.

She knew that her father, who was the one who guided Morgan in the ways of the Christian Faith when she was little, was in heaven now, looking down at her. And that Joe could no doubt see from the balconies of heaven how Morgan's heart was so light and pure now that she had even said a prayer asking God to have mercy on Deacon Embers's soul for taking her dad from her. That was how much Morgan had grown as a person and let go of the bitterness and torment that plagued her even before Joe Carter was killed. She was completely at peace now, with the exception of the matter with the love of her life, Anthony. And what made matters even more gut-wrenching for her on that subject was the fact that Morgan knew that her beloved father would've approved of Anthony, who had walked his own path of redemption and almost died twice in saving her life.

Joe Carter would not only approve of and commend such a man, but he would also most certainly give his blessing to the two of them being together.

At this point, Morgan was just dying to see Anthony again, and even though she had never held him in her arms before, the idea of such a possibility made her hug every one of the fifteen pillows on the bed in the Bauers' guest room. Pretending she was embracing A. J., Morgan rolled around on the mattress, getting tangled up in all those übercomfortable German quilts.

Finally, after hours of tossing in bed as her mind raced in only one direction, she eventually succumbed to the sandman while lying on her back and embracing a big soft pillow wrapped in a clean pillowcase that smelled like Downy Infusions Liquid Fabric Conditioner.

She was only able to sleep for two hours this night, but during that time, Morgan had one of the most vivid dreams she had ever had in her life.

As she drifted off to sleep, she heard Anthony's voice somewhere in the distance.

*****

Morgan was standing on the balcony of a beautiful two-story white stone building that was located in a luxurious but small Italian or Greek village by the sea. Every building in this heavenly place was made of pure-white stone. It was not marble but matte stone so white that it looked as if every structure was constructed from white chalk, but the kind of miraculous white chalk that did not come off onto your hand when touching it. The village shined incredibly bright not only because sunlight showered every nook and cranny of it, but also, it seemed as if each building had its own glow that emanated outward from the inside of the white-chalk walls. And whoever built this dream place must have used Roman architecture as a template since stone pillars and finely detailed columns held every building's balcony in place. Some of the pillars were sculpted with beautiful white horses in them, and the artisan who sculpted these horses was clearly a master of his craft because every muscle and fiber of hair from each horse's mane was beautifully depicted in the white stone canvases.

The village was built into a hill, and starting at the top of the it, each row of houses went one step lower and further out from the hill than the previous one as they got closer to the sea. Majestic white steps and winding alleyways made the tiny town look more like a breathtaking maze you would find in paradise rather than anywhere else in this world. The buildings at the bottom of the hill sat on white sand that itself spilled into clear ocean waters that surrounded the village on three sides like a peninsula.

Morgan stood on the balcony of a building located at the top of the hill, and she heard Anthony's voice calling to her from the beach. She saw him walking on the white sand below, and she quickly and frantically ran down the steps descending from the balcony. On reaching a white stone courtyard, she lost sight of the beach. Knowing that in order to get to Anthony, she had to gradually descend toward the ocean, she ran down many steps and through numerous alleyways and courtyards that snaked throughout the mazelike village like white anacondas of various sizes.

Yet no matter what she did, it seemed like Morgan could not get any closer to the ocean. It seemed that way to her because every time she reached a courtyard where she could visually see the beach again, it looked just as far away as it did when she stood on the balcony of the first building, at the top of the hill. She kept running and running, but despite the fact that she had been going toward the ocean for what seemed like an eternity, the water never looked any closer. In fact, sometimes it even looked farther away. Morgan was trapped inside a truly beautiful nightmare.

Every so often, as she rounded the corner of a building, Agent Guardavaccaro, dressed in a pitch-black suit (which was in high contrast to the sea of white stone that surrounded her), was either standing or sitting in a beautiful courtyard and looking at her, smiling. When he was standing, he was smoking a cigarette; and the smoke he exhaled was highly exaggerated, mirroring some sort of human steam whistle. And when he was sitting, it was always at a small round table made of white stone. As he sat at the small table, he drank hot coffee from a chalky-white cup with an ornate handle. The steam from the beverage was also highly exaggerated as it danced upward into the sky. Guardavaccaro's taunting smile was the only way he interacted with Ms. Carter as he never tried to stop her from attempting to make progress toward the beach. Morgan easily jogged past him every time but either ran into a dead end shortly after or into a courtyard that showed the beach to be just as far away (or farther away) as it was when she started her descent from the top of the village.

This futile exercise went on and on and on as Morgan scrunched her eyebrows into a frown while sleeping in the Bauers' guest-room bed. Beads of sweat were forming on her forehead as her face twitched from time to time in disapproval of the events in her dream.

She continued desperately running down steps, from courtyard to courtyard, and from alleyway to alleyway without ever getting any closer to the beach. On reaching the peak of desperation, she stopped in her tracks and started crying. Her despair over-whelmed her, and she even said *no* out loud while sleeping in Anna Bauer's guest-room bed. She went on crying for a little while with her face in her hands when all of a sudden, she picked her head up and realized that she was on the beach with the white sand.

Her joy was quickly interrupted when she looked up toward the hill village she had just come from and saw Anthony on the same balcony at the top of the hill where she initially was. He was stand-ing on the balcony, clothed in a white Roman-style toga garment, while drinking from a white porcelain cup, when the most beautiful woman that Morgan had ever seen walked out onto the balcony with him. Her gorgeous, long red hair flowed in the wind as she embraced and kissed Anthony on the lips for what seemed like an eternity. Morgan felt what she could only guess was an invisible steel dagger enter her heart, and she partially opened her mouth to speak, but no words came out. The longer the kiss went on, the longer the woman's red hair became as it wildly floated in the wind, wrapping itself around the embracing couple.

The wind then picked up as rain clouds rushed into the sky above, which had been clear until that moment. Thunder and lightning were heard and seen as the sunny skies became dark, and torrential rain started to pour down on Morgan, who could no longer see more than ten feet in front of her through the storm.

*****

She woke up and immediately sat up in bed, completely drenched in sweat. A feeling of dread overtook her even though she realized it was just a dream. She looked over to the window and discovered that it was now light out.

She forced herself to get out of bed and into the shower that was in the bathroom connected directly to the guest room, but even in the shower, she could not shake the feeling of dread she woke up with. She got dressed; and while heading downstairs, she walked past Johann's room, where the young boy was playing video games. He greeted her good morning as she walked past his door, but Morgan barely responded since she was completely wrapped up in the bad feeling the dream gave her.

After forcing herself to smile and greet Mr. and Mrs. Bauer good morning, Morgan packed her belongings into her suitcase, put Pepp in her pet carrier, loaded everything into Dietrich's cab, and said goodbye to Anna and Johann.

Mrs. Winter shouted, "Thank you!" from her driveway as she waved her autographed copy of the *To Hell and Back* DVD case at Morgan, who smiled back and mouthed *you're welcome* from the back seat of Dietrich's cab while waving goodbye.

Dietrich started the engine, and they were off toward the general store.

Dietrich (smiling): So, young *fräulein*, today you finally see your long-lost boyfran, yah?
Morgan: Oh, I truly hope so, Dietrich. I *really* hope so, but...

Morgan looked at the floor of the cab.

Dietrich (concerned): What iiis iiit, *fräulein*?
Morgan: I had a very bad dream last night, and even now, I just have a really bad feeling about this.

Her eyes became glazed over as tears filled them.
Dietrich stopped the cab at a stop sign, turned around, looked Morgan in the eyes, and said with the most serious tone he had used since meeting Ms. Carter, "Morgan, what iiis supposed to be...vill be."
Morgan understood his point, and she nodded as the cab started moving again. Within ten minutes or so, Dietrich's car turned onto Mc Quillan Street and parked a little ways down from the general store as the time on the car's dashboard said 9:47 AM.

Dietrich: I tink ze store opens at ten.

Morgan nodded her head and agreed to sit and wait until 10:00 AM.

*****

Directly ahead of them, approximately seven parking spaces up, on the opposite side of the street, special agents Guardavaccaro and O'Neil sat in a black Cadillac rental that had been there all night.

Frank Guardavaccaro nudged Frank O'Neil with his elbow and motioned toward Dietrich's cab with his head. On seeing Morgan sitting in the back of the cab, O'Neil smiled and said, "Well, would you look at that? You gotta give it to her, Frank. She's a regular Shirley Holmes."

Frank G. looked at him as if to say, "That's not funny," and he then recognized that Frank O. was right.

Guardavaccaro: Yeah, she's pretty good, kid. Might just offer her *your* job.

O'Neil stopped smiling. "That's not funny, Frank."

Guardavaccaro smiled at him for the fourth time since they had met.

The two special agents sat there in silence, waiting for Morgan to get out of the cab and go into the store, where they could easily apprehend her, as O'Neil tried to figure out a way to bring up what he wanted to say without angering Frank or giving himself away.

O'Neil: Hey, Frank. I've been thinking…
Guardavaccaro: Have you, now?
O'Neil: Well…it sure seems like we are wasting a *lot* of time and resources following these two around, Frank. Couldn't we just slap them with a gag order, which, in this case, would be punishable with jail time, and just let them be? If either one of them brings attention to Black Rock Mine in any way, they go to prison. We can still bug their phones and all that, but at least we don't have to follow them around all the time. I'm kind of getting sick of it, to be completely honest with you, Frank.

Guardavaccaro stared off into space while nodding.

Guardavaccaro: Let me tell you something, kid. The only way that will *ever* happen is if I am no longer an FBI agent. And I might be old, but I'm not into my golden years yet. I won't even reach legal retiring age until March of this year.
O'Neil: Frank, that's in a few days.

O'Neil laughed.

Guardavaccaro: Yea, well, just because I'm old enough to retire doesn't mean that I *have* to retire, kid.

Besides…it's a matter of *principle* with these two now. Especially after that little cupcake lied to my face in the diner in Sky Haven and made a fool of me when she switched places with the bartender's wife at her house. Now I'm definitely gonna see this case through to the end, and then *maybe* I'll think about retiring.

O'Neil: Live and let live, Frank. Live and let live.

Guardavaccaro: Live and let live? That's cute. Did you learn that in college, kid?

O'Neil: Yea, I did, Frank. I can say it in three languages too if you'd like me to, including Latin.

Guardavaccaro: Woooow! Latin, huh? Fancy. [He paused.] I bet you can, kid. You're a smart cookie. All you need now is experience. Then you'll be the complete package in all that is the FBI agent.

O'Neil laughed.

O'Neil: Thanks, Frank. But…I know more than you give me credit for sometimes. Maybe not all the time, but once in a while, I'm right on top of things. I might even surprise you, old man.

Guardavaccaro: Yeah? Well, c'mon, kid. Surprise me. Show me what you got, Potter!

O'Neil: Yea?

Guardavaccaro: *Absolutely!* Bring it on, kid.

O'Neil: Okay, Frank. How about the fact that your little spiel about retiring is straight up BS?

Guardavaccaro: Oh, is that so?

O'Neil: Yea, Frank. I heard you tell Director Ricketts that as soon as you wrap this case up, you're retiring and moving to Florida.

Guardavaccaro smiled for the fifth time since knowing O'Neil.

Guardavaccaro: You been spying on me, kid?
O'Neil: Spying? Frank, you told Ricketts that as I was in the shower at the Tonopah Motel. Their walls are made of some form of grits, for cryin' out loud.

Guardavaccaro laughed again, marking the sixth time in two years.

Guardavaccaro: You got me, kid. You're right. I've had enough of monitoring and chasing idiots all over the country. Not to mention that some of the supernatural or just plain unnatural things I've seen over the last four decades of doing this job have turned my hair gray. This job is a young man's game. And, to be honest, I think you're ready, kid. If you ever decide to finally harden up that li'l bleeding heart of yours, that is.

O'Neil wanted to say something smart-alecky, but he couldn't as the thought of not having Guardavaccaro as his partner deeply saddened him. He had known about it for a couple of days now, but hearing Guardavaccaro finally admit it to him just hit differently. He stared at Dietrich's cab as his eyes started to water.

Guardavaccaro noticed, and his first instinct was to make fun of O'Neil. But on realizing he was not tearing up at being told he had a bleeding heart but because he would miss his partner, he stopped himself from ridiculing Frank O.

Guardavaccaro: Aw, c'mon, kid. You'll be a great FBI agent on your own. I don't know any other second-year rookie who has a level 5 security clearance. I mean, you managed to disarm, kidnap, and successfully interrogate a veteran agent, earning yourself an advanced security clearance, for crying out loud! How many rookies can say that, kid? You have the skills, the brains, the intuition… And the killer instinct will come to you the more you're in the field, bustin' heads and covering up the existence of things that the public shouldn't know exist.

O'Neil nodded and remained silent with tears in his eyes.

Guardavaccaro was not good at these types of moments, and he was not sure what else to say. He looked at the time on the dashboard and saw that it said 9:55 AM. "It's almost that time," he said to O'Neil, who wiped his eyes and got his head in the game.

O'Neil: You really wanna split these two up, huh, Frank?

Guardavaccaro: You have no idea, kid. I'm going to split them up if it's the last thing I do! Oh, look!

He pointed to a balcony above the general store where Vincent Falcone was now standing and drinking coffee from a white porcelain cup. He was wrapped in a white sheet, having most likely just rolled out of bed.

*****

In Dietrich's cab, Morgan and Dietrich were talking when suddenly Bauer blurted out, "There he iiis!"

Morgan did not look forward through the front windshield to see what Dietrich was pointing at, but she immediately got out of the cab and looked at the balcony above the general store.

At this moment, all her dreams came true as she saw Anthony alive and well, standing no more than seventy-five feet from her, on his balcony. Her entire body felt like it was lifting off the ground, and she experienced what felt like one million tiny needles in her arms and legs. A release of serotonin and endorphins, the likes of which she had never experienced in all her life, hit her like natural heroin dispatched through her body's biochemical processes. She would have ran, screamed, or shouted, but she could not as her heart was pounding harder than Jean-Claude

A. TRICERATOPS

Van Damme's in his final match against Tong Po. All Morgan could do now was slowly put one foot in front of the other as she moved toward the general store. Her eyes were fixed on Anthony as tears intermittently rolled down her cheeks. Slowly she moved forward. Slowly she made progress toward him. He looked just like he did in Morgan's dream the night before. She could not believe this was real life.

Out of the corner of her eye, she saw two federal agents get out of a black car on the opposite side of the street, about thirty-five feet away from her. Guardavaccaro buttoned his suit jacket up as he nodded at her and smiled. Suddenly all feeling returned to Morgan's body, and she tried to make a run for it toward the store. She got no further than three full strides and stopped dead in her tracks. So did the special agents who had started running toward her.

A stunning red-haired woman who was also wrapped in a white bedsheet walked out onto the balcony right behind Anthony, who had not yet seen Morgan or the FBI agents. The gorgeous redhead hugged Anthony from behind him, placing the side of her face on his back. He smiled and turned around, and she embraced him again and kissed him on the lips as the dry Nevada morning wind tossed her extremely long red hair to and fro, wrapping her and Anthony in it. Morgan recognized the red-haired woman as the same woman she saw working at the front desk of the Ramada Inn when she first arrived in Tonopah—the very same woman Morgan complimented on her diamond butterfly brooch and who

Morgan thought was so beautiful that she could easily get a perfume deal with Chanel.

The invisible steel dagger from Morgan's dream entered her heart, and her mouth opened slightly, but no words came out except for a slight anemic squeal. She found enough strength to turn around since she was unable to bear the sight above the general store. She was trembling and very close to fainting but somehow mustered up enough strength to slowly walk back to the cab, where Dietrich was making a shocked face while covering his mouth with his hand. She got in the back seat of the cab and burst into full-blown tears. Through her enormous tears, she said, "Take me to the airport, please!"

Up the street a ways, Frank G. and Frank O. were both shaking their heads while walking back to the rent-a-car as they could not help but feel sad for Morgan, who just had her heart broken in front of them.

Dietrich started the cab's engine; and in his anger at the situation, he stepped on the gas hard, inadvertently peeling off from the parking spot, causing a loud tire screech, which Anthony heard and looked toward. Seeing the car pull off in that manner, he watched it speed up the street and drive right past Frank G. and Frank O., who were getting back in their rented Cadillac.

*****

The beautiful red-haired woman had stopped kissing Anthony moments before he saw the federal agents because he gently pushed her off right after Morgan turned her back to the balcony. Releasing Anthony from her embrace, the redhead apologized: "I'm sorry. I shouldn't have done that. I just really wanted to thank you for letting me sleep on your couch last night. I would have had nowhere else to go after Ernesto broke up with me and threw me out of my room at the Ramada Inn."

Anthony: Oh, don't mention it. What are friends for, Amber? And it's okay. I'm not mad that you kissed me or anything, it's just… I have a girl-friend, you know?

Amber: I know. You're right. I'm sorry, Vince. Forgive me?

Anthony: Water under the bridge, kiddo. C'mon, let's get you some breakfast.

They both walked back inside Anthony's apartment as Amber dropped the bedsheet she was wrapped in, revealing her white pajamas, which were covered in small butterflies of different colors.

*****

Inside Dietrich's cab, Morgan was bawling her eyes out as Bauer did his best to console her on the way to the airport.

Dietrich: I'm so sorry, *fräulein*. Pleeez don't cry. Iiit iiis going to be okay, I promiiise.

Morgan could not hear what he was saying as she shook uncontrollably from crying, and she swore she could hear her chest rattle from how many pieces her heart had shattered into. She continued to cry all the way to the airport, where Dietrich helped her buy a ticket back to Pennsylvania and check in to get a boarding pass. He offered to wait with her until her flight time, but Morgan thanked him and let him know that she appreciated his offer but that it was not necessary.

Morgan: You have done more than anyone could ask for, Dietrich. Please tell Anna and Johann and the little ones I said I will never forget them. I think I just need to be alone right now. I'm sorry.

Dietrich understood and gave Morgan a big hug and a kiss on the top of her head; and then he went back to his family, leaving her holding her suitcase and pet carrier in the middle of the airport terminal by herself.

After a few minutes, she tried to pretend she didn't have a broken heart and wiped her tears. Knowing she had about thirty minutes before her flight boarded, she went over to the Auntie Anne's shop and got herself a soft pretzel and a Pepsi since she had been too nervous to have breakfast earlier.

A. TRICERATOPS

Morgan found an empty table in front of Auntie Anne's, sat down, and ate her pretzel with the saddest look on her face that anyone had ever seen.

*****

"Poor kid. I can't imagine what she must be goin' through right now," said Special Agent Guardavaccaro as he and Special Agent O'Neil watched Morgan from across the terminal while they sat at a table in front of Burger King.

O'Neil: I know, right? That poor girl has been through so much, Frank. And in the end, it wasn't even anything *we* did that will prevent her and Tricerra from being together.

O'Neil shook his head.

Guardavaccaro: Yeah. I think it is safe to say that she will never come back here again, kid. We don't even have to relocate him because I guarantee you she wants nothing to do with him now after seeing him with that redheaded fox on his balcony. Wow! Tell you what, Potter. That kid has great taste in women, though. Sheesh!

O'Neil wanted to be sympathetic to Morgan but could not help himself.

O'Neil: I know, *right?*

The federal agents looked at Morgan, then at each other and felt a little embarrassed about their immature and insensitive reactions to Amber while Morgan was still so visibly upset.

Guardavaccaro cleared his throat.

Guardavaccaro: Well, anyway, kid, once that poor, brokenhearted girl boards that flight back to Pennsylvania, this case will be over for me, and I will officially retire. Within a week, Ricketts will assign you a new partner, and I will be nothing but a memory.

O'Neil: Actually, Frank...

Guardavaccaro: Yeah, kid?

O'Neil: I have tickets to see Juventus play the MLS all-stars in Cleveland in May. You, uh...wanna come along?

Guardavaccaro looked at O'Neil and smiled for the seventh time they had known each other.

Guardavaccaro: Kid, I'm Italian. *Of course*, I wanna come along!

O'Neil smiled back at his partner while giving him the ol' finger gun and side-mouth click. Guardavaccaro patted him on his shoulder twice, signifying he would be interested in remaining friends after he retired.

A. TRICERATOPS

A voice came over the intercom, announcing, "Now boarding flight 57 to Philadelphia. Please head to gate 7. Thank you."

The two federal agents watched Morgan as she finished her Pepsi, crumpled up her Auntie Anne's wrapper, and then threw everything in the trash can closest to the pretzel shop. She picked up her pet carrier, and with a sad and defeated tone of voice and facial expression, she said, "Well, Pepp...ready to go back home?" The fat, soft, and friendly cat meowed once. Morgan gave Pepp half of a broken smile, picked up the suitcase with her other hand, and started heading toward gate 7.

The federal agents stood up as well, and having had nothing to throw away since they had ordered nothing to eat or drink, they started following her, making sure not to get spotted. Morgan reached gate 7 and found herself in a very long line of people who were one by one walking up to a man standing by the entrance to the gate, waving them in after he checked their IDs and boarding passes.

Since the line at gate 7 was extremely long, Frank Guardavaccaro grabbed a seat at a table outside of Chili's, realizing they were going to be there for a while. A cute young girl with dark hair, pretty blue eyes, glasses, and a name tag that said "Hannah" came over to their table and asked if she could start them off with some appetizers, to which Guardavaccaro replied, "Just two coffees, hon. Thank you."

She politely replied, "No problem" and walked away from their table. After a few minutes, she returned with two coffees and placed them on the agents' table. "Will that be all?" she asked.

"Yes, hon, thank you," replied Guardavaccaro.

The cute girl with glasses placed a check for $9 on the table and walked away.

Guardavaccaro: Can you believe this? Nine bucks for two coffees. What is this world coming to, Potter?

O'Neil laughed.

O'Neil: Don't worry about it, Frank. I got it.
Guardavaccaro: John D. Rockefeller over here.

O'Neil laughed again and took a sip of his coffee. So did Guardavaccaro. They continued watching Morgan slowly move up to the front of the long line at gate 7.

O'Neil: Tell you what, Frank. I just can't wait to get outa here and go home for a little while. I need a nice shower and a good night's sleep in my own bed. This case has really taken a toll on me.
Guardavaccaro: Yea, well, nobody told you to go AWOL for three months, kid.

O'Neil smiled and nodded, then took another sip of his coffee. So did Guardavaccaro.

O'Neil: Which part of Florida are you going to retire to, Frank?

Guardavaccaro: Well, Nurse Jenkins and I were thinking Palm Beach would be nice, but—

O'Neil: Whoa, whoa, whoa, back up… Did you say Nurse Jenkins?

Guardavaccaro: You bet your sweet ass, Potter!

O'Neil burst into laughter and followed up with "Why, Frank Guardavaccaro! Dating the beautiful Black nurse, are you? Well, good for you, Frank!"

Guardavaccaro: Thanks, kid. Now like I was saying, Palm Beach would be nice, but I wouldn't mind spending some time in Key West too. I've always wanted to go to the world-renowned Sloppy Joe's on Duval Street. I heard they have great music and great food there.

O'Neil: I went there once with my parents when I was a kid. Great BBQ pork sandwiches.

Guardavaccaro: Oh yeah?

O'Neil: The best.

O'Neil took another sip of his coffee. So did Guardavaccaro.

Guardavaccaro: You know, kid…I'm not one for sentimental talk and all that, but I meant everything I said to you back in Sky Haven. You know…in that abandoned house on Church Street. That wasn't a con job.

O'Neil looked at Frank with appreciation in his eyes.

O'Neil: I know you did, Frank. And I won't forget it.

Guardavaccaro stopped any tears that might have tried to make their way through his tear ducts and into his eyeballs and changed the subject.

Guardavaccaro: Man, this freakin' line at gate 7 is moving so slow!

O'Neil: Tell me about it.

Guardavaccaro: Well, at least it'll be over soon. These two kids have dragged my old ass all over the country. [He paused.] But you know…at least *one* good thing has come from all this.

O'Neil: What's that, Frank?

Guardavaccaro: That godforsaken thing in Black Rock Mine. Without anybody to feed it, it will finally die. Something that should have happened a long time ago!

O'Neil: Amen to *that*, Frank!

A small section of silence took place as the federal agents watched Morgan make her way to the front of the line with the speed of Michelangelo before radioactive goo spilled onto him, turning him into a ninja turtle.

O'Neil: I can't help but feel bad for Morgan, Frank. That poor girl has come a long way, both literally and figuratively. And she has lost so much in such a short time.

Guardavaccaro: You're right, kid. I feel bad for her too, if I'm being completely honest. Nobody should lose a parent at the hands of a sociopath. And now this thing with Tricerra? It's a tough hand she's been dealt. And…

He paused, unsure if he should say it.

O'Neil: What, Frank?

Guardavaccaro: She's not a bad kid. She made huge mistakes in her life, she really has, but you're right. She has definitely come a long way. This girl has a good heart, and she is certainly not that same bratty snob from Hollywood anymore, that's for sure.

O'Neil: No, no she's not.

The agents sipped their coffees in unison as they watched Morgan say something to Pepp that they could not make out as she was standing in line. Slowly she moved closer to the gate.

O'Neil: I never expected Tricerra to move on so fast. I honestly thought he loved Morgan.

Guardavaccaro: Yea, me too, kid. To be honest, I was pretty shocked when I saw him with that red-head myself. I would have never expected that from him. When I talked to him in the hospital room and told him the relocation plan, I really got the impression that he would die for that girl. I'm very rarely wrong when reading human character, kid. But I got this one wrong. Very wrong.

O'Neil: You and me both, Frank. You and me both.

Both men took a sip of their coffees in unison once again, but this time Guardavaccaro spat his out. "I don't believe it!" he said while looking toward gate 7.

*****

As Morgan was about to walk through the gate, she saw Anthony standing there, out of breath, blocking it and looking at her with a mixture of despair and ecstasy in his eyes as he panted for air. He had, no doubt, been running to several gates to check them for Morgan before finding her at gate 7. Without thinking, Morgan just reacted, running toward him and jumping into his arms. He caught her and spun her around for a good five seconds. Morgan did not know exactly why she was so eager to run into his arms after seeing him with the redhead, but it was probably a combination of being completely in love, instinctual reflex, and being so happy to see him alive and standing no more than ten feet from her.

Morgan (looking into Anthony's eyes): But how did you know?

Anthony: I had no doubt you would figure out I was alive and find me somehow after receiving the missing sapphire and seeing my handwriting on the envelope. And I saw "our" FBI agents on my street as a cab sped past them. I figured you were in the cab and that the two agents could only be here to stop you from finding me, but since you probably saw me with Amber, it wasn't necessary for them to intervene anymore. And I figured you were very upset after seeing us on the balcony and most likely just wanted to catch the first flight out of Nevada to go home.

Morgan: Great powers of deduction, townie. But who is—

Anthony: The redhead is a friend I let sleep on my couch last night. She kissed me against my will, and now she's having breakfast at my house by herself. Apart from when she kissed me today, I have never touched her. She means nothing to me, nor does any other woman on this planet because I only have eyes and room in my heart for you, blondie.

Morgan knew that Anthony did not lie—nor had he ever lied—to her, and the two of them immediately kissed as no other explanation was needed. They belonged to each other, and nothing would or could ever change that. A recreation of Mount Vesuvius in AD 79 took place simultaneously inside both their hearts as neither one of them thought this moment would ever come. Their souls intertwined and became one at that exact moment, knowing that neither one would ever abandon the other for any reason until the end of time. Both of their prayers had been answered, and after a long road filled with much heartache, they were finally together. A little boy standing next to them got the most cinematic view of the event because he had headphones on, and the chorus of "I Don't Care" by Justin Bieber and Ed Sheeran was playing in his ears during the beautiful moment of the couple's passionate embrace.

*****

Frank Guardavaccaro stood up from his seat at the table outside of Chili's, but Frank O'Neil gently grabbed his arm as he remained seated, looked at him with a serious look on his face, and with a soft but authoritative tone said, "Hey, Frank. Let's just get the hell outa here, huh?"

Guardavaccaro looked at his partner, then back at Anthony and Morgan, who were still kissing while locked in their embrace, then back at his partner, then back at Anthony and Morgan. After a few seconds of really thinking things over, the old man slowly sat back down at the table and took another sip of his coffee. O'Neil smiled at him, but Guardavaccaro rolled his eyes and mumbled something about bleed-ing hearts.

*****

A. TRICERATOPS

Anthony and Morgan finally released each another, then each put one arm around the other after Morgan grabbed Pepp's carrier in her left hand and Anthony grabbed Morgan's suitcase in his right hand. They headed toward the airport's exit while holding each other in this manner, smiling from ear to ear. One their way out, they passed by the federal agents' table out front of Chili's and made eye contact with them. O'Neil smiled and nodded, quite proud of himself (for obvious reasons), while Guardavaccaro shook his head and rolled his eyes at them, then continued to drink his coffee. Anthony and Morgan understood they were free, and they laughed, filled with relief and joy. They pulled each other even closer as they continued to walk toward the exit. Morgan silently mouthed the words "thank you" to Frank O'Neil while Frank Guardavaccaro was looking down at his coffee, and O'Neil winked with his right eye, acknowledging her gratitude.

*****

O'Neil: You're a good man, Frank!

He touched the $9 coffee bill with his left hand while reaching for his wallet, which was in the back pocket of his pants, with his right hand. Frank Guardavaccaro touched him on his left hand to stop him while reaching into the inside pocket of his own suit jacket with his free hand.

Guardavaccaro: Allow me.

He pulled a $20 bill out of his inside pocket and put it on the table, with Andrew Jackson's face down.

The hairs on the back of O'Neil's neck stood up, and three full seconds passed before he looked up directly into his partner's eyes. Guardavaccaro winked with his right eye and walked away from the table, heading toward one of the airport's other exits.

O'Neil sat there, staring at the $20 bill for a full minute nervously, then grabbed it and turned it over, discovering that four words were written on Andrew Jackson's face in blue pen. He read the words, made big eyes, then smiled with a newfound respect for Guardavaccaro as he got up and went after him.

The cute waitress with the black hair, beautiful blue eyes, and glasses came over to the table after the special agents had gone and picked up the $20 bill they left her. On seeing that four words were written on it, she read them out loud with her cute, pleasant voice: "*Vivere et vivere sinere.*" (Latin for "Live and let live.")

The End

www.atriceratops.bandcamp.com

ABOUT THE AUTHOR

In a galaxy far from our own exists an ancient solar system similar to the one found in the Milky Way. Within this solar system is a planet, the name of which cannot be properly pronounced by human vocal cords. On this planet lives a race of beings who are the ancestors of our very own triceratops dinosaurs.

This proud race of extraterrestrials once had a falling out with one of their own and banished him from their galaxy because of his abrasive and obnoxious personality.

After searching the cosmos for another life-supporting planet to call home, this ostracized being settled on Earth; but upon entering our atmosphere, his spaceship malfunctioned and crashed in a mountainous region on the East Coast. Soon after, massive seismic tremors buried his ship beneath hundreds of tons of volcanic rock, where it remains today as the unplanned prison of A. Triceratops.

Despite being trapped deep within Earth, this mysterious creature somehow managed to get his codex to the outside world, and now it has made its way into your hands.

You have been chosen to read his manuscript. Congratulations, human. And good luck…